I've travelled the world twice over,
Met the famous: saints and sinners,
Poets and artists, kings and queens,
Old stars and hopeful beginners,
I've been where no-one's been before,
Learned secrets from writers and cooks
All with one library ticket
To the wonderful world of books.

© JANICE JAMES.

OF MASKS AND MINDS

James Allister is a brilliant composer who is going mad. His wife, Mary, is distressed beyond words by the tragedy which threatens her husband; but should she agree to an operation which, in curing him, could destroy not only his personality but his genius as a composer? Tortured by her husband's black moods, harassed by relatives who can see no reason against the operation, Mary grasps at the hope of a third alternative—only to find her dilemma deeper than ever . . .

Books by Frederick E. Smith
in the Ulverscroft Large Print Series:

THE DARK CLIFFS
OF MASKS AND MINDS

FREDERICK E. SMITH

OF MASKS AND MINDS

Complete and Unabridged

ULVERSCROFT
Leicester

First Large Print Edition
published April 1990

British Library CIP Data

Smith, Frederick E. (Frederick Edward)
Of masks and minds.—Large print ed.—
Ulverscroft large print series: general fiction
I. Title
823'.914

ISBN 0-7089-2178-7

Published by
F. A. Thorpe (Publishing) Ltd.
Anstey, Leicestershire
Set by Rowland Phototypesetting Ltd.
Bury St. Edmunds, Suffolk
Printed and bound in Great Britain by
T. J. Press (Padstow) Ltd., Padstow, Cornwall

To

MY WIFE AND PARENTS

to whom I owe so much

Thursday Evening

1

WINTER came early to North Devon that year after the war. One Thursday, two weeks before Christmas, a bitter wind came from the grey Atlantic and brought up leaden clouds that hid the blue-ice sky. And in the afternoon, slowly at first and delicately, came the snow. First a single flake, falling, swooping, hovering—as graceful as a ballerina and as reluctant to come to earth. Then another, and another . . . until the dance became a great ballet of white, swirling arabesques against a slate-grey backdrop.

In two hours the frozen earth was white. The trees, so stark and black earlier in the day, became shapes of rare white filigree against the leaden sky. In the town of Rombury the cathedral had every delicate line of its tracery limned in snow. Before the evening its northern transept, so rich in trefoiled and lancet windows, stood up like a sparkling sheet of frozen lace.

3

Under the white roofs, families huddled round their fires. In Iveston, the village seven miles from Rombury and on the coast, the cold seemed more intense. To anyone approaching it over the whitened road, the wind grew wilder with every passing minute. The road led to the cliffs and then along them, passing a bleak, grey house that stood back on the cliff edge. The wind was merciless here. It drove the ponderous waves forward, hurling them in attack after attack against the grim, towering heights. In the village, a mile down the road, the dull shock of combat could be heard. To those living in the bleak, grey house on the cliffs, it could be felt. . . .

The house was Georgian in appearance, with a wide central doorway, dormer windows, and a plain, hipped roof. The approach from the highway was a narrow, tarred road running by two huge elms, between two lawns, to emerge finally into a broad gravel frontage. This gravel, a pepper-and-salt mixture in the snow, forked into two paths that ran round either side of the house, the left-hand one leading to a double garage. Behind the house, and bounded by a stunted privet hedge, the garden stretched almost to the cliff edge. Like the front garden it was mostly snow-covered lawn with an occasional flower-bed. A cluster of rose bushes huddled for shelter behind the hedge, their few late blooms frost-nipped and capped with snow.

The house itself was large and draughty. Behind the wide front door stood a roomy, panelled hall. On the right were three doors: one leading to the lounge, the second to the dining-room, and the third to a room reserved for the maid's personal use. On the left was a drawing-room, a library, a study, and a large back room with french windows commanding a view of the garden. At the end of the hall, to the right of the staircase, was a door leading to the kitchen quarters, which were situated behind the maid's room.

Except in two of the bedrooms, the furniture of the house was generally heavy and old-fashioned—massive pieces of carved mahogany predominating. Efforts had obviously been made here and there to lighten the sombre respectability of the house—they showed in an occasional bright curtain, a cheerful cushion, a vase of flowers. . . . But the house would have none of them. It had been built in the days when respectability and gravity were synonymous. A gentleman did not wear a gay tie with his broad-cloth; nor did he interpose frivolous witticisms into his conversation. In the grim, disapproving atmosphere the trifles wilted, to fade and merge their banal personalities into that of the bigoted old house.

In one of the two modern bedrooms, Mary Allister sat at her window looking down the main road that led to Rombury. The light was not switched on, and the room behind her could be seen only dimly. Even so, its modernity could be established. The furniture was compact and neat, without ornateness: the twin beds were built low in the modern fashion; the shaded lamps were hung on wall brackets; the thick pile carpet was light in colour. Even in the dusk the room had a tasteful appearance, a look of wealth without ostentation.

At the sound of a distant car engine, the woman at the window stirred and leaned forward eagerly. She saw its headlights approaching and waited, tensed and expectant. The lights came closer, glowed in her eyes a moment as the car swung round a bend, and then came down the road swiftly.

Too swiftly. She could not see the car pass the front of the house—her window was at its side—but the sound of the receding engine told her it had gone past. With a sigh she sank back, turning her eyes to the Rombury road again. The minutes passed slowly by. . . .

Although tall, and with a good figure and carriage, Mary Allister was not a beauty in the accepted sense. Those who thought she was failed to realize that her attractiveness lay not so much in the shape of her features as in the tranquillity of them. Perhaps it was her eyes that lent her face its greatest charm. They were beautiful eyes, serenely grey and steady, and their appearance was not delusive. She was a woman of unusual composure and seemed to carry with her an aura of restful charm. Her dress, of excellent though simple cut, was a royal blue that toned with her black hair, which she wore brushed back over her ears and softly curled. She was a woman in her early thirties.

Tonight, however, in the loneliness of her room, Mary Allister looked the anxious woman she was. Apprehension showed in every movement of her restless hands. For the tenth time in as many minutes she glanced down at her watch. Twenty minutes to six, and she had expected them back by four o'clock at the latest. She kept telling herself that their delay could be caused by a hundred insignificant things, and still her anxious mind refused to be consoled. Perhaps it was due to the snow. . . . She shook her head. It had stopped falling and could be little more than an inch deep at the moment. More would fall during the night—the heavy sky made that threat apparent—but as yet the roads were clear. No; it could not be the weather. . . .

In vain she tried to reassure herself that her fears were groundless. A man like James did not lose his mind. She was being foolish. . . . His excitability was an integral part of his temperament—a man could not be a great artist and have the balance of an ordinary man. Sickness had accentuated this hyper-sensitivity, bringing irritation and fretfulness. Rest and time would surely restore his balance. . . .

The very arguments she used as consolation brought her new fear. If a man could not be a great artist and have the stability of an ordinary man, was that not the same as saying a price must be paid for genius? Was this perhaps the price James had to pay. . . ? Her cold lips moved in the darkness. No; it could not be. It must not be. How could a mind that could take eight simple notes of an octave and arrange them into chords and melodies of unearthly beauty lose its grasp of the simple things of life, the smiling, the laughing, the crying, the loving things. . . ?

He will be well again, she told herself desperately. We will go away; we will laugh again, swim again, lie in the warm sun and I will see him smile and know the nightmare is over and he is well and mine once more. . . . And her inward cries were shouted to drown the toneless voice that whispered other things.

Her tortured eyes looked out again from

the window. The road was still deserted. How cold it looked as the wind came and lifted the snow! She shuddered. A mental picture of the two men driving back in the car came to her. James would be silent and brooding, sullen at having had to leave his work for an afternoon; and John Evans, his doctor and her friend, would be driving and talking, trying to cheer him up. Dear, dependable John; what would she have done without him these last few months? Without his understanding she felt she would have lost her own mind. He understood the tremendous strain under which she had laboured as from day to day she watched the disintegration of a brilliant mind. The slow, awful inevitability of it, watching the person one loved suffering the hell from which there is no escape— the hell of a sensitive mind struggling, fighting, screaming in despair against its own decay.

And, like an animal in pain, turning viciously on those who tried to comfort and help. How impossible not to feel raw pain at such moments. How impossible to comfort oneself that the angry looks, the cruel, biting words, came not from the man but from the disease possessing him. How impossible not to feel pain as sharp as a knife thrust in the body. Impossible because how could one know where sanity ended and insanity began? After hearing him compose music so gifted that it made one strangely breathless as in spring at the first glimpse of laughing, dancing lilac, how could one, how could she, believe that a mind capable of such creation was not capable of knowing the things it said to her? It was not easy.

Not that he was always like that. Sometimes, she told herself, with the bewildered expression of a lost child in them; and each time it happened she would tell herself that the long nightmare was over, that the morning was in sight. He would be gentle with her, tender, as if he remembered the harsh things he had said and was trying to win her forgiveness. She would hold on to those bitter-sweet moments with febrile strength, her brief happiness haunted by the knowledge that at any moment some trivial incident might cause him to turn on her as if she were his hated enemy. Then his eyes would burn her with their dislike. No word would pass between them for days; if she approached him she was met with sullen curses. And yet, without cessation, his work would go on. Although his music had changed in theme, although it was wilder and more elemental, it had lost nothing of its greatness. And so, in moments of despair, she could not help wondering if she were the cause of his moods—whether he would recover and be normal again if she were to go away and leave him.

She had wanted him to see a doctor five months ago, but the very mention of one had caused a violent outbreak of temper. Only when his headaches had grown so severe that they interfered with his work had he given in. Then she had called in John Evans, the friend to whom she had already been for advice. After his examination of the composer, John had come to see her.

"I'm making an appointment for him to see a consultant psychiatrist," he had told her.

A cold hand had clutched her heart at his words.

"What is it, John? What is wrong with him?"

His voice had remained non-committal. "Now don't start worrying. It may be nothing serious. But I can't tell you anything definite until I have had the advice of a psychiatrist. By the way; what was the name of that military hospital he was in at the end of the war?"

"Darley Hill, just outside Portsmouth."

"Exactly how long was he there?"

"Ten months. He came out in April this year. Why do you want to know?"

"The psychiatrist will want a full report of his case history. I shall have to write the Army medical authorities to find out the treatment he received. Tell me; did they ever ask him to go back for observation? Don't look so frightened, Mary. . . ."

She had tried to keep her voice steady. "Yes; they did. But his discharge had come through and he refused point-blank to have anything more to do with them. They gave him the chance to apply for a pension, but he refused it. I don't know what they did to him in hospital—he would never talk about it—but he's terribly bitter towards doctors. I had a frightful job persuading him to see you."

13

He had smiled ruefully. "I can believe it. I had a frightful job persuading him to see a psychiatrist. Anyway; he has finally agreed. Now there is just one more thing I would like to know. Did he ever have a breakdown in his youth?"

She had not known and had asked Frank, his brother. To her surprise and alarm she found out James had had a nervous breakdown in his 'teens that had kept him from school for nearly six months.

With this knowledge before him, John had sent the composer to a psychiatrist, and then to a neurologist. The outcome of these examinations had been treatment in a private nursing home. James had gone with the utmost reluctance, and then only under the persuasion that his work would benefit when the cause of his headaches was removed. Mary knew nothing of the treatment given him, nor did John tell her; but six weeks after his admittance he had returned home of his own accord in a blind rage and flatly refused to return to the clinic. It was then Mary became fully aware of the seriousness with which John regarded his condition. The doctor had come round to see her on the same day as James's unauthorized return home.

"We can't leave it like this, Mary," he had told her. "He must see Sir Miles Hartley. He is one of the foremost neurological surgeons in the country, and James must go to him."

"Surgeon! What is it now, John? You don't think he has a tumour, do you?"

"No; I don't think it is that. But he must see Hartley."

"But I daren't ask him, John. I don't know what they did to him in the nursing home, but the very mention of doctors and further treatment seems to send him off his head. I can't ask him to see yet another specialist."

"He must go, Mary. It is imperative."

In some way, she never knew how, John had persuaded James to agree. And once permission was granted, the doctor moved swiftly. The very immediacy of the appointment frightened Mary with its implications. It was made for the following morning, for Thursday, at Sir Hartley's rooms in Exeter. For ten-thirty. And now it was nearly six o'clock, and the journey back should have taken little more than an

15

hour. Allowing for lunch, which John had planned to take in Exeter, they were still well over two hours late.

Why were they taking so long? Was it a tumour? Had the specialist sent James straight to hospital; was his case so urgent? But then John would have 'phoned. . . . She was being ridiculous. Probably the appointment had been delayed, or possibly their car had broken down—there could be as many simple, harmless explanations for their lateness as there could be for James's headaches. She was growing morbid, she told herself with recrimination. Yet the shudder that ran through her was not caused by the cold, bitter though it was in the bedroom.

With a last, wistful look down the road, Mary Allister rose stiffly and went over to her dressing-table. Switching on the light, she examined herself critically in the mirror. Satisfied at last that the face staring back at her did not reflect the anxiety she felt, she walked from the room and made her way slowly downstairs.

As she approached the drawing-room, she could hear the high-pitched, complaining voice of her mother-in-law issuing from it.

"It's just on six o'clock, and Mary said they would be home by three. With all this ice on them, the roads will be terribly dangerous. . . ."

Hesitating a second outside the door, Mary opened it and entered the room. In front of an electric fire, both seated in armchairs, were Mrs. Allister and her only daughter, Ethel. Mrs. Allister was a woman of sixty-eight with wispy white hair and a thin, bowed body. She had an indecisive face, with a weak mouth and chin. Her pale, blue eyes, myopic behind thick spectacles, added to her general appearance of irresolution and vacuity. A habit of sniffing gave the impression she suffered from a permanent cold.

Ethel, her daughter, was cast in a similar mould, having the same shape of face and light-coloured eyes. The Allisters, indeed, went quite contrary to the popular concept that sons take on their mother's appearance and daughters resemble their father. None of Mrs. Allister's sons seemed to resemble her in the least—her daughter was the only child to whom she could point with pride as a production in her own right.

Even so, Ethel was a poor facsimile. Apart from her larger and squarer build, her mouth was thinner and more determined, with a look of waspish spite about it. Her hair was a dull, uninteresting brown and she was drably dressed. She could have been any age between thirty and forty-five.

On her arrival at the house, Mary had offered to redecorate it; but, with the obstinacy of the weak, Mrs. Allister had clung to her old associations. The drawing-room was typical of the house, being gloomy and heavily furnished. A massive sideboard stood against the wall opposite the window; in the centre of the room was a large round table. The chairs and suite were covered in faded cretonne. Two militant gladiators with upraised swords defended the sanctity of the fireplace. A huge marble clock on the jutting mantelpiece wound itself up ferociously as Mary approached the fire, and then delivered itself of six abortive, tinny chimes.

"Ah; here you are," Mrs. Allister muttered, looking up short-sightedly from the pullover she was knitting. "I was just saying to Ethel how late James is. You said they would be back about three, didn't you?"

"Yes; I thought they would be," Mary confessed, seating herself in the high-backed settee. "The appointment was for ten-thirty, and Doctor Evans said they would come straight back after lunch."

"Oh, Doctor Evans," the old lady sniffed. "You should have got someone older. I've no faith in these young doctors."

"He's thirty-five," Mary said, smiling in spite of herself. "And he has a very good reputation."

Mrs. Allister made a petulant gesture of irritation. "Oh; I know you think a lot about him. But I would rather have had someone with more experience."

"I agree with mother," Ethel broke in. Her voice was a stronger edition of her mother's. "It's only natural you will defend him—he is a friend of yours." There was emphasis on this last sentence. Then, to pacify: "It would be strange if you didn't. But we see things differently.

We would both feel more confidence in an older man."

Mary knew what was behind the words. She knew what Ethel was hinting. It was no secret that she and John were friends, good friends. She had known him much longer than she had known James. John had carried her books from school years before the Allisters had come to Iveston. She and he had grown up together. But it was nonsense to suggest that she had chosen John because of her friendship alone. He was a young doctor, energetic, enthusiastic, and up to date with his knowledge. She had confidence in him. And she knew that because of his affection for her he would do his utmost for James. But all of this would be wasted on Ethel.

Hearing a car on the road outside, she rose and went to the front window, drawing the heavy curtains aside. The car went by. Feeling the others' eyes on her she dropped the curtains self-consciously and returned to her seat.

"Where have Stella's friends gone this afternoon?" Ethel asked, her voice hostile with the subjects of her inquiry. Stella was the widowed wife of the Allisters' youngest son who had been killed in an air-raid over Germany in 1944. Stella and Ethel had never been friends.

"They have gone to Rombury," Mary told her. "They have some friends there, I believe."

"Didn't Stella go with them?"

Mary shook her head. "No; she said she had a headache. I think she is upstairs in her room reading."

"They haven't mentioned anything yet about going, have they?" Ethel asked grimly.

Mary turned to her in surprise. "The Ashburns? No. Why should they? Stella invited them here for Christmas. Didn't you know?"

"Of course I knew," Ethel said impatiently. "She must have been crazy to do such a thing with James the way he is. But surely, now they have seen for themselves, they'll have the decency to go. They can hardly expect us to entertain them in the circumstances."

"I don't think they expect us to entertain them," Mary said with a faint smile. "They are Stella's relations—she is taking

21

care of them. And they really haven't been any trouble—"

"That's all beside the point," Ethel broke in aggressively. "As I've been saying to mother, it isn't nice to have strangers about the house with James . . . well, with James the way he is. If Stella had any sense of propriety at all, she would never have invited them at a time like this. It isn't as if James had been taken ill suddenly. He has been growing worse for months, and Stella knows it."

Mary was silent a moment. Then she spoke slowly. "It must be dull here for Stella, Ethel. She wasn't brought up in the country, and she is full of life. And it's natural for her to want her own relations around her at Christmas-time. She hasn't any parents to go to. Mrs. Ashburn is her half-sister, her nearest relation—"

"Oh; I don't care what you say!" Ethel snapped. "It's inconsiderate of her to invite them, and that's the end of it. It's certain to make James worse. Mother tells me that the three of them were up until midnight the other night, drinking and singing bawdy songs. I'm surprised you don't want it stopped yourself."

"What can I do? I'm not Stella's keeper."

"You're James's wife," Ethel retorted. "And you're responsible for his welfare. You should drop Stella a strong hint. She might take some notice if you start on her."

Mary smiled wryly. "She would probably tell me to mind my own business, and frankly I wouldn't blame her. She isn't a child, you know, Ethel. She is a woman of twenty-five who has a perfect right to invite friends to her home."

"Her home!" Ethel exclaimed. "She is lucky to be here at all. If it hadn't been for mother she would still be cooped up in some dingy London basement."

"She is our sister-in-law," Mary said quietly. "And she could hardly be left to fend for herself after David . . ."

The mention of her deceased, youngest son was an opportunity for Mrs. Allister to enter the conversation with good effect. She did not let it pass.

"Poor David," she wailed, raising her handkerchief. "Oh; it was cruel. The youngest of the three, only a baby. . . .

Thank heaven your father never lived to see it happen. . . ."

"Now don't upset yourself, Mother," Ethel said hastily. She turned back to Mary. "I know we had to do something for Stella. But in return I think she might consider our feelings. I'm thinking about mother. It isn't pleasant for her to have strangers in the house at a time like this. You have a good excuse now that Doreen is off sick—you can tell her there is too much work without a maid, which is true. You won't catch Stella soiling her hands with housework."

"Doreen should be back before Christmas," Mary said. "We had a letter from her mother yesterday. She is hoping to start work a week on Monday."

"It gives you an excuse," Ethel snapped. "I don't know what you are all afraid of. If no one else has the courage to tell her, I shall do it myself one of these days."

Mrs. Allister raised her face anxiously from her handkerchief. "Now, dear; be careful what you go saying to Stella. She has a terrible temper."

24

"I'm not afraid of her," Ethel said grimly, squaring her shoulders.

Mrs. Allister sniffed uneasily. "No, dear; I know you're not. But let's wait a little longer and see what happens. Perhaps we can do something when we know what is wrong with James." Her myopic eyes peered at the marble clock on the mantelpiece. "Oh, dear; they are so late. I do hope nothing has happened. Why did it have to snow today? The roads will be like glass. . . ."

"Dr. Evans is a good driver," Mary said soothingly. "I shouldn't worry about that."

Ethel sniffed at her words, then rose. "I think I'll go and put the kettle on for tea. It's no use waiting any longer for them."

"Don't bother," Mary said, rising eagerly. "I'll go. . . ."

She passed down the hall into the kitchen with relief. A few minutes more in the drawing-room and she felt she would have screamed. It was always the same, she thought, when Ethel was in the house; she was a natural mischief-maker. Although married and living with her husband, Dick Cawthorne, in Iveston, she spent as much time in her mother's house as in her own. She and Stella were well-established enemies. It could hardly have been otherwise with two such diametrically opposite temperaments: Stella, sophisticated, beautiful, devil-may-care; Ethel, prim, dowdy, unbending and sanctimonious. Between them there was literally nothing in common; they were like oil and water and came together with equally unsuccessful results.

For that matter, there was no love lost between Stella and Mrs. Allister. The old lady had never approved of her youngest son's choice, but after his death she had felt herself duty bound to extend an invitation for the girl to make her home with them. Frank, the eldest son, may have added his weight to her decision. He had been invalided home from the Army with an amputated leg a year before James's return. Stella had been released from her work in the Food Ministry at the end of the war, and had joined the family a few months before Mary and James.

Financially, there was no problem. Although Mrs. Allister had only a moderate income from her deceased husband's estate, James's royalties from his highly successful compositions were more than enough to keep the whole family in comfort, quite apart from Frank's salary and Stella's own war pension.

Mary filled the electric kettle but did not switch it on. James and John would want tea after their cold ride; she would wait a few minutes more. She set out cups and saucers, putting them down gently so their noise would not drown the sound of the door-bell. She did not hurry; she moved slowly, postponing the moment when she would have to go back into the drawing-room again. As she stood there her mind wandered back, recapitulating their life together, lingering on the happy moments, wincing at the sad . . .

When had it begun? February 1943? Yes; that had really been the beginning. They had known one another for two years before that, but February had been the month of their marriage. She was in the nursing services at the time, and James had been commissioned in the Army two months earlier. They had married and had one full week together before the war had dragged them apart again. At that time James was in England, waiting for the invasion, and the year that followed had brought them brief but deliriously happy meetings. But at last, with awful inevitability, D-day came and James vanished somewhere in the maw of the titanic battles that raged over the channel. A month went by without news and then she received a communication from the War Office. "Missing, believed captured. . . ." Another week . . . a month—she was never sure how long—and then verification. James was a prisoner-of-war.

An endless year passed before the European war was over. Even then another ten months had to drag by before he was able to finally come home to her. A shoulder wound he had suffered before capture had begun to suppurate again and his general state of health was such that he needed prolonged medical treatment. Although she had realized his nerves were bad, she had not realized at the time the full seriousness of his condition. He had been put into the military hospital and it was Spring 1946 before he was discharged. During that time Stella, now alone in

London after David's death, had been invited by Mrs. Allister and Frank to make her home with them—an offer the girl had accepted.

Thus, at the end of the war, the bleak, grey house on the cliffs had been occupied by Mrs. Allister, Frank, and Stella. Only three people in so large a place. . . . As Mrs. Allister had pointed out, there was plenty of room for another family. It was then Mary had made a great mistake; it was bitterly clear to her now. She should have demanded her own home—James might have given it to her then; it would have been a natural request. If only she had known then what she knew now!

But she had not known. When Mrs. Allister, a constant visitor to the hospital, had suggested James should return home on his discharge, Mary had made no demur. At the time it seemed a reasonable enough thing to do. All James's things: his piano, his books, his music, were there, and the house was large enough for them all. It was natural, too, that his mother would want him with her a little while. Mary had thought of that. . . . The old woman's husband had died during the early years of the war, later her youngest son had been killed—she would want her two remaining sons by her side until she had fully recovered. They did not have to stay long. A few months, which would also give them a breathing space to look around for a home of their own. . . .

So they had come. On the surface all had seemed well. James's study was as it had been in the past, his piano had been dusted and polished with loving care. All had appeared well, and yet they had barely crossed the threshold when Mary had felt a premonition of unhappiness to come.

It had begun as a shadow at her side that vanished as she turned to face it, but it rapidly darkened and grew as the weeks went by. Something—she did not know what—but something was terribly wrong. The doors creaked of it; the very floorboards groaned their warning.

In the beginning Mary's fear had been a formless thing. Although she had not known James before the war, she had gathered from his family that he had always possessed a volatile temperament. In their short life together she had noticed it: how he would be up in the clouds one day and unaccountably depressed the next. Yet it had not been in itself anything unusual; she had known many other normal people of a like temperament. To her, probably because of the dissimilarity of their natures, it had added to his charm.

With this knowledge, she had not worried unduly at first about the change that had come over him. Brusque and moody, quarrelsome and ill-tempered though he now was, she had put it down to his war experiences, his captivity and his wound. Now he was back in familiar surroundings, back to the work he loved and with plenty of good food and rest, she had never doubted that he would make a complete recovery.

But, as the weeks turned into months, she had watched his rapid disintegration with growing fear. He had thrown himself into his work with all the desperation of a man trying to escape from life itself. At first she had attributed this to a natural reaction from his mental starvation over the last two years; but as the months went by he had shown no signs of satiation. He would come out from his study after ten, twelve, sometimes fourteen hours of work

31

with his eyes dark holes in his white face. His temper would explode at the slightest provocation. He had a bed made up in his study and sometimes he would stay in the room for days on end, having his meals by the piano and sleeping at its side. The strain had grown on everyone. On Mary it felt as if her nerves were violin strings, and each day the pegs were being tightened and tightened.

When she had realized the danger she had tried to get him away, but by then it was too late. The house had him. His piano was there, his music, his books, his study: they were all there, reinforcing the pull of family ties he had never broken. All the thousands of invisible things from the past were tugging on a mind now morbidly sensitive and neurotic. And their attraction was irresistible. When, in his rare rational moments, Mary had pleaded with him to go away on holiday with her, to take a rest and change of surroundings, he had reminded her of his family, of his mother, how cruel it would be to her, how she needed their financial assistance. . . . How the familiar old house helped his

composing with all its memories and senti-
mental promptings. . . .

And so that year had gone by. Time for
Mary Allister was not measured by day
and night, by sunlight and darkness. Day
for her lay in James's moments of lucidity,
and night in his black rages and melancholy. And because the former were few
and the latter many and often, the months
passed like a long Northern winter for her,
the brief moments of light only accentuating the endless hours of darkness. Black
rage after rage, and nearly all of them
directed at her. She felt she could have
stood anything but that, with all its implications. Cruelly the pegs were twisted,
tightening the strings—until the creak of
a board at night would bring her awake
with pounding heart and trembling limbs.

But the crisis was nearly here. She felt
it, as her mind brought her back to the
present. Soon she would know the truth,
the final and irrevocable truth. And so she
waited, one half of her mind longing to
end the suspense, the other terrified at
what that end might be.

2

ETHEL stared after Mary with irritation. She watched her leave the room and then turned to her mother.

"I can't understand why she sticks up for Stella," she grumbled. "They've never seemed very friendly to one another."

"They don't quarrel, dear, if that is what you mean."

"They aren't friendly in the way you'd expect two women to be who live in the same house," Ethel insisted. "They never go out together, for example."

"That's Stella's fault," Mrs. Allister said. "I've often heard Mary ask her if she would care to go into Rombury with her. Of course, now and then they have gone. . . ."

"Oh; now and then. . . . I know that," Ethel grunted. "But nothing like as often as you would expect. They aren't friends, and that's why I can't understand Mary taking her part."

34

"They're both such strange people," Mrs. Allister wailed. "Mary's so quiet—she never comes to chat with me any more. And Stella only thinks of having a good time. . . ."

"I can't think why Stella ever came here in the first place," Ethel said. "She's the last person to live in the country."

"She's a lucky girl to be here," Mrs. Allister declared in a sudden huff.

"I know that. But I am surprised she has stayed here so long."

"She's clever enough to know when she is well off, that's what it is," Mrs. Allister said, gripping her knitting-needles firmly. "She would never have been able to live in London off poor David's pension—not with things the price they are today."

"She could have got a job. Other women do."

"Well, she isn't the type that likes work. That's clear enough. But we had to ask her to come—there was nothing else we could do."

"I'm sure James doesn't like her," Ethel declared. "He goes out of his way to avoid her."

"It isn't a question of anyone liking

35

her," Mrs. Allister said with petulance. "We didn't ask her for her own sake—at least I didn't. It was poor David I was thinking of. . . ." She raised her handkerchief again.

"I'm sure if James had known, he wouldn't have agreed to her coming," Ethel went on, pursuing Stella relentlessly. "Unless"—bitterly—"unless he found her as glamorous as all the other men seem to find her. They're all alike; all they want is a body. Even David must have been the same."

"I can't think why he did it," Mrs. Allister wailed. "The least he could have done was to have brought her here first, so that we could have seen her and given him advice. . . . But he never said a word about her until they were married. . . ."

"I suppose she seduced him," Ethel said bitterly. "She's the type who would. She's all legs and sex."

Mrs. Allister thought it time to look shocked. "Ssh, dear; you mustn't talk of her like that. She was poor David's wife, and for his dear sake we must make the best of things."

Ethel's blunt-fingered hand came down

inflexibly on her knee. "I don't like her and I don't care who knows it. The house hasn't been the same since she's been here. I don't know how you stand it. There's a bottle of brandy in every cupboard you open. I'm always glad to get home. I don't see any reason at all why we should all have to suffer for what David did."

Mrs. Allister began to snivel again. "Please, dear; don't say any more. I can't stand it. Your poor father would turn over in his grave if he could see his house today. Poor soul, it's just as well he has passed away. Frank lamed for life, David gone, and now James. . . . Oh; it's too much. . . ." She wept profusely into her patient handkerchief.

Ethel appeared quite unmoved by her mother's tears.

"Now stop getting yourself worked up. You must count your blessings. You've got two of them back. All I was talking about was Stella . . ."

She paused at the sound of a latch-key being introduced into the front door. A tap on their door followed a second later and Frank Allister peered round it. Seeing they were alone, he came forward. He was a man of medium height and build, with a lined, rather sardonic face. His hair and eyes were dark, the former flecked with grey. He was dressed in overcoat and trilby hat, and was carrying a brief-case. He walked towards the two women with a pronounced limp.

"Hello, you girls. Having a nice, quiet bit of scandal?" he grinned. Then he noticed his mother's tears and his face became serious. He turned questioningly to Ethel.

"What's the news of James?" he asked.

"We don't know," she told him. "They haven't got back yet."

He shrugged. "Oh, well; that's nothing to worry about. Specialists never see one on time. That's their privilege. Cheer up, Mother. They'll be back soon."

He went out into the hall, removed his hat and coat, and returned to the room, warming his hands before the fire.

"Is this the best you can do?" he asked, making a disparaging gesture towards the electric fire. "You need a coal fire these nights."

"There is one in the lounge," his

mother muttered. "We put it there for the others. . . ."

"That's another thing," Ethel broke in triumphantly. "The coal ration. If you go on using up your coal in the lounge you won't have enough to last through the winter." She lifted her acid face to her brother. "Mother and I have been talking about these dreadful friends of Stella's. Don't you think they should have the decency to go now they see how ill James is?"

Frank shrugged, turning to warm his back. "I don't know. Stella invited 'em for Christmas. You can hardly expect them to alter their arrangements now. It isn't their fault James is ill."

"You must have been talking to Mary," Ethel said tartly. "She talks the same way. Or has Stella been getting round you with her big, green eyes?"

The faint flush died quickly on Frank's face. He smiled cynically. "What have you got against 'em, anyway? You don't live here. It wouldn't be because you don't like Stella, would it?"

"I wasn't thinking of myself at all," Ethel snapped. "I was thinking of James.

39

If more of us did that, the poor boy might be better in health than he is today."

"Has he grumbled about the Ashburns to you?"

"You know perfectly well that he hardly ever opens his mouth to anybody these days. But it stands to reason it can't be good for him to have strangers about the house."

"I should let Mary decide that," Frank yawned. "She knows better than any of us what is good for him."

Ethel bridled. "His own family probably know a good deal more. I'm surprised at your defending Stella. You're only doing it to be awkward."

"Look," Frank pointed out patiently. "They're our guests. We can't be rude to them. And they haven't been much trouble as far as I know."

"*Our* guests!" Ethel shuddered. "I should hate to think we invite people like that to our house. Mother says they have parties until all hours of the morning."

"You can't stop people having a bit of fun. In fact we need some in this dismal hole. They don't seem a bad couple to me."

40

"They're common," Ethel snapped. "That man—he's nothing but a drunken beast."

"He's rich," Frank grinned. "Perhaps he'll buy you a nice Christmas box. You should be careful what you say."

Ethel snorted and jerked her head away in disgust. Frank watched her in amusement, then turned to his mother.

"Where's Mary?"

"She went into the kitchen a few minutes ago to put the kettle on," Mrs. Allister muttered. "We haven't seen her since."

"How is she taking it?" Frank asked.

The old woman looked up at him vacantly. "Taking it. . . ?"

Ethel answered for her. "She's all right. It's mother I'm worried about. She's far more upset."

"Don't you believe it," Frank grunted. "Mary is worried to death about James. But she keeps it all to herself. She's that type."

"If she is so worried she should talk to Stella about those friends of hers," Ethel said stiffly. "Things can't go on this way any longer."

Frank turned to her sardonically. "Why don't you tell Stella? She's sure to listen to you."

Ethel looked at him with dislike. "If none of you has the courage to do it, then I shall. Someone has to look after mother's interests."

Frank leaned forward and patted her on the shoulder. "Good for you," he nodded seriously. "Let me know when you do it. I want to be around at the time."

"I'm not afraid of her," Ethel snapped.

Frank winked in mock admiration. "That's the spirit. But don't forget to tip me off. I'd hate to miss it."

Ethel's lips compressed. Mrs. Allister gave a sigh and rose unsteadily.

"I'm going to look at the dinner. I can't stand all this quarrelling," she quavered. "I don't know what is coming over you all. If your poor father could see you . . ." With another sigh she gathered up her knitting and shuffled unhappily from the room. Frank sank promptly into the vacant armchair. Ethel eyed him coldly.

"Now you've upset mother. Her nerves are getting into a dreadful state. She'll be having a breakdown if things go on like this much longer."

"She'll last the pace," Frank grinned. "She's tougher than she looks."

"You're callous," Ethel accused. "You haven't a scrap of sympathy in you."

Frank nodded absent-mindedly. He eyed the marble clock with a frown.

"I wonder why they are so late," he muttered, drumming his fingers on the arm of his chair.

Ethel turned towards him sullenly. "You don't think he has a tumour, or anything like that, do you?"

Frank shrugged. "I don't know what's wrong with him."

"It's very strange," Ethel muttered uneasily. "He never used to be like this before the war."

"I wouldn't say he had the best of tempers then," Frank grinned. "You were always quarrelling with him. Remember?"

"That's not true. I know he was a bit hasty-tempered, but it was soon over. He was never like this."

Frank sat silent. What she said was true.

Ethel lowered her voice. "Sometimes he acts as if he were out of his mind. If anyone outside the family were to see him in that state, they'd think him insane. That's one reason I want those dreadful friends of Stella's to go. If they once see him in a tantrum, it'll be splashed all over the newspapers in a couple of days. They're the type who'd only be too happy to spread a bit of scandal."

"Don't talk rubbish."

"I'm not talking rubbish," she snapped. "Someone must think of these things for the sake of the family."

"Of course. We mustn't have any scandal, must we?" Frank said softly.

Ethel flushed. "I'm not thinking of myself, if that's what you mean. You forget that James is a celebrity; that anything which happens to him is news. It's up to us all to see everything is hushed up until he is cured again."

Frank shifted restlessly. "Oh; for God's sake stop exaggerating."

"I'm not exaggerating. I'm not saying he is out of his mind; I'm only telling you what others might think. Personally I think he should be made to take a complete rest, and there I blame Mary. She is the one who should insist on that."

"How the devil can Mary stop him working? Wild horses couldn't keep him out of his study. Besides, he always liked work. He used to flog himself nearly as hard before the war, and it didn't do him any harm."

"Well; what else is it, then?" she demanded.

Frank shrugged. "Have you ever given the war a thought? Quite a few of us used to be different before it. Me, for example. I used to play football once." He stared down with distaste at his maimed leg.

"Oh; I know that," Ethel said impatiently. "But this is different. You don't fly off the handle at everyone who comes near you. You don't go raving about the place like a lunatic. Your nature hasn't changed."

"Hasn't it?" Frank murmured.

"You know it hasn't. You swear more than you used to do, and you are much ruder than you were, but at least we can understand you."

"I'm most relieved to hear it." This with immense sarcasm.

Ethel went on, ignoring him. "That's why I feel it can't be just the war that has upset James. It might be something quite different, you know."

"Such as?" Frank asked grimly.

She hesitated a moment, then went on defiantly. "Well, marriage, for example. Some men should never get married, and sometimes I think James is one."

"What do you mean? What are you hinting at now?"

"I'm hinting at nothing," she snapped. "All I'm trying to do is find out what is wrong with James. He's my brother and I'm worried about him."

"What has that to do with his marriage?"

"Well, I can't help noticing that he always goes for Mary when he is in a temper. Doesn't that suggest that he bears her some hidden resentment, that they're not suited to one another?"

"So now it's Mary's fault," Frank scowled. "Is that what you are getting at?"

"Not Mary's fault," Ethel said conciliatingly. "I don't necessarily mean that. It might just be that they get on each other's nerves. Some people do, you know."

"I know," Frank said dryly.

"One has to consider these things. It is

up to us all to find out exactly what is wrong with him, and then help him get over his difficulties. . . ."

"We won't help him by pulling his wife to pieces," Frank growled. "He's a lucky devil to have a wife like Mary, and you know it as well as I."

Ethel tossed her head impatiently. "Lucky! For the last six years James has been regarded as the finest composer in Britain. Do you realize what that means? He could have had almost any girl in the country."

"And he got Mary," came the reply. "That's why I say he is a lucky devil."

Ethel stared at him scornfully. "Most women who were married to a man as rich and distinguished as James would consider *they* were fortunate."

Frank laughed cynically. "He never takes her out, he sulks and grumbles at everything she does for him. . . . Fortunate! I think she leads a dog's life."

"Now you're talking nonsense," Ethel snapped.

Frank shook his head in despair, then rose impatiently. "Let's drop it, for heaven's sake! Stop blaming innocent people for James's vile moods. No one knows what has caused them, but certainly Mary is the last one to blame. She has more patience with him than the rest of us put together. The only reason he snaps so much at her is because she is with him more than we are. There's nothing more to it than that. . . ."

The telephone in the hall rang at that moment.

"That might be Evans now," Frank muttered.

Ethel started up to answer it, but, in spite of his limp, Frank was first at the door. He entered the hall and picked up the receiver, with Ethel close at his heels.

"Hello; Allister here," he called. "Oh; hello, Doctor. Yes; she's been waiting for you. Good news, I hope? All right; I'll call her. Just a moment. . . ." He was turning to go down the hall when Mary appeared at the kitchen door. She came forward, her grey eyes wide and questioning.

"It's Doctor Evans," Frank told her.

"Thank you, Frank." She gave him a half-smile as she took the receiver from him. He noticed the violent trembling of her hand. He stood back, almost colliding with Ethel, who was standing by the open drawing-room door. Taking his enraged sister by one arm, he guided her back into the room, leaving Mary alone in the hall.

Mary found herself shaking almost uncontrollably. She took a deep breath and made a great effort to compose herself.

"Hello. Oh, hello, John. Thank heaven. . . . Yes; I'm all right. What did he say. . . ?"

Stella Allister lay on her bed reading. The soft glow from the shaded bedside lamp threw a pool of light around her, setting off her beauty like an illuminated picture against the shadowy background.

Stella Allister was a rare beauty. Her long hair, copper beech in colour, swirled like dark fire on the blue of her satin bedspread. Her skin had not the pale debility so often found in those of her colouring—hers was strong, almost bronzed in appearance. Her features were perfect, with eyes of turquoise green and firm, full lips. She was tall and graceful, with a superbly proportioned body. Reclining elegantly on the bed in the warm pool of light, she made a picture with all the richness of a Titian oil.

In spite of her beauty, however, she gave no appearance of contentment. There was cynicism in her every expression, a permanent discontent behind her eyes. Yet this sulky sophistication did not, as it would have done with many other lovely women, dim and mar her beauty. Rather it mixed in some mysterious way with the aura of sex that surrounded her, and added sullen fire to its smouldering appeal.

Unrest showed in her eyes now as she glanced down at her wristlet watch. A furrow appeared between her eyes. Throwing her book impatiently aside, she reached out to the chair at her bedside and took a cigarette. Lighting it, she shook out the match and dropped it into an ashtray where half a dozen cigarette-ends lay charred and cold.

Lying back on one elbow, she inhaled deeply. Her beautiful, hard eyes were sombre; anxiety rough-grained with bitterness lay behind them. She lay staring into the shadows beyond the light while the ash on her cigarette lengthened.

The distant ringing of a telephone

brought her to life again. She moved suddenly, her lithe body bringing her to her feet in one swift movement. Crushing her cigarette in the ashtray, she gave herself a quick, automatic look in her mirror. She smoothed her dress, hesitated at the door for a moment, and then made her way down into the hall below.

Half-way down, on a bend in the stairs, she paused. Below her Mary was picking up the receiver. She saw Frank draw Ethel back into the drawing-room, leaving Mary alone. She drew back into the shadows, listening.

Mary's voice came to her clearly, tight now and under control.

"Yes; I'm all right. What did he say? Oh; thank God for that. What else did he say? Later on—yes, of course. Is James there? Yes; I'd like to. You say you'll be home in half an hour? Do hurry. Thank you, John."

The tensed body of the listening woman appeared to relax. She softly descended two more stairs, pausing as Mary spoke again.

"Hello, dear. How are you feeling? Never mind; you'll soon be home now.

51

Yes; there's a fire in your study. All right, dear. Don't be long."

As Mary put the receiver down, the drawing-room door was flung open and the irate face of Ethel appeared. Stella drew back into the shadows again.

"I want to know what's wrong with him," Ethel flung back through the door. "He's my own brother; I've every right to know." She swung round on Mary. "Well; what does the specialist say? From the way he is behaving"—pointing to Frank who was just emerging from the room—"one would think it a state secret."

"He doesn't think James has a tumour," Mary told her quietly.

Ethel stared at her. "Then everything's all right, isn't it? If he hasn't a tumour, all he needs is rest and peace. That's what I thought all along. Now it's up to us all to see he gets it." She paused, looking curiously at Mary. "What's the matter? You're not looking very pleased."

"Of course I'm pleased."

Ethel nodded doubtfully, her pale eyes searching Mary's face. Then she turned. "Well; I'll go and tell mother. The poor soul is half-crazy with worry. Then I must go home and get Dick's dinner ready. I'll come back later to see James."

She started down the hall, her square-toed, utilitarian shoes stepping out with purpose.

Frank waited until she had disappeared before speaking.

"Congratulations," he said.

Mary started, then smiled at him. "Thank you, Frank."

He noticed the slight hesitation in her voice and looked at her in surprise. "It is good news, isn't it?"

"Oh, yes. Yes; of course it is."

"Then what's the matter?" he asked gently. "You're not looking quite as happy as you might look. Is it reaction?"

"No; it's not that. It was something in John's voice. . . ." Her words were low-spoken—the woman on the stairs had to strain her ears to catch them.

"In his voice. What do you mean?" Frank asked curiously.

"Oh; I'm being foolish," she said, trying to laugh. "It's probably only my imagination. But"—and the frown came back on her face—"John didn't sound happy about it. He didn't say anything, but you know how it is—when you've known someone for years, you can tell so much from the tone of their voice."

Frank nodded doubtfully.

"Oh; I'm being stupid," Mary said impatiently. "I should be grateful." She turned away. "I'd better go through to mother now, and tell her. And I must help her with dinner. They'll be home in half an hour."

"It's reaction," Frank told her. "And voices often sound queer over the 'phone."

She threw him a grateful smile. "Of course. That's all it is. I'll realize how lucky I am in a few minutes."

"That's the spirit," Frank smiled. He watched her thoughtfully until she had disappeared into the kitchen, then turned back to the drawing-room. Remembering the electric heater, he grimaced and crossed the hall to the lounge opposite. He opened its door, grunted with satisfaction at the sight of the coal fire, and entered. As he limped towards the fireplace, he heard a tap-tapping of high heels in the hall. He turned, his face lighting up with pleasure as Stella appeared in the doorway.

"Hello," he greeted. "Come and get warm beside a real fire."

She sauntered carelessly forward. "Thanks. I will." Her voice was low-timbred, husky and appealing.

Frank drew up an armchair for her. "It's a stinker of a night. Your relations must be getting a poor opinion of our Devon climate. Are they coming home for dinner?"

"Yes," she said without interest, seating herself gracefully. She watched Frank limp over to his chair. "What's the latest news of James? That was Evans on the 'phone a few minutes ago, wasn't it?"

"Yes; it was." Frank fumbled in his pocket and pulled out a short-stemmed, large-bowled pipe. "He told Mary the specialist thought there was no tumour."

"That's good news, isn't it?" she asked. "Mary must be relieved."

He nodded, packing his pipe carefully. "It's good news, all right. But there's always a time lag with these things. You know how it is. . . ."

"You mean Mary isn't satisfied?"

His dark, shrewd eyes examined her a moment as he lit his pipe. He blew out the match and tossed it into the fire before answering her.

"She's very worried. She's had this thing on her mind so long now that it's difficult for her to believe in such a thing as good news. She felt Evans was holding something back."

"What could he be holding back?" she asked abruptly.

Frank shook his head. "I don't know. Probably nothing. It may be just her imagination."

"One thing I'm certain he will tell her— to keep him away from that damned piano. That's at the back of his trouble, I'm sure of it. No one could keep at it the way he does without cracking up sooner or later."

Frank did not bother to argue this time. Ethel, his mother, Stella: they all seemed of the same opinion—that James's condition was due to his excessive work. He shrugged and puffed at his pipe.

"It's nothing but overwork," Stella said sullenly, when he did not reply. "Anyway; they'll make him rest now."

"They'll have a job on their hands," Frank grinned. "He'll probably make up

56

the time he has wasted today by working half the night."

"You should all make him rest," Stella muttered.

Frank nodded inattentively. Through the haze of tobacco smoke he was studying her. She was staring moodily into the fire, a cigarette held in one long, tapering hand. She was a picture of elegance: Frank had never seen her other than perfectly groomed. She wore clothes with a natural grace, her slim body displaying them to perfection. The firelight seemed to reach out and touch her hair, where it smouldered darkly. His gaze moved to her eyes. They were fixed on the fire, sombre and sullen. She lifted her cigarette to her lips, inhaled deeply, and blew out smoke in one sharp exhalation. It appeared an act of exasperation, a minor explosion of frus- trated desires. It could also have been the outward expression of a sudden mental rebellion, perhaps directed against the life she was now having to live, he thought.

Feeling Frank's eyes on her, she turned suddenly towards him. Her look was hard, almost challenging. He did not meet it. He gazed down at the bowl of his pipe, and with one finger pressed down on a rising flake of burning tobacco.

There was the sound of a car on the gravel outside.

"That'll be Mervyn," she muttered. "I'll go."

Rising, she went outside. The front door opened and Frank heard voices in the hall.

"How was Rombury today?" That was Stella.

A man's voice, loud and hearty, answered her. "Oh; as dead as usual. My God; it's bitter outside. Hope you've got a good fire going."

"There's one in the lounge. Stick your coats on the hallstand and go in."

A few seconds later Stella returned to the lounge, followed by her relations, Gwen and Mervyn Ashburn. The man waved an arm to Frank.

"Hello. You've got the right place here. It's fifty below outside."

Frank rose with a grin. "Come over and thaw out."

Mervyn Ashburn took his wife's arm and led her forward. He was a man of about forty-five with a florid, slightly puffy face. He had a well-fed appearance, with smooth skin, stoutish body, and receding fair hair. His clothes, while of expensive material, were a trifle flashy. His general appearance suggested a hedonist and a man with more money than taste.

His wife, perhaps two or three years younger than he, was very definitely over-dressed. Her fingers were armoured in rings and her hair obviously peroxided. She had sharp features that had been pretty fifteen years earlier. She was of medium height, and her thin, almost emaciated body suggested an over-zealous attention to her diet. Her lean legs tapered off into a pair of shoes with extremely high heels, on which she balanced precariously. Obviously highly strung, she showed in every movement and gesture an acute hypochondria regarding her age. With every aid and artifice money could buy, Gwen Ashburn clung desperately to the last of her youth.

Frank offered her his chair, and with Mervyn's help pushed forward the settee. Stella waved Mervyn to the other armchair.

"You can sit there," she yawned. "I'm warm enough."

Mervyn hesitated only a moment, then seated himself. "Thanks," he said, holding his hands in front of the fire. Frank joined Stella on the settee.

"So you don't think much of Rombury?" Stella mocked.

Gwen Ashburn answered. "It gets deader every day." She had a shrill voice with a very faint Cockney accent.

Mervyn chuckled. "Cathedral cities have never appealed to Gwen's aesthetic tastes."

His wife replied tartly. "Listen to 'Arty 'Arry talking. Since when have you gone in for culture?"

Mervyn drew back a little from the fire, throwing a heavy-lidded wink at Frank.

"It takes all types to make a world," he grinned. He looked around, eyeing Stella and Frank hopefully. "How about us all having a little drink before dinner, eh?"

"You've had enough," Gwen broke in sharply. "You're always the same when you've been with Bill Henson." She turned to Frank. "Is your brother back yet?"

"Not yet," Frank told her. "But his doctor 'phoned through to Mary. There's nothing organically wrong. There isn't a tumour."

"Good show," Mervyn interrupted heartily. "Glad to hear it. Probably just his nerves, then."

"I know it's none of my business," Gwen went on. "But really I'm not a bit surprised his nerves are bad. No one can expect anything else if they work the way he does."

"It's true," Frank confessed. "But he has always been like this. These artistic temperaments, you know. . . ."

"Well, thank heavens I'm not married to one of 'em," Gwen said. "He'd soon get blazes from me if I was neglected the way he neglects your sister-in-law."

"You see how lucky you are," Mervyn said, winking at Stella.

"Yes; thank God you're no genius," came the tart reply.

Stella laughed at the expression on Mervyn's face.

"Never mind, darling," she comforted. "You have a genius for making money, haven't you? And without working too hard for it, either."

"It's nice to have someone appreciate

me," Mervyn grunted. His eyes were twinkling as he spoke, but Gwen's lips suddenly tightened.

"You poor thing. You lead such a dog's life, don't you?" There was a sharp ring in her voice. Frank rose at that moment with a yawn.

"If you'll all excuse me, I'll run along and clean up," he said. "I'll see you all at dinner."

"Of course." Mervyn half-rose as Frank limped out, then dropped back into his chair with a grunt. Gwen looked across at him.

"It's time we did the same," she said, rising.

Mervyn stretched out his legs. "Um. I suppose so. But this fire is grand."

Gwen stared down at him. "Well; aren't you coming?"

"In a moment," he said with sudden impatience. "When I've thawed out a bit more."

She gave him a pointed look, and then walked out without another word. Mervyn watched her go with a frown of irritation.

"Confound it," he muttered, when her footsteps were well up the stairs. "She won't leave me alone a minute. She's always round my neck. I don't know what's wrong with her these days." He looked eagerly at Stella, who was eyeing him with amusement. "You are coming out with us this evening, aren't you?"

Stella stretched, aware of his eyes flickering over her. "I don't think I had better," she yawned. "It'll look rather bad. I'd better wait with the rest of the family to hear just what is wrong with James."

His face dropped. "It isn't going to help him if you stay here brooding," he muttered. "You heard what Frank said— he hasn't a tumour or anything like that. So what are you worried about? Come out with us tonight. It'll do you good."

"No; I'd better not."

"Confound it," he muttered. "I haven't seen anything of you all day."

Her voice mocked him. "Poor darling. How you must have suffered."

"What's the matter with you these days?" he complained. "You used to be a darn sight different during the war."

"I'm a hoary old widow," she said. "You forget that."

His heavy-lidded eyes wandered down her long, slim legs. He stirred restlessly. "It's must be this place that has got you down. It's like a confounded mausoleum."

She turned her eyes from the fire and stared at him. "That sounds as if you're pulling out."

"You know I don't mean that," he said thickly. "As long as you're about I'm happy enough. But I'm not seeing enough of you—that's the trouble."

She eyed him quizzically. "I don't quite know what you expect me to do, darling. You've got a wife upstairs, you know. A wife with very sharp eyes."

He scowled at the reminder, then looked at her recklessly. "I'm crazy about you," he muttered. "And you know it."

"I'm beginning to know it," she mocked. "I wondered why you hinted in your letter for an invitation here for Christmas."

He grinned. "You didn't think I wanted to come to this dead-and-alive place for the scenery, did you? Or just to see the Hensons? Hadn't you guessed why I wanted to come?"

"I thought you were interested," she

said coolly. "But I thought you had more intelligence than to bring your wife with you on a hunting trip. So I was a little surprised."

"I couldn't very well leave her behind, could I?" he muttered.

"Not very well," she agreed. "But as she is here, you'd better remember it. She's looking a bit acid these days. I don't want any trouble while you are here. Do you understand?"

His eyes were busy wandering over her as she was speaking.

"Do you hear?" she said sharply.

"I can't help feeling this way," he muttered. "You do things to me. . . . I'd give you a good time if you'd let me. . . ."

Footsteps sounded on the tiled floor of the hall. Mervyn sat up in alarm.

"You'd better go upstairs before Gwen starts getting ideas," Stella murmured.

Mary appeared at the door at that moment. Mervyn rose as she came forward.

"Good evening, Mr. Ashburn," she smiled. "Frank said you were back. Will you be going out this evening?"

"We were thinking of going to a show," he said.

"Then we'll have dinner early," Mary told him.

"That's very kind of you. By the way, Frank said you've had better news about your husband. Congratulations."

Mary hesitated, then smiled. "Thank you very much. I expect him home soon. Do excuse me now. I'll see you have dinner in good time."

"That's very nice of you."

Mervyn watched her go out, then turned to Stella. "By Jove; that's a charming woman. She's got the real stuff in her."

Stella nodded without speaking. He looked down appealingly at her.

"Change your mind and come out with us tonight," he pleaded.

She shook her head impatiently. "Can't you take no for an answer? I've already told you I can't go. Now go upstairs before Gwen starts causing trouble."

He turned discontentedly to the door. "All right," he grunted. "I'll try you again tomorrow. And for heaven's sake cheer up."

He stalked moodily from the room and

up the stairs. Stella was reaching for a cigarette when the sound of a car engine came from up the drive. A moment later headlights gleamed briefly through the curtains as the car swung round outside.

Stella went to the front door. As she reached it Mary came out anxiously from the kitchen. Stella met her questioning glance, and nodded.

"They are here now," she said.

3

"NOT much longer now," John Evans said cheerfully as the lights of Rombury receded behind them. "We're nearly home. Sorry we're late, but it couldn't be helped."

The brooding man huddled in an overcoat beside him did not answer. He sat staring with fixed eyes through the windscreen of the speeding car.

"That's Hartley's one fault," Evans went on, ignoring the other's silence. "He is never punctual. But he is a good man otherwise. How is the headache now?"

James Allister lifted a hand to his head. His voice was thick and unsteady. "Very bad," he muttered.

"Never mind," Evans said. "I'll give you a sleeping draught tonight to take away the pain. All this travelling today will have made it bad. . . ."

"No." James Allister turned his deep-set eyes on the doctor. "I don't want any more drugs. I must work when I get back. Let me alone, will you?"

"All right; if you wish it." Evans shrugged conciliatingly. "But I shouldn't work tonight. I'd have an evening off. Mary will feel like a chat when you get back."

Irritation sounded at once in the other's voice. "Confound it, man; why does everyone try to stop me working? Are you in the conspiracy, as well? Has Mary been talking to you?"

"Work if you want to," the doctor said in an even, disinterested tone. Slowly James Allister's fists unclenched and his taut body relaxed. His eyes lost their angry glow and turned moodily back to the white road over which they were passing. In seconds he lapsed back into the torpor in which he had dwelt the whole afternoon.

"Cigarette?" Evans asked, holding out his case.

The composer made no sign of hearing, and Evans did not press him. Holding the steering-wheel steady with his elbows, he took one himself and slipped the case back into his pocket. He struck a match, noticing without moving his eyes how James started at the sudden flare of light.

They reached the coast road a few minutes later and turned down it. The wind came like a wild thing over the cliff, buffeting the car half-way across the road. In front of them the powdered snow eddied, forming weird shapes that sidled, leapt and writhed like things in torment. John Evans saw the brooding eyes of the man beside him watching them, and something near a shudder crawled down his back.

They did not speak again until they reached the house. It appeared on their left, a black shadow against the sky with two eyes of light staring from it. The doctor slowed the car, turned up the narrow road and came to a halt on the gravel frontage. Pulling on the hand-brake, he turned to James.

"Here we are," he announced cheerfully. "I hope they have a big fire going inside."

The composer did not reply. He was fumbling clumsily with the door-handle. Evans jumped out, walked round the car and opened the door for him.

A rectangle of light shone on the snow

as the front door was thrown open. Mary stood silhouetted against the light for a moment, then ran out to meet them.

"Hello, darling. Hello, John," she called breathlessly. "You must both be freezing. Hurry inside—we have tea waiting."

She slipped a hand through her husband's arm, her eyes meeting those of the doctor. He smiled reassuringly in return, and joined her at the other side of James.

"What do you mean by coming out without a coat?" he admonished her. "Do you want to catch pneumonia?"

"I'm all right," she smiled. They entered the house—James pulling away irritably from Mary as they stepped into the hall. Ignoring Stella, who was standing by the front door, he pushed by her on his way to the hallstand, where he began removing his coat. Mary followed and helped him take it off.

Stella looked from James to the doctor, who had followed the others into the hall.

"Hello," she said. "You must have had a cold trip."

He smiled at her. "Good evening, Mrs. Allister. Yes; it's a bleak night."

She nodded towards the lounge. "Go inside and warm up. There's a useful fire in there."

He hesitated. "I must be going, I'm afraid. My surgery is at seven—I'll be late as it is."

Mary, who was leading James into the lounge, stopped at his words.

"Oh, don't go yet, John," she pleaded. "Stay a little while. Tea is almost ready."

He saw the disappointment in her eyes and knew how much she was longing to hear his news.

"Only five minutes, then," he said. "I mustn't be any longer."

They entered the lounge. After the subdued light of the hall, the lounge seemed brightly illuminated, and James winced and shaded his eyes. Seeing his distress, Mary switched off the main lights, leaving on a soft, standard lamp by the fire. James muttered an exclamation of relief, pulled away from his wife, and slumped down into an armchair. Mary stood back uncertainly, then turned to John.

"I'll go and get the tea now," she said nervously. "I won't be a moment."

He nodded, trying to express his sympathy in the look he threw her. She gave him a half-smile in return as she left the room.

John moved nearer the fireplace where the composer was staring morosely into the fire. Stella, who had crossed over to the sideboard to collect her cigarettes, looked at James and then at him, lifting her slim shoulders expressively. Embarrassed by her unspoken question, John spoke at random.

"It looks as if we are going to have a white Christmas this year, Mrs. Allister."

"That will be nice," she murmured, sauntering over towards him. "Do have a cigarette."

"Thank you."

After accepting his light, she moved with grace towards the composer.

"Cigarette?" she asked.

James looked at her blankly, then shook his head. "No, thanks." His reply was curt, and John noticed her bite her lips. Recovering quickly, she turned back to him with a laugh.

"Don't stand over there. Be human and come near the fire. Have a drink."

John laughed with some embarrassment as he approached her. Shy by nature, he had always felt ill at ease in Stella Allister's sophisticated presence. In spite of this he could not help admiring her. She moved and spoke with a casual ease that was refreshing. In her grace she reminded him of a sleek and lovely cat. But his trained eyes noticed the same restlessness in her tonight that he had noticed on the other few occasions they had met. A restlessness and something else that both puzzled and eluded him.

"I'd like a drink very much," he confessed. "But I still have my surgery, and if one of my old woman patients smelt alcohol on me the news would be round Rombury in a flash."

"I always thought old women liked their doctors slightly on the naughty side," she mocked, her eyes examining him. Tall, fair, well built with good shoulders, there was something typically "country" about him. It showed in his ruddy healthy face, his blue eyes, and sounded in his slow, reflective speech. There was no sophistry about John Evans; a lie would sound like a lie on his lips, it would be taken for nothing else. But there was nothing insensitive about his pleasant face: there was intelligence in his high forehead, and both humour and kindness in the wrinkles round his eyes and mouth. Stella's summing up was characteristically brief. An attractive man, and a strong one; but appallingly shy. . . .

"I've never been quite sure what women do want of their doctors," he was saying ruefully.

"Really," she murmured. "I must talk to you about it sometime. They don't want curing, of course. That is *most* unsatisfactory. They never come to young doctors for that. All they ask for is understanding —if you give them that they'll be quite happy and you'll be a fashionable doctor in no time. Perhaps you are one now."

"I wish I was," he smiled.

"Didn't they tell you all this at medical school?" she asked innocently. "Never mind. It's never too late to learn."

"I'll try to remember," he promised, trying to match her banter.

"You should," she said, giving him a

long, mocking look under her black eyelashes. Then she turned to James in an effort to bring him into the conversation.

"How are you feeling now?" she asked. "Any warmer?"

He moved, as if irritated by the question. "I'm all right," he muttered. He swung round in sudden temper. "Where is that tea? I haven't all the night to waste. Why are they taking so long?"

"I'll go and hurry them up," Stella said lightly. She gave the doctor a glance as she passed him on her way to the kitchen, and he found himself trying to analyse the expression. Exasperation, annoyance, anxiety: it could have been any or all of these.

Any of them and more, he thought, gazing down at the brooding figure of James Allister who, after his outburst of temper, had lapsed again into his posture of sullen dejection. Melancholia such as this was a monster whose shadow must sooner or later fall on every person living in the house. No one, however self-possessed, could go unaffected for long. Nerves would tighten; tempers would fray as daily the strain grew. And to those who loved a man as cruelly affected as James Allister, the tension would grow unbearable. Mary came inevitably into his thoughts, and he winced as he remembered the news he had to give her.

He studied the figure in the armchair, trying to see him not as a patient but as a man, a great musician. In the soft lamplight, helped by the deeper glow of the fire, he saw a pale, sensitive face with deep-set black eyes overshadowed by a broad, high forehead. James Allister was thirty-eight, three years older than Evans himself. He was a man of medium height, small-boned, with the hands of an artist. He bore a resemblance to his brother Frank, except that his face had not the cynical, weather-beaten lines of the latter, being smoother and more aesthetic in appearance. His eyes were the outstanding features of an extremely handsome face. They were an intense black, and in animated moments shone like polished jet. The very flame of creation itself seemed to burn behind them. At his best, the composer possessed an unusual charm of manner.

John Evans had never known him well

in the past, yet at their few meetings had been impressed by the immense, restless vitality of the man. True, his history showed a strain of instability: there had been that breakdown in his youth and he had been subject to moods of depression when all was not going well with his works, but these indications alone were not enough to explain his present state. No one who had known him before the war had regarded his moods as anything extraordinary but merely the temperamental displays one expects occasionally from the artistic mind. And at his best he had been gay, vital, and tremendously confident—the very antithesis of the disconsolate, brooding neurotic he had now become. Women had found his charm irresistible, and he had been greatly in demand at social gatherings. His famous Night concerto and his Second symphony, both published in the first year of the war, had established his virtuosity and brought him world renown.

None of this fame and distinction appeared to have changed him. He had not even bothered to move his headquarters to London, being quite content to work at home and keep a small flat in the West End to accommodate him during business trips. In taste he seemed to have been both moderate and well judged.

Such was the composite picture of the musician that the doctor had built up, partly from his own knowledge and partly from the expositions of others, in particular Mary. Now, as he gazed on the musician's moody face, he wondered for the hundredth time what the exact cause for such a degeneration could be.

Could it have been his war experiences? He had been wounded and captured and had spent a year in a prison camp. Could that have caused it? No; that was not enough in itself although the wound would have lowered his level of general health. But his treatment in the military hospital had been chiefly for his mental condition —John had established that from the Army authorities. Then had he undergone some other worse experience of which his family knew nothing?

He would have seen his share of horror and suffering and his mind would have been affected to some extent. From the doctor's own experiences—he had served with the 14th Army in Burma—he knew that no man came back from war entirely unchanged. There was always some effect. In James's case it was the degree of that effect that was in question. It was no argument to insist that other men, millions of them, had returned home comparatively normal. Minds were not all alike in their structure. What held for one mind, for ten thousand minds, by no means held for the mind of an artist. The resistance of the cliffs below the house to the pounding of the great waves tonight would depend upon their substance. Where it was insensitive rock, they would emerge from the ordeal unharmed, but where there was soft and fertile earth the waves would hungrily bite and suck. So it was with the brain. The brutal, gouging fingers of war could find little in the dull brain to damage, but among the hair-sprung, delicate mechanism of the genius there were many cogs to strip, many spindles to break. . . .

And yet John, without knowing why, did not believe the war was wholly to blame for James's present condition. Unless—and he made this mental reservation—unless he had passed through some abnormal experience. But it was all supposition, he thought wearily. The cause he did not know but the cure had been given him, and the nature of it he had to pass on to Mary before the night was over. He winced again at the remembrance.

There was a patter of feet down the hall and Mrs. Allister hurried into the lounge. John turned.

"Good evening, Mrs. Allister," he said.

The old woman's myopic eyes were all for her son; they barely brushed the doctor before settling on the armchair. Her voice was equally abstracted.

"Oh; good evening, Doctor."

She shuffled anxiously by to James, who looked up at the sound of her voice.

"Hello, Mother," he muttered. John noticed a flicker of interest in his eyes. The old woman leaned over him solicitiously.

"I'm sorry I wasn't here to meet you, dear, but you came just as I was upstairs changing my dress. How are you feeling now?"

James shifted irritably in his chair. "Vile," he complained. "My head's splitting. And I want to start work. . . ." He twisted round in his chair, scowling at the door. "Where is that confounded tea? Mary said it was ready."

"They're coming through with it now," his mother soothed. "But you mustn't work tonight, dear. You've done quite enough for one day. Have your dinner, have a nice read in front of the fire, and go to bed early. Don't you agree, Doctor Evans?"

John cleared his throat, choosing his words carefully. "I certainly wouldn't work. But then I'm not a composer."

"He shouldn't, should he?" the old woman insisted. "Didn't the specialist say he must have plenty of rest? He must have said so," she went on irritably when John hesitated. "It's as clear as crystal that he is working too hard."

John was relieved of making a reply by the arrival of the tea-wagon. Mary wheeled it in, followed by Stella.

"This will make you feel better, dear," Mrs. Allister declared, fussing over the cups. As she was pouring the tea John caught Mary's eye and motioned her to follow him. He moved unnoticed into the hall. A few seconds later she joined him.

"I must go now, Mary," he told her.

"I'm late as it is. I'll come back tonight and talk to you. Will that be all right?"

"Of course. And you'll tell me the treatment for James. . . ?"

He nodded. "Yes. And please—when I come—arrange for me to see you alone."

Her hand lifted involuntarily to her throat, and her cheeks paled. He cursed inwardly.

"What is it, John?" she whispered.

"Now don't be frightened. It is just that one has to discuss these things in private."

"Very well," she said quietly, her eyes searching his face anxiously. "What time will you come?"

"About nine. Now cheer up. Everything is going to be all right."

"Is it?" she whispered.

"Of course it is. Keep your chin up."

"Hurry back, won't you? And . . . thanks for everything."

He smiled at her, then went to the lounge door.

"Good night," he called to those inside the room. "I have to go now. Please excuse me."

"Aren't you staying for tea, after all?" Mrs. Allister complained, turning to him.

"You can't go yet. You haven't told us what to do for James."

"I'll see to all that," John smiled. "Good night, all."

He came back to Mary who was standing by the front door. "Good-bye for now," he whispered. "Don't worry."

She nodded, trying to smile. He paused with one hand on the door-handle, then ran out into the darkness.

Mary closed the door. She listened to the sound of his receding car before returning to the lounge. Mrs. Allister turned towards her as she entered.

"That's a very off-hand way to treat people," she complained. "It's no use, Mary. I can't help feeling you should have got an older doctor. He seems so young and irresponsible."

"He looks anything but irresponsible to me," Stella drawled. "I should say he was very competent."

Mary threw her a grateful glance but the old lady turned on her petulantly. "We've been waiting anxiously all day for news of James and now he goes dashing off without saying a word. I don't see anything competent about that. . . ."

"He's coming back later tonight to see me," Mary said.

"But why can't he tell us now? Don't we matter at all?"

"He has his surgery, Mother. He's late for it now."

Mrs. Allister turned to James, who was sipping his tea morosely, taking no notice whatsoever of their conversation.

"Don't work tonight, dear," she said in coaxing tones. "Have a rest, for my sake."

At the mention of the word work, his head lifted. "I must work," he muttered. "You don't understand. . . ."

"But you mustn't, dear," his mother wailed. "You'll only make your head worse."

"I'm going to work," he said sullenly.

Mary drew nearer. "There's an excellent play on the wireless tonight, James. One of Ibsen's—*The Lady from the Sea*. Wouldn't you care to listen to it?"

His face suddenly contorted. He brought his cup down on its saucer with such violence that the china cracked. He directed the whole of his fury at Mary.

"What is the matter with you? Why are you always trying to stop me working?

Don't you like my music? That's the reason. I know. I know. . . ." His voice rose into a scream.

The blood drained from Mary's face. "I'm sorry, dear," she whispered. "Of course it isn't that. You know I like your music. I only want you to rest—just the same as mother does."

"Leave me alone," he shouted. "Keep your advice to yourself. I don't want any of it. And keep out of my study tonight."

With a muttered curse he jumped to his feet, pushed by them and stumbled into the hall. They heard his study door close with a slam.

Mary reached for the arm of a chair and leaned against it. Her whole body was shaking violently, and she felt sick with shock. Stella made a movement towards her, then crossed over to the sideboard, where she pulled out a bottle of brandy and two glasses.

Mrs. Allister stood gaping at the door. Her pale eyes were enormous behind her thick lenses. Slowly she sank into a chair, fumbling for her handkerchief. A few seconds later the sound of her weeping filled the room.

Stella raised her eyes to the ceiling in mute supplication. She half-filled a glass with neat brandy and brought it over to Mary.

"Drink it," she snapped as the other woman shook her head. Mary obeyed at last, grimacing at the strength of the spirit. Colour slowly came back to her cheeks. She drew in a long, shuddering breath.

Stella turned to the old woman. "Do you want one too?" she asked.

"You know I never take drink," Mrs. Allister wailed. "Oh; the poor boy. . . ."

"I thought you might think this a good time to start," Stella said unfeelingly. She looked at Mary. "Has it helped?"

Mary smiled her thanks. Stella returned to the sideboard, filled the other glass, and swallowed deeply.

"It has its uses," she said bitterly.

Mrs. Allister's sobs became more assertive. "Oh; the poor boy. He must be in awful pain. He can't rest . . . his nerves are in a dreadful state. What are we going to do?" She dabbed at her nose, then raised her tear-stained face to Mary.

"You must try not to annoy him," she wailed. "You mustn't try to persuade him against his will. I've told you before—it only makes him worse."

"My God!" Stella said.

Mary did not answer. Her face was white again. She turned and walked from the room like an automaton. Stella heard her footsteps, walking as far as the stairs and then breaking into a run. She made as if to follow her, then drew slowly back. She picked up her glass, stared at its contents with bitter eyes, and in one swift movement drained it dry. It was a gesture almost of abandonment. Then, without a backward glance at the weeping woman, she walked from the room.

4

AN hour after dinner Frank came out from the library with a book under his arm. From the study alongside the sound of James's piano could be heard, and he stopped to listen a moment before walking across the hall into the lounge. The fire had burned low, and he built it up with loving care before settling down into an armchair. With a sigh of satisfaction, he lit his pipe and settled down to his book.

A quarter of an hour passed, and then the door opened. Frank looked up and rose to his feet. Mary was standing in the doorway.

"Come in and sit down," he said. "You're looking all in."

"I don't like disturbing you," she smiled. "You're looking so comfortable."

He waved aside her apologies and drew up the other armchair. "There'll be a rattling good fire in a few minutes," he told her. "I've been building it up scientifically."

"You do like your coal fires, don't you?" she laughed, seating herself.

"Those effeminate electric things don't get through my thick hide," he grinned. He did not ask her what she wanted of him. It was better to let her choose her time, he decided. He offered her a cigarette.

"Have one," he said. "It will help to drown the smell of this thing"—pointing to his pipe.

She took one and accepted his light with an air of preoccupation. He could see she was listening. The sound of the piano came louder for the moment and she started slightly. Then she saw his gaze on her, and inhaled deeply on her cigarette to cover her embarrassment.

Frank inclined his head to the door. "He's at it again, I hear," he said.

She nodded slowly.

"What is he working on now?"

"A symphony," she told him quietly.

"How is it going? Is it nearly finished?"

She moved her hands despairingly. "I don't know, Frank. He never discusses his

90

work with me these days. I hear a good deal of it, of course."

He nodded grimly. "I know you do. During the nights, in that bedroom of yours. It must be murder there, right over his study. You should move into one of the spare rooms."

"I don't mind," she said slowly. She did not tell him that she could not have borne to be anywhere else. To lie at nights and not know what was happening. . . .

He puffed thoughtfully at his pipe for a few moments. "You know, it's queer when you come to think of it. Here I am, with a brother hailed as the leading composer in the country, and I'm hardly able to appreciate a note he writes. It's funny, isn't it?"

"We can't all be musical," she said quietly. "Perhaps it is just as well."

"You love music, don't you?" he said abruptly, looking at her. "The kind he writes, I mean."

She nodded without speaking.

"It must be rather wonderful for him to be able to write music that holds you spellbound. There can't be many husbands lucky enough to have such a hold over their wives."

She smiled at him. "It's a very romantic thought, Frank; but I really don't think husbands write music for their wives, do you? I don't think they know they have wives when they are working."

"I don't see why they should not," he reflected whimsically. He paused and looked at her curiously. "Am I imagining things or is his music beginning to change? I don't know what you call it professionally, but lately it has sounded different. . . . Have you noticed it?"

He had said the wrong thing. He saw the pain in her eyes, and went on hastily.

"I don't mean it isn't as good. As a matter of fact, in one way it sounds more alive—it has more body in it, if you know what I mean."

"I know what you mean," she said quietly. "It's quite true. It is wilder, more passionate music. Wonderful music, but desperate. It frightens me. Sometimes it sounds so reckless and abandoned, as if he were trying to run away from himself and the world about him. . . . The symphony he is writing now is a perfect example of it."

Frank shifted uncomfortably. "Not all his music," he protested. "Some of it I like. There is one thing—I haven't heard it for some time—that even I can appreciate. I don't know what you'd call it, but it has a slow movement and a very attractive melody. It's sad, but it's very beautiful. I wouldn't call that piece reckless or abandoned."

"That's a new concerto," she said softly. "It is beautiful. I love it, although it sometimes sends a shudder through me. It's so terribly sad and lonely. . . . But I love it because it is not wild like the symphony. It's sane. . . ." Her voice was a bare whisper as she finished speaking. Frank did not look at her. He kept his eyes on the fire.

"It's not finished," Mary went on. "Somehow I want him to finish that one piece of music more than anything else in the world. But he seldom plays it now. I think he realizes he can't complete it."

"Doesn't that prove his music isn't deteriorating?" Frank argued. "If he can make me like something he has written, he must be improving."

She tried to smile. "Oh; it isn't that I think his music isn't as good as it used to be. It may even be better in its way. But it has changed—it is more elemental, more Wagnerian. That's what frightens me."

"The concerto isn't wild," he insisted. "You've just said so yourself."

"Not the concerto," she agreed, smiling wistfully. "That's why I love it so much. But I never hear it nowadays."

He coughed and knocked his pipe against the hearth. "Don't worry too much. You'll hear it again. He'll complete it one of these days, perhaps sooner than you think. I shouldn't worry. Ill health can play the devil with one's nerves. When I was in hospital I was gloomier than a London fog. If I'd have been a composer there would have been some pretty weird stuff put out. Probably all he needs is a couple of months' rest and a change of scenery."

Mary stared down at the cigarette in her hand. "I wish I could believe it, Frank. But look at all the treatment he has had since the war. None of it has made a scrap of difference. In fact he is ten times worse now than when he came out of the prison camp."

"I know," Frank muttered. "But don't give up hope. He's in good hands and they'll put him right. I'm as worried about you as I am of him. Much more of his nonsense and you'll be having a breakdown. Stella tells me he went for you again before dinner."

She nodded. "Yes; he did." She looked at him pleadingly. "That's what I can't understand, Frank. Why does he attack me more than anyone else? Tonight I only added to what mother had said, and yet he flew at me. Sometimes I think he hates me."

"You bother with him too much," Frank growled. "When he takes a bite at me, I tell him to go to hell, and leave him to work it off. You try to pacify him, and the ungrateful devil takes another crack at you. I'm not sure you treat him the right way by giving in to his moods. A good dressing-down might do him the world of good."

"No, Frank. He is very ill. And"— her voice almost broke—"he doesn't remember anything about these moods afterwards. That's the most frightening thing of all."

Frank nodded slowly. "Well; we'll see what Evans has to say. He is coming tonight, isn't he?"

"Yes; at any time now. He said about nine o'clock." She hesitated, then turned to him. "Do me a favour tonight. John asked if he could see me alone, and I'm afraid mother will come dashing through as soon as he arrives. Will you try to—?"

"Hold her down?" Frank broke in with a grin. "Leave that to me. Ethel's back and the two of 'em are in the drawing-room now. I'll keep 'em both in there until you have finished."

She smiled her thanks. Frank looked at her reflectively. "You know, you're a lucky person to know a chap like Evans," he said. "He seems a good type to me. I like the way he is taking all this trouble over James. You have known him a long time, haven't you?"

"We grew up together," Mary told him. "You didn't see much of him before the war because he left for university just after you all came to live here, and during the war he was out in the East for four years."

Frank nodded, eyeing her whimsically. "I don't think father did him a good turn when he brought us all here. You wouldn't have met James otherwise, would you?"

"No; I don't suppose I would."

"But because of father, you did, and bang went Evans's dream. He is in love with you yet, you know."

Mary started, then flushed with embarrassment. "No, Frank . . ."

"He is," Frank said with conviction. "But there's no need to feel ashamed about it. It isn't your fault, or his, for that matter. It's just one of those things. I like Evans."

"I believe he is a very good doctor," Mary murmured.

"I shouldn't be surprised. He took over his father's practice, didn't he?"

Mary nodded.

"I don't envy him," Frank said. "The older people will always think of him as a little boy. You see it with mother. She probably saw him as a university student, and still thinks of him as one."

"It is true," Mary agreed. "He has told

me he runs into a good deal of that prejudice."

"It's always the same," Frank grunted. "These old stodgers never change. Talking of stodgers"—and he grinned—"do you know Ethel has been priming mother to get rid of the Ashburns?"

"Oh, yes; I had all that earlier," Mary said wearily.

"Do you think they worry James?"

"It's so hard to say. . . . He hasn't grumbled yet, so I don't think they can do. I sometimes wonder if he knows they are still here. Most of the time when he is not working he seems to be in a stupor."

"I don't think they have worried him," Frank said. "In any case, we can hardly tell 'em to go. They've only been here a week."

"The thing I'm most afraid of is that they do annoy him one night, and he comes in and insults them. That can happen at any time, of course."

Frank grinned. "Well; don't go worrying about that. That's Stella's baby. In any case, I think the Ashburns have pretty thick skins. There wouldn't be any permanent harm done."

He was watching Mary's hands. They were picking nervously at the fringed surround of a cover that lay over the arm of her chair. He saw her eyes stray again to the grandfather clock that stood near the door. It was ten minutes past nine. He leaned forward, trying to keep her mind off the waiting.

"Stella seems pretty jumpy these days," he said. "Have you noticed?"

Mary looked at him in surprise. "Stella? I can't say I have. I've noticed she seems bored, but I haven't noticed anything wrong with her nerves."

"She's as jumpy as a cat," Frank declared. "It might do her good to have these relations here for another couple of weeks."

"What do you think is wrong with her? Is she lonely?"

Frank shrugged. "Country life, perhaps. She's essentially city-bred. But every now and then I get the idea it's something deeper than that."

"She may be missing David more than we think."

Frank frowned. He looked down at his pipe, then up at her wryly.

"Do you believe that?"

"What do you mean?"

"I wouldn't say this to anyone else in the house," he said softly, "but do you think David and Stella were suited? You met David a few times—you know the kind of boy he was."

Mary hesitated. "I don't know. It's hard to say."

"I knew David well—he was my kid brother. Oh; a nice lad, but not strong enough for her. She is all fire and dash and devil, and he was only a shy, gentle boy. He could never have managed her. That's my opinion, anyway."

"Yet they married," she reminded him.

"Oh; in wartime everyone goes crazy. He was a good-looking boy and his nice Air Force uniform probably did the rest. She probably was fond of him. But it wouldn't have lasted if Dave had come through the war."

"You don't know," Mary said quietly. "And you mustn't ever say this to mother. She would turn on Stella immediately."

"Don't worry; I'm not such a fool. In any case," he went on quietly, "I like

100

Stella. It wasn't her fault any more than his."

"You're only guessing this, aren't you? How do you know they weren't happy?"

"I didn't say they weren't happy," he corrected her. "I said they weren't suited, and if they had lived together long enough it would have shown up. David hadn't a pair of reins strong enough to hold Stella, and she would have broken loose sooner or later. But neither of them was to blame. Their marriage was no more of a mistake than thousands of others during the war."

He wasn't doing at all well tonight, he thought grimly as he watched her sad eyes staring into the fire. He could follow her thoughts as clearly as if they were being read out aloud to him. She was seeing her own marriage as another wartime failure. He could see it in the droop of her shoulders, the sad veiling of her eyes. He shook his pipe at her sternly.

"Get that bee out of your bonnet, Mary. It has nothing to do with James's affection for you. It is just that you see more of him than we do; and so he has more opportunities to snap at you. If you were to go away for a few weeks, he would be screaming his head off for you."

Longing shone behind her eyes as she smiled at him. "You are being very nice, Frank. It's very mean of me not to believe you. I'll try. Really I will."

"The two of you should never have come back here," Frank said gruffly. "This is no place for a chap like James, either. He belongs to London; he should be among gaiety and culture. I know you came for mother's sake, but it was a mistake."

"I know," she murmured. "But it is too late now. He won't hear of moving."

"Never mind. Evans may have something to say about that. If he says you must both go, James will have no alternative."

"I'm not sure he will go even then," Mary said anxiously. "I'm not sure he will take any notice of John. And mother is sure to try to hold him back."

"Well; I'm on your side," Frank said grimly. "I'll get him out if I have to pitch his piano into the snow."

Mary smiled her gratitude. They sat in silence for a while. Frank stirred the fire, making the flames leap up brightly. Outside, the wind growled and blustered. From the grandfather clock where the gaunt figure of Father Time swung his scythe with infinite patience, came a steady tick-tock, tick-tock. Frank saw Mary glance at it again.

A car engine sounded at last on the drive outside. Both relief and apprehension showed in Mary's eyes. She nodded to Frank's gesture.

"Yes, this will be John," she said, a faint breathlessness in her voice. "Excuse me a moment."

She was at the front door before the doctor reached it. She threw it open, shivering at the inrush of bitter night air. John ran up the steps.

"Sorry I'm late," he said, closing the door behind him. "But I had a large surgery tonight."

"Take off your coat and come into the lounge," Mary told him.

He obeyed. As he entered the room he saw Frank rising from his armchair.

"Good evening," he greeted. "How are you?"

Frank grinned. "If you're asking me

professionally, I'm limping as well as ever. Otherwise I'm fine, thanks." He drew nearer. "I believe the news about James was encouraging?"

John's hesitation was almost imperceptible. "There doesn't seem to be anything organically wrong with him."

"Good. Well; I suppose you'll be wanting a chat about him with Mary, so I'll run along now," Frank said, moving to the door. "Give me a call when you've finished, and I'll fix up coffee for you."

John replied apologetically. "That's very kind of you, but I doubt if I'll be able to stay long. I have a confinement coming up later tonight."

Frank shook his head. "It's badly arranged—the way women have their kids after working hours. Isn't there anything you can do about it? You don't think a campaign in the newspapers might help?"

"If there was any way of stopping it," John laughed, "we should have done it already. That I can assure you."

"I bet you would," Frank chuckled. "Well; cheerio." He went out, half-closed the door; then called back to Mary:

"Don't worry about the interference. I'll handle it."

"Thanks, Frank," Mary smiled.

John turned away as the door closed and approached the fire, making a pretence of warming his hands. Mary's eyes followed him, noticing his ill-concealed air of discomfort as he stood upright and fumbled in his pocket for his cigarette-case. As she approached he held out the case to her. She shook her head. He took a cigarette himself, taking an excessively long time to light it. She put one hand lightly on his arm, speaking quietly.

"What is it, John? What have you to tell me? I know it is something rather unpleasant. . . ."

Surprise showed on his open face. "Know? How can you know?"

Pain at the confirmation of her fears made her wince slightly. "Your voice on the 'phone this afternoon; your appearance now. . . . When you have known a person for a long time, John, it isn't easy to keep things from them."

"No," he muttered. "I suppose it isn't." He inhaled deeply on his cigarette and moved restlessly across the room. "How has he been since he arrived home?"

"Not too good," she told him quietly. "I asked him to rest tonight, and he turned on me. He is in his study working now."

John's lips tightened. "What did he say?"

"Oh; the usual thing. That I hate his music; that I'm always trying to stop him working. His mother asked him to rest and he said nothing to her, but the moment I spoke . . ." She shook her head wearily. "But don't worry about it. Tell me what the specialist said."

He shifted restlessly. "You'll have to take more care of yourself. If you aren't careful, you'll be cracking up next."

"John," she said quietly. "What is it? Why are you so afraid to tell me? Is it so very bad? I'm ready to hear, you know. I've been waiting for this ever since you 'phoned. And I can't bear to wait much longer."

He moved back to the fireplace, put his arms on the mantelpiece and laid his forehead on them. He stood there, staring down.

"It's hard, Mary. It's hard to be both a friend and a doctor."

She closed her eyes for a moment. "I know. I know how hard it must be. But, whatever happens, I want you to know this. That I would rather trust him with you than anybody else."

"Thank you." His voice was low, unsteady.

"Now please. . . . Tell me everything."

He raised his head and turned to her. "Very well. It isn't as much what Hartley said this afternoon, Mary, although he confirmed it. It is the verdict of all the psychiatrists who have examined him recently. They have sent in their signed case notes for me and Hartley to read. James hasn't a tumour, but he has to have an operation—a leucotomy operation."

Her face paled. "An operation! But why? Why, if there is no tumour?"

"He has a severe mental disorder, and the only chance of clearing it is by operating on him."

She shook her head faintly, in bewilderment. "Go on," she faltered. "Tell me everything."

His words came quickly now. "It's a

fairly modern operation but is being performed quite frequently in mental hospitals today. It is an operation on the pre-frontal lobes of the brain to free the patient of tension and depression."

"Is it dangerous?"

"With Hartley operating, James should be safe enough."

"And afterwards? Will it cure him?"

"We can't make any guarantees, Mary. No one can with brain operations. But all the specialists are very hopeful that it will clear his trouble."

"And if it does cure him, will he be normal in every way?"

John lifted his cigarette to his mouth and sucked on it deeply. "It all revolves round that word normal, Mary. James is no normal man. He is a great musician; I think we can call him a genius. Normality in him would be abnormality in others. That is our problem."

"I don't understand you. What are you trying to tell me?"

He shook his head unhappily. "It's not easy. I've been trying for days to find words to explain it. It is my duty to warn you of all the risks of the operation before it is performed, and yet I am not sure of all the risks, for that matter neither are the specialists. Doctors are not prophets, Mary. Much of their knowledge is obtained from trial and error. From the results of previous operations they can base their theories on those to follow. But how many world-famous composers require leucotomy operations? That is the trouble; James's case is almost unique."

"Are you telling me that his chances of recovery are less than an ordinary man's?"

"No. It isn't that. What I am saying is that, after a leucotomy, a patient is sometimes left with a lethargy and if this happened to James it would destroy his creative ability. But even without that lethargy it might still affect it to some degree. I have to warn you of that."

She stared at him in horror. "Why, that would be like death to him. Music is his life; it would be murder to take it away. He would be deaf and dumb and blind without it. You can't do that to him. You can't risk it."

"We have no alternative, Mary," he said sadly. "Everything else has been tried and has failed."

"But he'll never agree to it when you tell him. You know he won't."

John winced as he answered. "I'm afraid he must not be told. The shock might be too much for him."

"But he must be told. You can't carry out an operation with risks like that without warning him."

His voice was very gentle, very sad. "You are going to have to be very brave, Mary. You see, it isn't James who has to give his permission; it is you. James is too far gone to make decisions for himself."

Her lips were ashen. "You're not saying. . . ? Oh, no. No; you can't mean that."

"This is going to be a terrible shock to you, Mary. It is the reason I had to get him to Hartley." He took a deep breath as he turned and faced her. "In the considered opinion of all the specialists who have examined him recently, James is already insane. . . ."

5

THERE was a sudden hush in the room. The hiss of gas from a burning coal in the fire sounded like an indrawn breath. Mary took one blind, faltering step forward.

John watched her anxiously. "I'm so sorry, my dear," he muttered. "I would have given anything to have spared you this."

The thing he had said was like acid—it took time to eat through to the sensitive core of her mind. Her eyes widened in sudden agony.

"Insane! Oh, no. Dear God, no!"

John took her arm and led her to a chair. "Sit down. Please. I'm very worried about you, Mary."

She turned from him to the fire and stared blindly down into it.

"Insane," she breathed. Panic surged up within her and made her clutch his arm for protection. "I'm dreaming all this, aren't I?" she sobbed. "I'll wake up in a

111

moment to find it has all been a rather dreadful nightmare. Won't I, John?"

A deep shudder ran through him. It was the feel of that tremor through his arm that pulled her together. She stood motionless for a few seconds, then looked up at him apologetically.

"I'm sorry, John. I'm making it very diffcult for you, aren't I? I'm all right now. I won't be foolish again."

"I want you to be foolish," he said harshly. "I want you to cry. After this, I want you to go to your room and to cry as hard as you can. Don't try to be brave. Do you hear?"

She was not listening to him. Suddenly she took a deep breath and turned fiercely on him. "I don't believe it. It's not true. How could he talk to us, even the way he talked tonight, if he were insane?" Then she drew back at the expression on his face, her voice hushed. "You don't agree with them, do you?"

"I do, Mary. I'm sorry, but I do. I know how hard it is for you, but you must believe it."

"I'll never believe it. How could an insane man write such music as he is writing now? Some of it is wonderful. There's a piano concerto—it is so beautiful it tears at your heartstrings. How could an insane man do such work?"

He sighed. "That is no proof of his sanity, Mary, I'm afraid. But even that has been affected. You yourself told me his music had changed. This symphony he is working on—isn't it wild and elemental?"

Her shoulders sagged for a moment. "Yes. It is. . . ." Then her voice rose vehemently. "But it is still great music. It's full of the sea and the wind, the sky and the earth. It may be primeval, but it's magnificent. It may turn out to be the greatest thing he has ever done."

"I know it is hard to understand," he answered slowly. "The mind is so infinitely complex. Perhaps, when it suffers most, it touches the stars. Perhaps all great art comes from great suffering. None of us can say."

"But how could he talk the way he does if he were mad? He isn't always in a rage or depression."

"Insanity isn't a clear-cut thing, Mary. There are many degrees of it. I know he has lucid moments, but they are very infrequent now—you've often admitted it. Most of the time he is over the borderline and stumbling about in the shadows. Up to the present he has not gone too far into the darkness, but one of these days he will, and then it will be the end. Because somewhere back there in the darkness is a bottomless pit, and once he falls into that he is gone for ever. That is why he must have this operation, and have it quickly. It may be his last chance to avoid permanent insanity."

"Isn't there anything else you can try?" she begged.

"Everything else has been tried. Frankly, Mary; I had a shock the first time I examined him. I had no idea his condition was so serious. I wrote the Army medical authorities and they sent me a full case history of the treatment given him in Darley Hill. It had been most exhaustive and thorough, and yet he had shown no improvement. As you know, he left on his own insistence, but actually they had already given up hope of improving his condition with clinical methods. And, don't forget, his condition was not as serious then as it is now. That was why the psychiatrist and neurologist I called in, although both eminent men, were not in the least optimistic of getting any better results, although they tried hard enough."

"What did they do; what did they give him?"

"Immobilization, drugs. . . ."

"What drugs?"

"Drugs such as sodium amytal, ether, pentothal. The psychiatrists use them to lull the patient's conscious mind. Then they ask questions to find out if there is some deep-rooted repression which is causing the disorder. Sometimes it works, but not always. So much depends on the patient's will-power, the quality of his mind, and, of course, the degree of his desire to keep his repression secret. They had no success with James. They could get very little from him under anaesthesia, and what they did get was no use. He has no ordinary brain."

"What about this shock treatment I have read about?"

"Yes. That was tried here too, in the short time he gave them. But he had already been given a thorough course of it in the Military Hospital without success.

He has had everything, Mary. Although he walked out of the nursing home, the psychiatrists had already decided it was useless to continue on clinical lines. They had decided his mind had gone too far and that a leucotomy was his only chance. That was the report submitted to Hartley and he confirmed it."

"So you think he has some repression?" she asked, trying to keep her voice steady.

"Yes. They all say his condition is psychological. It's a terribly difficult case, Mary. In almost every way his mind is different from the average mind. It is more perceptive and sensitive, and also more fragile. That explains his genius but it also may explain his condition today. Some types of shock might have a more profound effect on him than they would on others. But quite apart from his state of mind, there is his bodily health to consider. His wound, his imprisonment, all the work he does, and then his mental condition: they have all taken a tremendous toll."

"If his condition is low, won't the operation be dangerous?"

"No. I'm not worried about that."

"Try rest," she pleaded. "Surely a few more weeks cannot make so much difference."

John shook his head grimly. "No. His mind wouldn't be resting, whatever his body was doing. In fact it would be worse; it would be fretting to work. His case is urgent, Mary. It is imperative you realize that."

"But, John; think what you are asking me to do. To agree to an operation that will take from him the thing he loves most in life. How can I agree? What right have I?"

"It may not take it away. It may not affect him at all."

"Oh, yes, it will. I feel it will. And it's cruel—viciously cruel. Why must it be that one thing—the thing that has brought such beauty into the world? Why must that be the price he has to pay?"

"He may not pay that price. It may never happen. But it is my duty to warn you of all the dangers."

"What do you think?" she demanded. "Do you think it will?"

He made a few uneasy steps across the room before answering. "There is a

117

chance, I admit. It is the fineness of James's mind which gives him his creative gift, and leucotomy does sometimes have a coarsening effect. But James is an almost unique case—no one can say one way or the other."

"It will destroy it," she said dully. "I feel it will."

He walked towards her and put his hands gently on her trembling shoulders. "Mary; you mustn't look upon this as something to which you can say yes or no. You have no alternative. If he doesn't have the operation he will grow rapidly worse until . . ." He finished the sentence with a hopeless shrug of his shoulders.

"Until he goes permanently insane," she breathed.

"You have no alternative," he said again.

She moved like someone in a nightmare. "I haven't, have I? Either way I destroy his mind."

"The operation won't destroy his mind. We are all very hopeful that it will cure him."

"Without his music he will be dead. Music is his life."

"If it were to go, it wouldn't be the end of everything. There are other things in life worth living for. He would find them in time. He would be infinitely happier than he is now. He would have peace of mind."

"Peace of mind?" She laughed wildly. "When he had discovered what he had lost? He'd curse me, John. He'd hate me, and he'd hate me more as the years went by."

"No, he wouldn't. He would understand it had been done for his own good. Perhaps he would not even bother about it. Perhaps the desire to compose might leave him completely, so that he wouldn't care. . . ."

She shuddered. "Don't, please. That would be even worse. It would be bad enough to see the look in his eyes when he knew what I had done to him, but even that would show he had some emotion left. But to see nothing at all: to see the dumbness of a ruined brain that had forgotten its own greatness—that would be hell itself. I would feel like Delilah."

"Don't use the word ruined, Mary. It's too severe."

"Without music his brain would be ruined."

"But you have no alternative," he reminded her. "Therefore, even if this did happen—and it may not—you could never blame yourself."

"I can't believe it," she cried. "I can't believe there isn't some other way he can be cured. How long will it be before his mind goes permanently—a week, a month, a year?"

John shook his head. "No one can answer that, Mary. No one knows how long a man can wander among the fringes of insanity before going over for good. But Hartley wants the operation within two weeks. That will give you an idea of the urgency. You can't risk waiting. The dangers are too great."

"Two weeks!"

He nodded grimly.

"I can't believe he is as bad as that. Don't put the onus on me, John. It's too cruel. Wait until he is in a rational mood and then put the whole thing to him. He might listen to you."

"Mary; I keep telling you he is too far

gone for that. At the moment he is insane. I have to get him certified."

"Certified!" Her eyes dilated with shock.

"Of course. No surgeon would dream of operating on anyone, much less a person as eminent as James, without certification. Otherwise, when James has recovered, he might sue the surgeon for malpractice. The surgeon has to cover himself legally."

She leaned weakly against the fireplace, trying to digest all she had heard. John stood by helplessly, waiting for her to speak.

"You've hit me very hard tonight, John," she said at last.

He winced. "I know. And I've hated every minute of it. But it is my duty to tell you everything."

"James—to be certified. I can't believe it. I have to get used to the idea." She turned to him. "If he is certified, does that mean I need not give permission—that you can do it of your own accord?"

Even that pathetic plea was denied her.

"No, Mary. I'm afraid we should still need your signed permission."

"Have you done anything about the certification yet?"

"No, not yet. I thought it better to see both you and Hartley first."

She tried to clear her dazed brain. "What has brought it on, John? What has happened to him?"

He cleared his throat. "He has had a severe mental shock, probably during the war. And, of course, his history is unstable —that breakdown in his youth. . . ."

"What kind of mental shock?"

"I'd prefer not to answer that yet, Mary. There is a theory, but all the case notes of the psychiatrists are with Hartley at the moment. I shall be getting a report from him in a day or two. I'll try and answer you then."

"Then don't do anything until you see me again," she begged, clutching at the respite.

He hesitated, studying her. She had had more than enough for one night, he decided. After months of worry and strain this shock had been an almost unbearable one. It would be better to give her a little time. He could not safely ask more of her tonight.

"All right. I'll come round when I have Hartley's report, and we'll talk more about it then. But in the meantime I want you to be very careful. Don't do or say anything to upset James, and don't be left alone with him in the house. If he shows any change whatsoever, 'phone me at once."

She gave a sightless smile. "You're not saying that he might attack me, are you?"

"I'm telling you the dangers Mary. They are very real ones. Be careful."

"I will be," she whispered.

He smiled anxiously at her then turned towards the door. "I must go now. Heaven only knows how my confinement is getting on."

Mary followed him, hesitated, then touched his arm, almost shyly. "Tell me one thing more, John, before you go. Why does he turn on me so often? Why am I the one he always attacks? I want to know that very badly."

He took her hand between his own. "It is a cruel thing, I know, but sufferers of the mind do very often turn on the people they love best. That is the only comfort I can offer you, Mary."

"Dear John," she whispered. "Is that true or are you just being very kind to me? I'll never know, will I?"

He gripped her hand tightly, then released it as a knock sounded on the door. Stella entered, glancing at them casually.

"Sorry to butt in," she said. "But I left my cigarettes on the sideboard and couldn't hold out any longer for a smoke."

"Have one of mine," John said, offering her his case.

She paused, then approached him, the blue housecoat she was wearing swirling round her slim legs.

"Any more news of James?" she asked casually as she accepted John's match.

John hesitated, his gaze wandering to Mary and then back to the girl. "No doubt Mary will tell you later. I have to run along now."

Mary started at his words. "I forgot to ask you. What should I do? Have I to tell them or not?"

"It's difficult to say," he muttered. "You don't want any hysteria to make things worse for you tonight. His mother might take it badly. And you mustn't let any of them influence you. But it would be as well to warn them, in case they do anything to upset him."

Mary nodded. Stella stared from one to the other. "This sounds pretty mysterious. Is anything wrong?"

Mary turned to her in sudden decision. "Do me a favour, Stella. Please ask the others to wait in the drawing-room until I come through. Mother might be going to bed otherwise. Tell them I have some further news about James."

"But what's wrong now?" Stella muttered, a shadow appearing between her eyes. "I thought he was going to be all right."

"Please," Mary said quietly. "I'll tell you everything in a moment."

She shrugged. "All right. I'll tell them." She went to the door, gave them both a sullen stare, then went out. They heard her high heels tapping across the hall to the drawing-room. A chatter of shrill voices came to them as the other door opened, then died into silence.

John looked at Mary. "You should have waited until the morning," he said sternly. "You don't know how Mrs. Allister will take it, and you've had quite enough for one day."

She waved aside his protests. "I'd rather get it over now. Do you think I should tell them that you all believe he is already insane?"

He frowned. "I don't know, although they'll have to find out. If you do tell them, warn them to be careful what they say to others outside the family. We want to keep everything hushed up. And tell them to be most careful not to irritate him in any way."

She nodded, then took his arm and led him to the front door. "Don't make yourself late for me, John."

"I'll be round again as soon as I have Hartley's report," he told her. "Probably on Saturday morning. Now don't forget. Let me know immediately if anything unusual happens. And be careful."

He paused in the porch and gave her a bromide. "Take it tonight. Promise?"

She gave him a half-smile as she took it. "Don't worry. I'll be all right."

He gave her a last anxious look before turning away. She closed the door, hesitated a moment, then returned to the lounge. She needed a few minutes to gather herself together before facing the family in the drawing-room. Resting her head against the mantelpiece she stared down at the reddening fire. A coal fell with a sudden rustle on to the hearth. A flame leapt up from it brightly, faltered, flared up vainly again, and died. She watched the coal turning stark and grey with something near horror in her eyes. Wrenching herself away, she walked unsteadily towards the door.

6

"I SUPPOSE Mary will come and tell us the news." Mrs. Allister's voice was impatient and complaining as she broke off her chattering to Ethel for a moment and turned to Frank.

Frank lowered his book. "If there is anything worth telling us I suppose she will," he said evenly.

"I don't understand all this secrecy," Ethel broke in. "Why couldn't Evans have told us all? We've as much right as Mary to know what's wrong with James. Personally, I've always thought Mary had a nerve in the first place. She should have asked our opinion before choosing a doctor—not gone running straight to him."

Frank shrugged in amusement. "Seeing Evans is just about the only doctor in Rombury under seventy, I don't suppose she felt the need for it. He was a natural choice."

"She called him in because he is her

friend," Ethel said. "That was her only reason."

"And what better one could she have?" Frank asked belligerently.

"Oh; you'll stick up for her," Ethel retorted. "We know that. I think it's an insult we aren't allowed to hear what he has to say. Look at the time. Mary knows well enough I have to get back home to Dick. . . ."

"She'll forgive you if you run along," Frank murmured. "We can ring you in the morning and give you the news."

Ethel's thin lips set tightly. Her hands settled more firmly on her ample lap.

"I shall go when I have heard about James," she said grimly. "And not a minute before."

Frank groaned inwardly. Keeping Ethel and his mother out of the lounge was no mean assignment, he thought ruefully. A quarter of an hour more and he could see himself having to use brute force.

He himself was wondering what Evans was taking so long to tell Mary. In spite of his seeming optimism, inwardly Frank was as alarmed about James as Mary herself. To him, the change in his brother was incomprehensible, and as the minutes went by he could not stifle the feeling that Mary may have been right in her surmise that John Evans had been holding something back over the telephone that afternoon.

He thought of the James he had known before the war, trying to reassure himself with the memory. Apart from that one nervous breakdown during his schooldays, his brother had not been abnormally sensitive. He had been temperamental, yes—Frank used the word for want of a better one—but his moods and depressions had been only transient things. Then what had happened to turn him into the sullen creature he was today, this brooding enigma who brought the coldness of uncertainty and fear into every room he entered? He had now become a stranger to his own family. Every sentence spoken in his presence had to be weighed and considered first: at any moment an unthinking word might precipitate a wild rage in which the composer seemed to lose all control of speech and action.

The worst of these moods, however, seemed reserved for Mary. The rest of the family were unlucky if they received more than an angry retort or a door slammed in their faces; but Mary was spared nothing. At times, James appeared to have the obsession that she hated his work, that her every thought and deed were designed to prevent it; while in truth she was a music-lover and immensely proud of his talent.

The unfairness of it made Frank's temper rise and his anxiety recede. Surely the man could pull himself together. He must be aware of the things he did and said. If he would leave his confounded piano alone for a while and show more appreciation to those who were trying to help him, one could feel more sympathy. Any man who worked with intense mental concentration for ten and twelve hours a day had to expect to go off the rails sooner or later. He owed it to his wife, whose life he was making into a hell, to ease up and regain his control again.

Here Frank paused in his thoughts, remembering he had denied that very argument earlier in the evening. In the old days James had always worked hard when on some major composition but his health had shown no signs of being adversely affected then. Occasionally, through sheer fatigue or irritation at some hindrance, he might have lost his temper or become depressed, but such moods had been very short-lived.

Then what was wrong now? Was it a flaw in his nature that had been accentuated by the war, by something he had seen or experienced? Was it his general health, his state of nerves? Or was it his brain that was degenerating—burning itself out with its own exertions?

Ethel's acid voice came to him, pricking like a pin through the blanket of his thoughts.

"If she doesn't come through in another five minutes, I'm going into see Evans myself. Why, they've been in there alone for over three-quarters of an hour now."

"You'd better not, dear," Mrs. Allister said nervously. "We don't want to go out of our way to offend him."

Ethel sniffed. "If Mary doesn't tell us anything, I shall go to his surgery and ask him. I'm beginning to wonder if they are discussing James at all. He might have made a social call instead."

"Stop talking rubbish," Frank muttered.

They all turned sharply as Stella entered. The girl came towards them.

"I've just seen Mary," she said shortly. "She wants you all to wait here until she comes through. She has some news about James."

Ethel bristled. "Wait here, indeed! You tell her that I've been here, on and off, since three o'clock this afternoon waiting to hear news of my own brother."

"Tell her yourself," Stella yawned, taking a chair beside Frank.

Ethel threw her a glare of dislike. Stella lit a cigarette and blew smoke vaguely in her direction.

"Have one?" she asked Frank, offering him her packet.

"Thanks." He looked at her questioningly. "Did Mary say anything else while you were in there?"

"She asked the doctor whether or not she should tell the family. He said he thought it might be as well, in case you do anything to upset him. Then she turned to me and said she had some more news of

James and would we wait. She looked pretty pale. That's all."

"Oh; I knew it. I knew it all the time. My poor boy. . . ." Mrs. Allister buried her face into her handkerchief, her thin shoulders shaking.

A car engine started up outside. As they listened, the sound receded down the drive. Frank put down his unlighted cigarette and rose.

"Where is Mary now? In the lounge?" he asked Stella.

"I suppose so. They were both in there a few minutes ago."

"I'd better go to her," he muttered. He limped hastily into the hall and made for the lounge. As he entered Mary was approaching the door. He noticed the pallor of her face with alarm.

"What is it?" he asked anxiously. "Is he worse than we think?"

"I'm afraid he is," she told him quietly. "I'm coming through now."

He followed her into the drawing-room. Mrs. Allister lifted her tear-stained face fearfully. Ethel drew herself grimly upright. Stella drew deeply on her cigarette.

"Sit there," Frank muttered, pointing to his chair.

Mary declined, choosing to stand at the far side of the round table. Her hands rested on its dark, polished top, and Frank noticed her knuckles standing out white and rigid. Although pale, her face was composed. The others had all swivelled round in their chairs and were facing her.

"As you all know," Mary began in a low but clear voice, "Doctor Evans has been round tonight to give me the latest report on James. I'm afraid what he has told me is going to be a shock to you all." Her gaze was on Mrs. Allister, whose watery eyes were enormous behind her thick glasses. "James has to have an operation —a leucotomy operation."

There was a shocked silence in the room, broken by a sudden outcry from Mrs. Allister. "Oh; the poor boy," she sobbed. "I knew there was something seriously wrong with him. I knew it wasn't just his temper. I told you all that—"

"Mother, please," Frank interrupted. "Let Mary finish. What is the trouble?" he asked Mary gently. "What is a leucotomy?"

"It is a brain operation, Frank. It's to—"

"A brain operation!" Mrs. Allister let out a scream. "You said he didn't have a tumour. You said there was nothing wrong with his brain."

"For God's sake be quiet and let Mary finish," Stella snapped.

The harshness of her words brought a fresh flood of tears to the old woman. Ethel turned sharply, her eyes like gimlets. Frank gave the girl a level, steady glance.

Stella lowered her head. "I'm sorry," she muttered. "But we want to hear what is wrong with him. Crying and yelling isn't going to do him any good."

Frank leaned forward and patted his mother's shoulder. "Come on, Mother," he urged. "Mary hasn't finished yet. Try to pull yourself together." He nodded at Mary to continue.

"It has nothing to do with a tumour," she went on quietly. "There is nothing organically wrong with him. But this operation is necessary to take away his headaches and his moods."

Mrs. Allister's sobs died down somewhat. "Is it a dangerous operation?" she managed.

"No. It isn't particularly dangerous."

The old woman began to quieten down. Frank looked at Mary with some surprise.

"The operation isn't to remove a growth, or anything like that?"

"No, Frank. John couldn't go into many details tonight, but he said it was carried out on the pre-frontal lobes of the brain. It frees the mind of tension."

"I see," he said slowly. "And it is absolutely necessary?"

"The specialists say it is. Everything else has been tried without success."

"What about after-effects?" Stella asked bluntly.

A spasm of pain crossed Mary's face. She nodded heavily at the question.

"I still have to mention that. I'm afraid this will be another shock to you."

Mrs. Allister drew in a sobbing breath. Ethel's lips tightened further, white spots appearing at their corners. Stella lowered her face over her cigarette. Frank waited, his body tensed.

"John says that after the operation . . ." Mary's voice faltered for only a second,

". . . there is a possibility—I think it is a strong possibility—that James will not be able to compose again."

There was a hush in the room as the four listeners strove to understand her. Mary felt detached, unreal. Her eyes travelled almost in curiosity from one face to another.

Mrs. Allister looked bewildered, fearful at the implications of her words. Ethel's waspish face was a mixture of puzzlement and vague alarm. Frank looked shocked. Stella's expression was indefinable. There was something of both bewilderment and apprehension in her eyes.

Mrs. Allister was the first to break the silence. "You're not saying he won't be normal, are you?" she quavered. "That he won't be his old self again?"

"No. If it is successful, he should lose his depression."

"And regain his health, lose his headaches, and be better-tempered again? He'll become a normal man again?"

"He'll be normal in the way you mean, yes."

The faces of all the three women before Mary relaxed. Relief showed on them all.

Only Frank remained tensed. Mrs. Allister sank back into her chair with a muttered sigh.

"That's all I want to know. Never mind about the music."

It was Mary's turn to look bewildered. She looked down at the old woman's relieved face, and her voice faltered again.

"Never mind!"

"Of course not. What is music beside his health?"

"I agree." Ethel spoke for the first time since Mary had entered the room. "His health is the important thing—his health and peace of mind. What does music matter beside that? I've always said it was all this hard work that was pulling him down. He would never have been allowed to do it if he had been my husband. No one can expect a person to work day and night without their nerves going eventually. I'll be glad if he has to stop it. He'll get a normal job like Frank and Dick and finish at five o'clock the way they do." There was a note of triumph in her voice as she finished speaking.

"You do all understand what I have

said?" Mary asked slowly. "That the operation may finish his career?"

Ethel stared at her with hostility. "Of course we understand. It's a pity, naturally, but it might have been a thousand times worse. His health and peace of mind are far more important than his career. You needn't worry about the money. He has already made enough to keep you comfortable for the rest of your life."

Mary looked as if she had been struck across the face. Without another word, she turned and left the room. With a curse Frank rose and limped after her. He followed her into the hall, calling after her. She walked on blindly. He half-ran and caught her arm as she was ascending the stairs.

"For God's sake don't take any notice of her," he gritted. "The bitch can't help talking like that. I know what's worrying you. You know James will never agree to the operation. And he won't—not if he is told what it might do to him."

Mary turned her agonized face to him. "No, Frank; it isn't that. I didn't get a chance to tell them the rest of it. James mustn't be told, or the shock might kill him. I have to give permission myself."

"You!" His face paled at the implications of her words. "But why? Why can't they ask him?"

"Because they say he is already insane, Frank," she sobbed. "John says he will have to be certified."

"Certified! Good God; you don't mean it!"

"John says that is the opinion of all the psychiatrists. They say his only hope is for him to have the operation. It is his last chance. Legally the surgeon can't operate until he is certified and until I have given my permission. Don't you see now. . . ? James wouldn't agree if he knew—you have just said so yourself—and yet I have to say yes. I have to betray him."

He caught his breath in sympathy. "I understand."

"They don't," she sobbed. 'They never will. They think I'm worried about money. Money . . . oh, God, how can people be like that? How can they think such things. . . ?"

"To hell with what they think," he snarled. "To hell with Ethel. Don't worry about them. . . ." Then he paused help-lessly. "But if what Evans says about James is true, then I don't see what alter-native you've got. If his mind has already gone and they are going to certify him—if the operation is his only chance—then you haven't any choice. You must find your comfort there. That's the way you must think of it."

She shook her head dully. "That's what John tells me; but I don't believe James is insane. I don't believe he could write music the way he does if he were out of his mind. I'll feel I'm betraying him, Frank. If he knew the risks, he would refuse; and I'll feel like a traitor when I lie to him and tell him he is having the oper-ation done to cure his headaches—when all the time it may mean that the thing he loves most in life may be cut from him. Can't you see how horrible it is?"

"Of course I can," he said gently. "When does the surgeon want to do the operation?"

"As soon as possible. Within two weeks."

He winced. "So soon!" His voice rose in anger. "Why the devil did Evans tell you of these risks? If it has to be done, why drive you half-crazy with worry? I thought the fellow had more sense."

"He had to tell me, Frank. He hated doing it, but it was his duty. He couldn't take my signature until he did."

"You haven't signed yet, have you?"

"No; he's given me a little grace. He's coming to see me again when he has the latest report."

He eyed her helplessly. She gave a faint smile. "That's just it, Frank. There's nothing anyone can do. I'm going up to my room now."

"Try not to worry too much," he begged, then went on savagely: "And if any of these damned women bother you, let me know and I'll wring their scrawny necks. I'm ashamed of my own family tonight."

She smiled, moved to turn away, then paused. "Oh, Frank. This is most important. Please ask them to be very careful what they say to James. He must not be upset in any way."

"I'll tell them," he promised. "Now you go and get some rest, or you'll be the next one to crack up."

He watched her until she had vanished at the top of the stairs before returning to the drawing-room. The three women were still there. Mrs. Allister and Ethel had their heads close together. Stella was sitting apart, a newly lit cigarette in her hand.

The old woman peered round at Frank as he entered. "Why did she go stalking off like that?" she complained. "I wanted to ask her more about the operation."

"She went after Ethel hit her across the face with a whip," Frank said savagely.

"Ethel said nothing that wasn't true," his mother retorted. "She only said the two of them will have no financial worries if James has to stop composing. It's perfectly true."

"There was no need to say it to Mary. She isn't the type to worry about money."

"She seemed very worried about it a moment ago. It was she who brought up his career."

"She was trying to explain to you all what music means to James. Don't *you* know? You're his mother—you keep telling us how well you understand him."

"I haven't the slightest doubt that he

will be only too glad to give up his music if it means curing his headaches," the old woman muttered. "Not the slightest doubt. You'll see I am right when Evans asks him."

Frank smiled sardonically. "So you've no doubt, haven't you? Right. Now I'm going to tell you the rest of the story—the part Mary was going to give you before Ethel took a slap at her. It's imperative that none of us says anything to upset James. He's in a bad way—much worse than we've thought. He mustn't be asked about the operation or be told what it might do to him. He's too far gone to make any decisions for himself."

"Too far gone," Mrs. Allister breathed.

"What do you mean?" Ethel asked hoarsely.

"They have already decided that James is over the bend. Not permanently—they hope the operation will put him right again. But to operate they have to certify him and get Mary's permission. He has no say in it whatever."

"Certify him!" Ethel gasped. Mrs. Allister let out a scream.

"Now keep calm," Frank said. "The

145

certification is to cover the surgeon legally. I suppose it is really a formality."

Ethel was staring horror-stricken at him. "Does that mean everyone will find out; that it will go into the newspapers?"

"Of course it doesn't. They aren't going to shout it out over the housetops. Evans will see it is kept quiet, and as soon as James is normal again, it will all be put right. For God's sake stop worrying about a family scandal and think of Mary's position. She is the one who has to give permission for the operation; she has to take the full responsibility. Now do you think you can find the time to be decent to the kid?"

Ethel rallied quickly on hearing the certification would not become public knowledge. "It's a scandalous thing to suggest that James is insane. Evans must be crazy himself. I don't believe for one minute that the specialists said anything of the sort." She leaned over and patted her sobbing mother's shoulder. "Don't be upset, dear. You know as well as I do that James isn't out of his mind."

"I know he isn't," the old woman

wailed. "But it's such a wicked thing to say."

Ethel turned back to Frank. "I don't see why you're making such a fuss about Mary. If James needs the operation to cure him, then that is all there is to it. All this talk about his music is twaddle—absolute twaddle."

Frank scowled bitterly. "So you can't find any sympathy for her?"

She stared back defiantly. "She's no more upset than we are. We'll all be sorry if he loses his musical talent but our sense of values is better. We put his life and happiness first."

Frank turned his eyes in despair on Stella, who had sat in silence throughout the argument. She rose as he met her gaze, throwing her cigarette into the fireplace. Her lips twisted as she spoke.

"Sorry. I know what you mean about his music, and how Mary feels. She understands him better than anyone else here, I know that. But if the operation can cure him, then it's plain common sense for her to give permission. He can't be left as he is. He'll drive us all crazy. If something isn't done soon, music won't be much use to him." With that she walked from the room.

"Even she can see it," Ethel sneered. "If you go on like this, you'll encourage Mary into refusing the operation." She paused reflectively, her eyes narrowing. "Or is she already thinking of refusing? Is that what you're trying to tell us?"

Frank scowled at her and his weeping mother. "No one said anything about her refusing. The poor kid knows she has no choice. But you could both show some understanding and feeling. You haven't to make the decision; you haven't to face him afterwards when it's over and done. What if he can't compose; who will he blame? Not either of you—you'll see to that. You'll keep your noses clean by looking sidewards at Mary. By God; you both make me sick."

Mrs. Allister let forth a fresh flood of tears. Ethel sat stiffly upright, a picture of wronged dignity. Frank glared from one to the other, cursed, limped to the door, and slammed it heavily behind him.

7

UNABLE to sleep, Mary sat upright in her bed and pulled back the curtains of the window by her side. The cold finger of a moonbeam stretched out and touched the empty bed alongside her own. The rest of the room showed dimly. It was deathly quiet.

She held her watch into the moonlight. The time was one-thirty. She had read until midnight, and since then had been lying in the darkness, trying in vain to sleep.

She listened intently. There was still no noise from below. For hours the sound of James's piano had come to her almost unceasingly, the brief intervals of silence lasting only long enough for him to write down feverishly the products of his work. More than once the sudden harshness of a discord had sent a jangle of shock through her tensed body. She knew too well what they indicated. In her imagination she saw him poised with contorted face over the

149

keyboard, raging at his inability to find the note or chord he wanted and venting his fury by crashing his hands down savagely. With her nerves as tightly drawn as they were, the sudden dissonances sent them jangling in agonized sympathy.

Tonight, mercifully, there had been few of these outbursts of rage. He had worked unremittingly, but with more composure than usual. And now all was quiet, deathly quiet except for the sound of the sea; and she sat upright in bed, listening anxiously.

Suddenly, with infinite gentleness, the haunting melody of the uncompleted piano concerto came to her. With a sob of relief, she let her tensed body relax. Weeks had passed since he had last played it—it seemed as if its completion was too much for him. He had been working on his new symphony, and, although he had not discussed it with her, she interpreted it to be a work representing the growth of the world and its early, primitive life. It was great music, with a savage, even brutal, power. There was the sound of the earth before and beyond time, when white-hot lava bubbled and sucked, and jagged mountains were hurled up like great spears to pierce the crimson, bloody skies. Then followed music of tormented oceans and vast, wild forests; of primordial life, of monstrous things that snarled their hate and hurled their immense bodies into mortal and dreadful combat. Then music of the gods, with the Valkyries winging their awful way over the battlefields, with Vulcan forging his lightning spears and Thor hurling them with abandoned glee to the darkened, reeling earth below. There was Tyr wielding his great sword, Loki weaving dark spells of evil, and Hel moving silently, throwing her dark shadow of death on all things.

Magnificent music, all of it, but not music to be heard too often, or at night. . . . It had a paganism that was frightening. Sometimes, to Mary listening in the fanciful darkness, it seemed to possess a despairing agnosticism, almost an unholiness; as if its composer in the tormented delirium of his mind had turned in despair to the demon world. Time and again she had told herself that it was all fantasy on her part, that it was febrile imagination made morbid by months of strain and worry; but always without conviction. She could never hear it without a vague nameless fear clutching her heart.

But now, after the fierce and tumultuous chords that had preceded it, the limpid notes of the concerto came as sweetly as a young, clear alto in a cathedral. Sorrowful and full of loneliness though the music was, it was inexpressibly beautiful. But to the listening woman, used to the wildness of the symphony, it was more than beautiful. It was sane. . . .

With a shudder she turned and gazed through the window. Clouds, heavy with snow, were massing round the moon, their edges lined with silver. The cliffs and trees made a study in black and white. On the window-sill outside, particles of ice glittered like diamonds.

The music that welled up from below could have been written for such a night. As she watched the silver beam of light over her bed shifted as the clouds closed in on the moon above. Its radiance dimmed and out of the darkness came great flakes of snow that swirled by her window.

At the same moment the music ceased. The composer had played what he had written; the rest was unfinished. To Mary there was something symbolical about those clouds that now covered the moon. Was the sadness of his concerto visionary? Had he, when writing it, seen the dark clouds approaching and poured out his anguish in that haunting melody? Now, hidden in darkness, could he only write of storm and strife and terror?

She listened breathlessly. He had played again the last few bars and was now trying to continue the melody. The notes came hesitantly and off key. He tried again, and again the motif failed him. Mary found herself stiffening with renewed tension as she waited for the crash of discords that would cry out his agony of mind.

They did not come. There was silence again. A minute passed and her taut body slowly relaxed. Then she heard footsteps coming up the stairs and her heart began racing again. This was a nightly ordeal. As always she lay pretending she was asleep, never knowing the mood that possessed him.

With closed eyes she lay waiting. He reached the landing and a board creaked outside her door. Then he entered and

153

approached his bed. She listened for the click of his bedside light being turned on.

"Mary, are you awake?"

She listened, afraid to believe. Could this be one of the rare, bitter-sweet moments when his mind was clear? She lay trembling.

"Mary," he called again softly. She answered this time, in a voice she hardly recognized. He clicked on the switch then, and soft light flooded the room. He walked over to her bedside.

"I didn't want to wake you with the light if you were sleeping." His voice was pleasant, gentle.

"I . . . haven't been asleep," she whispered, sitting upright.

"Did I keep you awake?" he asked apologetically. "I'm sorry. I must get this floor insulated. It's the only bedroom in which you can really hear the piano. Why don't you use another room until I have it done?"

"I don't mind," she protested, feeling the happiness of the moment nourishing every starved corner of her being. "I don't mind at all. How is your headache tonight? Is it any better?"

His hands lifted to his head, almost

defensively. "It is easier tonight," he muttered. "I don't know why . . . By the way, did John Evans tell you about the treatment I was to have? He told me nothing, you know." Then a frown crossed his face. "Or if he did, I have forgotten. I forget things so easily these days. Sometimes I can't remember anything. It frightens me, Mary."

He sank down on her bed as he was speaking. She reached out gently, running her cool hand over his forehead.

"Try not to worry about it," she whispered. "You'll soon be all right again."

"It's been awful recently. I've had some terrible headaches, and I get nightmares . . . beastly things. I can never remember what they are about afterwards . . . but they must be pretty bad because I wake up in cold sweats."

She felt the sweat on his forehead now, icy with burning heat underneath.

"Don't worry, darling," she whispered again.

"What the dickens is the matter with me? I can't think; I can't remember . . . I hope I'm not going crazy." He laughed, a high-pitched, frightened sound.

"Don't think of such things," she begged. "You're just run down. You need a long rest."

"I suppose I do," he said. "We must have one as soon as I've finished this symphony. You need a holiday just as much as I do."

"Let's go now," she said eagerly. "Let's go and forget everything for a month or two. . . ." Her voice trailed away as she remembered what John had told her that evening.

His face was troubled. "I couldn't enjoy a holiday until this symphony is finished. It has a strange hold on me—it's like an obsession. I don't know what's happening around me when I'm working on it."

She saw his disquiet, and pain stabbed at her heart. In moments like this, when he was aware that all was not well with him, his fear was pitiful to see.

He laughed uneasily. "It's overpowering at times. I lose myself in it. I suppose it's rather ungrateful of me to grumble. A composer should be thankful when a work comes to him as easily as this one does to me. What do you think of it? You must have heard it plenty of times."

Her hesitation lasted only a second. "It's great music," she said slowly. "It is immensely powerful and impressive. But . . ."

"Go on," he said.

"Oh; I know there is no comparison in the work, but I like that concerto you were playing tonight. I think it is the loveliest thing you have ever written."

His eyes turned sombre. "I can't finish it," he muttered. "I tried again tonight, but couldn't put a note to it. It's maddening. I can't understand it."

She saw the anxiety behind his eyes, and hastened to comfort him.

"You will finish it," she assured him. "It will come one of these days."

"Do you really like it?" he asked.

Mary nodded happily. "Oh; I do. It's sad, but the melody is beautiful. I think it's wonderful."

"Then I must finish it, mustn't I?" he smiled.

Her eyes roved over him wonderingly. The soft light was smoothing the lines of strain from his face and showing to advantage its aesthetic qualities, with its broad, high forehead, slender nose and sensitive, mobile mouth. But it was to his eyes that her attention was chiefly directed. They were as black and lustrous as ever, but the light that shone through them was lambent again; it had lost its unnatural intensity.

A sudden rush of tears almost blinded her. "Oh, James," she whispered, clutching hold of his hand.

He stared down at her in astonishment. "What is it, darling?"

With a supreme effort, she fought back the tears.

"It's nothing. . . . Really it isn't."

"Aren't you feeling well?"

She laughed shakily. "I'm all right. Really I am."

"You're run down," he said with concern. "It's my fault. It must be impossible to sleep when I'm playing downstairs. Why don't you take another room?"

She could not tell him her reason. Torture though it often was to listen, what greater torture it would be to lie and wonder, and not know. . . .

"Don't worry about me," she said again. "There's nothing the matter."

"I shouldn't work at night, I know," he frowned. "But sometimes I find it easier.

Ideas come to me better. But it must be pretty awful for you."

"I don't mind as long as you are happy," she breathed.

"I'm always happy when I'm working," he said. Then he paused doubtfully. "At least I always used to be. Sometimes now I get irritable . . . these headaches make it so hard. . . . But it is a wonderful feeling to complete something and know it is good. It's the most wonderful feeling in the world." He laughed, and the sound was a nostalgic echo from the past. "One does know when one has done something good, you know," he smiled. "I suppose one shouldn't, but I always do."

"Good for you," Mary laughed back, glorying in the moment.

"It's a wonderful feeling—that feeling that it is all your own—that you made it from beginning to end. And to hear it played back by a full orchestra—I've never got over the thrill yet."

"I know," she whispered. "I know what you mean."

"I love it," he said passionately. "There are moments when I could chop the piano up with an axe, but for all that I wouldn't do anything else. I couldn't."

The pain took revenge for her forgetfulness, and the ache in her eyes became almost too much to bear.

"I know," was all she could whisper again. "I know. . . ."

James stood up, smiling down at her. "Well; I suppose I had better let you get some sleep. I won't forget about that concerto. I'll do my best to finish it." He raised his hands to his temples and frowned. "It's strange, but just at the moment I have lost all interest in the symphony. It happened downstairs a quarter of an hour ago. My mind seemed to clear, and I didn't want to work on it any longer. That's why I picked up the concerto . . ." He turned away slowly, his voice trailing off. "I suppose it will all be different again tomorrow."

"Will it?" she murmured, a shiver running through her.

His eyes darkened in shadow. "I expect it will."

She lifted her arms out to him. "James; listen to me. Leave that symphony for a while. Work on something else if you must work, but don't work on the symphony. You're not well, and that kind of music is too . . . too morbid. Try something lighter until your headaches are cured."

He stared at her with fear in his eyes and gave an uneasy laugh. "But I can't . . . I can't leave the damn thing alone. It's got a hold on me. This is the first night in weeks I haven't wanted to work on it."

"Make yourself leave it alone," she begged. "Put all your manuscripts of it away . . ." *Burn it,* she wanted to scream at him. *Burn every evil note of the thing.* . . . "Try to forget it for a while," her voice managed to finish.

"I'd like to, in one way," he muttered. "But it's not easy. . . . But anyway, we'll see about the concerto."

She dare not urge him further. He undressed quickly, put on his pyjamas, and then came over and kissed her.

"Good night, darling," he said.

"Good night, James. . . ." Her hand lingered on his cheek for a moment, then fell away. He gave her a last smile, then turned and slipped into his bed. The light clicked off, and she was alone again in the darkness.

Reaction from her few moments of happiness set in quickly. It was bitterly ironical that on the night she had been told of the operation he must have, and the loss he might incur, he should have one of his rare spells of normality and remind her what music meant to him. It was almost as if some instinct had warned and brought him to plead with her. . . .

She lay sleepless, watching through the window the falling snow, the fitful moon, and the dark, driving clouds. She did not want to sleep because that would bring the morrow to her more quickly, and she was afraid of the morrow. It would bring nearer the moment when she had to give her consent to the operation. It would bring her into contact again with Mrs. Allister and Ethel, who would carp and criticize her. And, worst of all, it would probably bring back the return of that monstrous symphony.

She found herself wishing the night would last for ever. For the moment James seemed hers again. After the first few affectionate words to her for weeks, he was lying peacefully asleep near her side. To many women it would have been little enough. To her, parched for affection, it had come like a water-hole to a wanderer in the desert. She had drunk thirstily of the few drops it contained, and was now resting. Tomorrow she had to face the wilderness again, and fear of what it might hold made her wish the red dawn would never come. But, in spite of herself, exhaustion overcame her at last, and her eyes closed into fitful sleep.

Mary awoke with a start at the sound of movement by her bed. For a moment, with her brain dulled by sleep and with the memory of James's late retirements impressed on it, she thought he was just coming to bed. Then she remembered, and her heart began racing. She lifted herself on one elbow, staring into the darkness.

"What is it, darling?" she called softly. She held her breath as she waited for his reply. It came softly, and she breathed again.

"It's all right, Mary. I'm just going down for a few minutes. I've got an idea for that concerto."

"You can put the light on," she told him, struggling upright.

James switched it on, and she saw he was clad in dressing-gown and slippers. He smiled at her sheepishly.

"Sorry to wake you up, but I woke up a few minutes ago with an idea or two running through my head, and I must get them down. I'd like to finish the thing for you."

She tried to conceal her anxiety. "You shouldn't bother now, dear. There's plenty of time."

He shook his head. "No, I'd rather go. It isn't often I think of anything but the symphony these days and I can't miss the chance. Don't stay awake. I'll play as quietly as possible."

"Don't be long," she pleaded. "You haven't had much sleep."

"I won't," he promised. "Shall I turn the light out?"

"No. Leave it on."

He threw her a smile that was almost boyish, then slipped from the room, closing the door quietly behind him.

Mary glanced at her watch. Five-thirty. He had slept four hours—as long as he ever slept these days. His behaviour on coming to bed had encouraged her to believe he might sleep the full night, but her hopes had not been realized.

She lay back, trying to assure herself that his conduct was not in itself unusual. From what his family had told her, she knew that before the war he had often risen at nights to work. Ideas could not be disciplined; they drifted into the mind at any odd hour, and unless they were secured at once they were as likely to drift away again, leaving the mind clutching vainly after them. But, although James had gone to work on the concerto, and that because he knew she liked it, she wished he had slept through to the morning. Whatever the morrow might bring, she would have liked this one night of stolen happiness.

Tensed again, she listened to his piano. He played the last few completed bars, then went on hesitantly. Note after note; bar after bar: each in perfect sympathy with those that had gone before. . . . Upright now in excitement she listened breathlessly, her hands clenched tightly as she mentally urged him on.

He faltered. A tentative note followed, then another and another. The listening woman flinched. The motif was lost. Again he tried, and again. In her mind's eye she could see him, bending with a frown over the keyboard, utterly absorbed in his concentration. Note after experimental note followed in rapid succession, but now the brief inspiration had gone and his efforts became merely those of trial and error. Like a man that had wandered from a narrow causeway in the darkness, he had lost the theme and his efforts to regain it were only leading him further away.

A quarter of an hour passed. In spite of the early morning cold, Mary felt perspiration cold on her hands as she heard the piano keys being struck with ever greater violence.

"Leave it now," her pale lips whispered in anguish. "You've done enough. Please leave it now."

Then the thing she had been fearing happened. There was a crash of discords as his hands drove down in fury upon the offending keys. The harsh noise tore through her body like an electric shock. It was followed by another and yet another, as if the composer were smashing his fists down on the keys in a frenzy of madness. Mary jumped out of bed, her trembling legs almost collapsing under her. Throwing on her dressing-gown, she ran downstairs and along the hall to his study.

He was sitting wild-eyed before the piano, his black hair falling over his face. As she watched he crashed both fists down on the keys again, cursing as he struck.

"Damn you!" he shouted. "You . . ."

The clamorous explosion of noise died into a dull murmur as the maltreated strings groaned their protest. In the silence that followed Mary could hear his heavy breathing. He muttered something unintelligible and seized the offending manuscript as if he were going to tear it to fragments. Mary ran forward.

"Give it to me, darling," she sobbed. "Don't get angry. Come to bed now, and you can start again tomorrow."

He turned his face towards her and her voice died away in terror. His eyes looked as if a mad fire were burning behind them. With a curse he hurled the manuscript into a corner of the room. She clutched at his shoulders, sobbing.

"James. Please, darling. Come and rest now."

He turned violently, hurling her arms away.

"What are you doing here? How many times have I told you to leave me alone when I'm working?"

His voice was thick with heavy enunciation.

"You were doing it for me," she sobbed. "I don't want you to tire yourself. Please leave it now."

His face contorted. "You're always doing it. . . . You're always trying to stop me working. You hate my music. I know what you want to do. . . . You want me to stop composing. . . ." His voice rose into a scream. "Well, I won't. I won't stop, do you understand? Get out of here. Get out, damn you. . . ."

"Oh, God," she whispered. "Dear God."

"Get out!" he screamed again.

Like an automaton she stumbled through the open door. He ran up and crashed it behind her. She walked blindly down the hall, not seeing Frank until he was at her side. He was in dressing-gown and slippers. He gripped her arm, his alarmed face staring at her.

"What is it?" he muttered. "What has happened?"

She shook her head dumbly, unable to speak.

His face set. He started grimly towards the study. "I'm going to have a few words with him myself," he said, tight-lipped.

In panic she ran after him.

"Don't, Frank. . . . Don't bother him any more, for God's sake! He's in a terrible temper. Please don't go in."

She pulled at him in fear. Unwillingly, he gave in and followed her.

"You won't go in, will you? Please, for my sake," she begged.

Frank examined her ashen face in alarm. "All right. Not if you don't wish it," he muttered. "You're looking terrible. Come into the lounge and I'll give you a drink of brandy. . . ."

She shook her head. "No. . . . I'm going upstairs. . . . I must. . . . But I'm all right. Really, I am."

She turned from him and ran up the stairs. On the landing above she encountered Mrs. Allister shuffling from her bedroom.

"What has happened?" the old woman wailed. "What have you been doing to the poor boy? Where is he?"

"He's in his study," Mary managed. "But don't go to him . . . you'll only make him worse. Please leave him alone. . . ."

"Make him worse! *I* don't quarrel with him. I heard what he was saying to you—that you are always disturbing him. I do think you should make an effort to appease him, Mary. You know how sick he is. . . ."

Mary did not know how she managed the last few steps to her room. Somehow she did, and locked the door behind her to keep out a hostile world. Until sunrise, and long after, coming in waves of mocking triumph that drowned her sobs, came the sound of that monstrous symphony. And outside dawn came like a deep wound slashed in the sky, and its reflection spread a crimson stain across the white of the snow.

Saturday

1

IT was nine-thirty on the Saturday morning and Gwen Ashburn was sitting huddled in front of a newly made fire in the lounge. The chill had not yet been burned out of the air, and her clothing was no protection against it. She was wearing a pastel-brown grosgrain dress, high-necked, with tapering sleeves and a full skirt. In other weather, and on a woman ten years younger, it might have been pleasing. With things as they were, it was neither attractive nor adequate. Round her thin shoulders—her only concession to the weather—she wore an angora scarf, and to this she clung as if her life depended on it.

She was alone in the large room. Cold though it was, she had left the door slightly ajar, as if to observe who entered or left the house. A book was lying on her knee but she was not reading. Nor was she listening to the wireless over which a woman's well-modulated voice was approaching the *dénouement* of a short story. Her thin, nervous features were drawn up in a frown. There were two deep grooves between her thin, plucked brows, and faint white lines down either side of her pinched nose. Her lips, dry behind their lipstick, were tightly drawn. Round her knees, which were barely two feet from the fire, her thin fingers twisted and tugged at her rings.

It was most apparent from her looks that her thoughts were anything but agreeable. Her eyes were continually narrowing, deepening the fine mesh of wrinkles around them. Fifteen years ago, when she had married Mervyn Ashburn, she had been a pretty woman. In those days her looks had served her well: they had captured for her a wealthy husband. Her mind had been as shallow then as it was today, but that had not mattered—he had not married her for her mind. But now, with her looks fading, she was growing conscious almost daily of her weakening hold on the susceptible Mervyn. By nature she was no more spiteful than most; in different circumstances she might have been a reasonably contented woman. As it was, conscious of her mental limitations and with no philosophy to turn to, she was rapidly growing embittered by jealousy. Huddled before the fire with her fears and misgivings Gwen Ashburn looked a lonely and pathetic figure.

Her thoughts, so often a helpless prey to her emotions, found it difficult to hold one theme long. They ran in spasmodic jerks. If only she could find some way of getting Mervyn out of the house! That Stella was a damned witch with men. Funny she had never thought of her and Mervyn. . . . She should have. There had been enough women before, God knew. But she had never thought of him and Stella. . . . Who would, anyway? Who would think of one's own half-sister? The little . . . In front of her eyes, too. They had been cunning, both of them, using Christmas as an excuse. The only thing they had forgotten was James's illness. She, Gwen, would have to play on that for all she was worth. If she didn't . . . Panic came like a stone hurled into water, throwing the pattern of her thoughts into a welter of confusion. It subsided gradually, but the silt from its impact remained to cloud her thoughts and leave her with a feeling of helpless dejection. Supposing she succeded in getting Mervyn away before things went too far, what then? There would be the next one, and the one after that. . . .

She tightened her lips, throwing off the mood. She would meet those problems when they came. The one at the moment was to get Mervyn away from Stella as soon as possible. She knew his technique well; he wasted little time once the preliminaries were over. And with Stella's encouragement . . . Her eyes narrowed in effort as she tried to come to grips with the problem.

Her thoughts were interrupted by the wireless. Some familiar name had been mentioned which had attracted her attention without registering consciously in her mind. She listened. An announcer was giving details of a programme to follow while an orchestra in the background was being gently faded in.

". . . renowned and distinguished composer who has proved as successful in the field of light music as in that of more serious and consequential works. The BBC studio orchestra is now to play six of James Allister's most popular, light works. These will be . . ."

Gwen did not hear the programme. Her mind, limited and unused to any form of concentration, had found itself an excuse to avoid the problem worrying it. Like a child, it had wandered off in search of more pleasant fields in which to play. Fancy hearing his name on the wireless like that! Fancy sitting in his house and hearing it! It made one feel a bit queer, it did. The renowned and distinguished composer, James Allister. You couldn't help feeling a bit of a thrill when you heard it, especially when you remembered he was a relation of yours. Distant, of course, but that didn't matter. And here she was, a guest in his house.

She remembered the envy of her friends when she had told them where she was going for Christmas, and the satisfaction it had given her. Something of it came back to her now. Not that she was a snob, mind. She hated snobs, she did; but it was nice to have a bit of art in the family.

She found definite comfort in this bath of reflected glory and felt warmer in its embrace as she listened to the music. The first piece was not in her line—she was no highbrow—but the second had a melody she knew and liked. Rising, she went to the set to turn up the volume. As she reached it, she heard footsteps in the hall outside. Turning, she saw James Allister standing at the door.

For a moment she felt nervous. Although the bedroom she and Mervyn were sharing was at the rear of the house, so preventing their hearing the quarrel the previous morning, Stella had told her about it; and she wondered for a moment whether the composer was still upset. A look at him relieved her fears. Although haggard in appearance, with a blue shadow of beard about his chin and face and still in pyjamas and dressing-gown, he did not look wild or dangerous. His expression was sombre and melancholy rather than moody. It was clear the music had attracted him to the door.

Gwen spoke unctuously, the announcer's words still sounding in her mind.

"Oh, good morning, Mr. Allister. How

nice to see you about. Isn't the music nice? Do come in."

He turned his gaze on her as if noticing her for the first time. His eyes were cloudy, dazed.

"Do come in," she urged. "Come in and listen to your music for a while. They're playing it divinely. I'm enjoying it no end. . . ."

Slowly he entered the room. Skittishly she took his arm and led him to a chair.

"Sit there," she coaxed. "It's nice and warm and you can listen to the music. There, that's right."

"Thank you," he muttered.

She went coquettishly to her chair and sat facing him.

"There we are," she said brightly. "Now we can listen in comfort, can't we?"

He nodded dully. Gwen chattered on, enjoying the moment.

"I think it's wonderful the way you write such beautiful music. I don't know how ever you do it. Of course, until I came to stay here I had no idea you worked so hard. I had no idea music was so hard to write. I thought you just sat down and dashed it off. Wasn't that silly of me?" Her laugh was high, affected.

His bewildered eyes moved from her to the wireless. He made no attempt to reply. She prattled on.

"You know, you've been so busy that I haven't had the chance to tell you how much I appreciate your letting us come for Christmas. Both Mervyn and I appreciate it no end, really we do. I wonder if you and your wife would come out with us over Christmas. We have some friends in Rombury who would be delighted to see you. Or else we could take a run into London and have a real slap-up party there. That would be great fun, wouldn't it?"

Her eyes gleamed at the thought. She wondered why she had not thought of it before. She'd make Mervyn dig deep, and they would throw a real party. She could invite all her friends and Mervyn could bring his business associates. It would be a leg up for them both to have James Allister as their guest of honour. Perhaps they could get him to play one or two of his compositions.

Her excitement grew at the idea. "You

will think about it, won't you?" she urged. "We'll both be so happy to entertain you."

He turned his eyes back from the wireless to her. "You're very kind," he muttered.

"Then you will come?" she asked in triumph.

He lifted a hand to his head. "I'll see. I shall have to ask Mary first."

"Oh, of course," she said, inwardly disappointed. "But I'm sure she'll agree. I'll talk to her myself."

She would, too, she thought. She'd point out that the change would do him good. Otherwise Mary might refuse. She was a quiet woman, that. You couldn't make her out easily.

She studied the averted face of the musician. They were all making a fuss about nothing, she decided. There wasn't anything wrong with him that food and rest from that piano couldn't cure. Maybe he had a bad temper, but he was all right if handled the right way. She was managing him, wasn't she? And he was a handsome devil. He ought to have been a film star. Those eyes of his . . . they made her all weak inside. No wonder he used to be a woman killer. . . .

The music stopped for a moment. She leaned forward.

"Doesn't it give you a thrill to sit here and hear your music being played?" Her voice was sycophantic.

He shook his head slowly. "It used to do. . . ."

"It still does," Gwen simpered. "You're just being coy. You still enjoy listening to it, don't you now?"

He frowned. "Sometimes. . . . But not often. I don't like some of the things any more."

The orchestra commenced playing again. Gwen recognized the tune at once. It was a waltz called "Delight" and had been extremely popular during the war years.

"This is one of the nicest things you ever wrote," she told him. "It used to be our favourite song. . . . Why, what's the matter?"

He was on his feet, staring at the wireless. His face was contorted in anguish.

"What is it?" Her voice was suddenly nervous.

He dragged the armchair out of his way and ran to the wireless. For a moment he looked as if he were going to drive his fist into it. He twisted a knob viciously, snapping the set into silence. The sound of his heavy breathing came to Gwen.

"What on earth's the matter?" she asked again, helplessly.

"Nothing," he muttered thickly. There were beads of sweat on his forehead, and even at that distance she could see the trembling of his fingers.

"It's nothing," he said again, louder. "Nothing at all. Some of that—filth—I can't bear to listen to it now. I must go. I must get back to my work. . . ."

He stumbled out of the room; the sound of his footsteps outside ending in the crash of his study door.

Gwen lowered herself back into her chair. Her heart was beating with a fear she did not understand. The others must be right after all, she thought. No normal man would behave like that on hearing a tune that must have brought him in a small fortune. That look on his face . . . it had given her the creeps, it had. It wasn't natural. . . .

Unless . . . Her eyes suddenly dilated, then narrowed. Was it possible. . . ? She sat a few minutes deep in thought, then shook her head in sullen disappointment. No, it couldn't be. It was a coincidence, nothing more. How could it be anything more?

With her temper exacerbated by the incident, she rose at last and went in search of Mervyn.

Stella swung down the stairs on her way to the lounge, to pause at the sound of the wireless. Keeping on the carpet runner down the centre of the hall, she quietly approached the half-open door. One glance was sufficient. She saw the narrow back of Gwen, and turned hastily away. That was one room too small for her this morning, she decided with a grimace. Damn. And it was the only room with a burning fire.

She wandered moodily along the hall and entered the large back room. It was a general-purpose room, suitable for large gatherings, furnished with an abundance of chairs and a big rectangular mahogany table. In the old days the family had used it as a music-room. A baby grand stood against one wall, and a radiogram with a cabinet of records against another. Two pastoral oils faced each other across the room.

Stella switched on an electric heater and stood before it, warming her hands. Through the large french windows she could see out into the snow-covered garden. The pale winter sun was shining fitfully, although the heavy clouds on the horizon still held the threat of more snow.

The door opened and Mervyn's face peered round it. His heavy eyes brightened as he saw Stella. He stepped inside closing the door behind him.

"So this is where you are" he said. "I've been looking all over the house for you."

"You're in the wrong room," she said caustically. "She's in the lounge."

"You've seen her there too, have you?" he grinned. "She shouldn't have left the wireless on—it gives her away. You are coming shopping with us this morning, aren't you?"

Stella flopped discontentedly into a chair. "No; I've changed my mind. I told Gwen earlier on. I don't feel like it this morning."

Mervyn's eyes were roaming over her as she was speaking. Her fashionable woollen frock clung to her every curve. His gaze slid down to the knees she had left carelessly exposed.

"Are those the nylons I sent you?" he asked.

She glanced down without interest. "I suppose they are. You can send me some more one of these days. You can't get them easily in this god-forsaken place."

"Don't worry," he grinned. "I'll fix you up. Come into town this morning and we'll have a look round."

She stared at him curiously. There was a smug air of triumph about him.

"You're looking pretty pleased with yourself. What's going on?"

"Come into town with me this morning and you'll find out," he said with a wink.

Her lips curled cynically. "I suppose you're going to buy me things with Gwen looking on. She'll just love that."

"Why shouldn't I?" he demanded. "I've plenty of cash, and you are my sister-in-law. I can give you a present or two, can't I?"

"As far as I am concerned, as many as

you like, my love," she said sarcastically. "But you're . . . er . . . forgetting Gwen."

He shook his head in disgust. "I can't take much more of her nagging."

"You'll get a damn sight more if she catches you giving me presents," Stella told him with amusement. "What has come over you this morning?"

He went to the door, opened it, stared down the hall, closed it again and approached her. She watched him with some astonishment.

"What on earth's going on . . ." she started.

He ran his tongue over his fleshy lips nervously. Stella moved, and he heard the sibilant hiss of her legs sliding over one another. What this woman did to him. . . .

"I want you to come in with us," he said thickly. "You needn't worry about Gwen. She's going to have her hair done. It'll leave us together for an hour." He lowered his voice mysteriously. "You won't regret it."

She rose, her every movement seductive, and walked to the windows. She stood staring out a moment, then swung round and faced him fully.

187

"What do you really want? A weekend with me? Is that it?"

Mervyn paused, taken aback by her bluntness.

"I say, that's putting it a bit crudely, isn't it?"

"That's putting it frankly," she sneered. "There isn't any point in beating about the bush. Isn't that the reason you want to buy me presents? Or are you one of nature's philanthropists?"

His florid cheeks flushed a darker hue at her sarcasm.

"I want you for more than a weekend. We can go away together. Anywhere— Paris, Vienna, Rome—anywhere you wish. What do you say?"

Stella lit a cigarette, studying him calculatingly through the blue smoke. In spite of his embarrassment at her cool reception to his proposal, his desire for her still showed in his heavy-lidded eyes. Desire— why not call it lust and have done with it, she asked herself contemptuously. He looked ridiculous, standing there like a middle-aged dog with its tongue out. Her eyes grew speculative. There was nothing wrong with his money, however. But there were . . . obstacles.

"And what about Gwen?" she asked grimly.

His face brightened at the implications of her question.

"Why worry about her?" he said eagerly, drawing nearer. "She wouldn't bother about you, if things were different."

"I don't suppose she would," Stella said with conviction. "But she does happen to be your wife."

He waved the difficulty away with a plump hand. "I'll fix all that up. Don't worry about it." He went on cajolingly. "You don't want to live in this dump for the rest of your life, do you? You'll never meet anyone here. You'll go like the others if you stay. Don't bother about Gwen. I'll leave her comfortable."

He put his arm clumsily around her waist and tried to kiss her. His breath was coming quickly, as if he had been indulging in strenuous exercise. She shook him off impatiently and wandered thoughtfully back into the centre of the room.

"You're nothing but a dirty old man," she told him.

He followed her, his eyes inflamed from his brief contact with her.

"I'm not so old. What are a few years in a man, in any case? I'm all right, I tell you. There's plenty of life left in me yet. . . ."

She did not answer. Her eyes were speculative.

"I'm crazy about you," he started again. "There isn't anything I wouldn't give you."

She spoke as if she had not heard him. "Gwen said something to me yesterday about your leaving. Are you going before Christmas?"

"Of course we aren't," he grunted. "She wants us to go this week—she says it is the only decent thing to do on account of your brother-in-law's illness. But that isn't her real reason for wanting to go."

"I know it isn't. She's suspicious, and that's why I keep telling you to be careful. I don't want any trouble here."

"She's got no proof, I keep telling you that. She's only scared of you. What wife wouldn't be?"

"So you aren't going yet?"

Mervyn shook his head vigorously. "I'm not going until you say yes."

She lifted her shoulders in sudden impatience. "Don't be in such a hurry. Give me time to think about it."

"If you agree, you won't regret it," he said thickly. "I'll make a queen out of you." He paused. "Then you will come into town this morning?"

"I will if you promise not to make a nuisance of yourself. I don't want a scene with Gwen in this house. Will you promise?"

"All right, all right," he grumbled. "But I keep telling you—she is going to the hairdresser's. We'll have an hour together. I've got something to show you."

"What?" she asked, curious in spite of herself.

He smirked. "Wait and see. It's a surprise."

"You're killing me," she said.

Mervyn was too pleased with himself to feel her sarcasm. "You'll be glad you came," he grinned. Then he looked at his watch. "I'll have to run along—I have a letter to write before we go. See you in about twenty minutes."

"I'll be ready," Stella yawned, "I've only to put a coat on."

His eyes flickered hungrily over her once more, and then he lumbered out of the room. With a puzzled frown, she sank into a chair. What was he up to now? she wondered. Probably he had seen something he wanted to buy her, and was going to take her to the shop when he got rid of Gwen. She shouldn't encourage him; she was being a fool. She shrugged. What did it matter? What did anything matter? Reaching over to the radiogram, she switched it on. She listened a few minutes, then heard a car being driven up to the garage alongside the house. Rising, she went to the french windows. A garage door slammed, and Frank appeared, coming along the gravel path that surrounded the house. He was making for the back entrance. As he passed the french windows he saw her and stopped. He tapped on the glass.

"Open up," he shouted, grinning at her.

She unlatched the doors and pushed

them open. A blast of icy air swept in, sending her recoiling into the room.

"Hurry up, for heaven's sake," she shivered. "It's as cold as step-sister's breath."

"I thought the expression was step-mother's," Frank grinned, stamping the snow off his shoes. He closed the door behind him.

"A slip of the tongue," she said.

His eyes swept round the empty room. "What are you doing in here— meditating?"

"You could call it that. Where have you been so early in the morning?"

He dropped into a chair before the fire and began warming his hands. "I had a few jobs to do in Rombury."

She sat opposite him, nodding to the wireless. "Do you hear what they're playing? They're giving a half-hour programme of his work."

Frank listened a moment, then shook his head moodily. "It's a bad business," he muttered. "And that sort of thing makes it worse, somehow. I ran into Evans this morning."

Her eyes lit with interest. "Had he

anything to say? Has he any fresh news of James?"

"No. Only that he had received the specialist's full report and would be coming round to see Mary later in the morning." He pulled out his cigarettes and threw one to her. "I wish to God I knew what had brought it on."

"Overwork," she said, in a tone that challenged denial.

He shook his head. "No. There has been something else. He must have had a worse time during the war than any of us realized."

"I don't see that. Surely anybody who works all day and night must go queer eventually. It stands to reason."

"I've argued all this before—he worked just as hard in the old days without ill effects. Besides, it takes more than hard work to unbalance a man; any doctor will tell you that. No; there's been something else. Don't forget he was a prisoner-of-war for over a year—and a year's a long time to be left alone with your memories, particularly if there's something in 'em you don't like."

"You're making it sound damned

mysterious," she muttered. "Why look for other reasons when you have a perfectly good one right under your nose? He's working impossible hours and his mind's cracking with the strain. What's impossible about that? Why make him sound like a criminal?"

"You may be right," Frank conceded. "But I'm beginning to think his working so hard is the symptom of his trouble, not the cause. I'm not suggesting he himself did anything wrong or criminal, but he might have seen or experienced something bad enough to cause this breakdown. Some pretty hellish and shocking things can happen in war, you know."

"It's overwork and this damned house," Stella muttered sullenly. "It's enough to make anyone neurotic. Mary was a fool to agree to come here. She should have made him buy her a place of her own."

Frank shrugged. "It's easy to talk now, but Mary had no idea then how things were going to go. I agree, she probably could have held out, although all James's manuscripts, books and things were here and you can be sure mother would use them to good effect. She wanted her two remaining sons back under her wing, and I think Mary gave in because she was sorry for her. Mary's that kind of a girl."

She met and held his gaze. "You think a good deal of Mary, don't you?" Her question was almost a challenge.

His eyes did not drop. "She is a brave woman and an intelligent one. James is lucky. There are few women who would have put up with him for so long."

A silence followed. Both were listening to the music. Emotion seemed to blur Stella's features for a moment, then leave them strangely frozen. She sat very still. Frank watched her, admiring the red-bronze swirl of her hair, the lovely chiselled lines of her face.

She came to life suddenly. Her face was hard. She rose and walked over to the wireless.

"I used to like it, once," she said, as if to explain. With an abrupt gesture, one of finality, she switched off the set and returned to her seat.

He did not answer. That would have been in David's time, he thought. Perhaps it had been one of his favourites. Suddenly he felt old, worn out.

They both started at the sound of James's uplifted voice, followed by the heavy slam of a door. Both of them sat tensed, listening. No further sound came and they slowly relaxed.

"We'll all go crazy with much more of this," Stella muttered.

Frank answered in a low voice, as if he were speaking to himself rather than to her.

"You know—it's a funny thing, this living with people. Take you and me, for example. We've known each other fifteen months—seen each other almost daily—and we think we know one another pretty well." He laughed soundlessly. "The truth is, of course, that we don't know one single thing of consequence about one another. All we know are the tricks the other one plays with his voice and face to keep his real thoughts secret. Our faces are masks we use to hide our real selves. But we don't know this until one day something unusual happens, and then we find the other person is just a stranger after all. It comes as a bit of a shock. . . ."

"What do you mean?" she asked harshly.

"Everyone is the same," he said quietly, as if to reassure her. "You and me, and everyone else. I don't know your secret thoughts and you don't know mine. . . ."

"I may know some of them," she asserted, with hidden meaning. "How can you be so sure?"

His eyes were suddenly anxious, uneasy. She felt them search her face. He moved more quickly to the point of his hypothesis.

"Well, take James and David—my brothers. You'd have thought I would have known them, wouldn't you? My brothers—they grew up with me from childhood. I should have some idea what is sending James over the bend, but I haven't. I haven't a single clue. And then there was David. He was my kid brother. A nice lad, but quiet and gentle. Those were my impressions, you understand. And what happens? He volunteers for a suicide raid; he becomes one of the death-or-glory boys. I couldn't believe it when I got the news. I still can't. Do you see what I mean?"

Stella jumped to her feet with an exclamation. "My God; you're starting it now.

I've always looked to you for a bit of humour. Does every conversation in this house have to be mournful? Doesn't anyone ever have a happy thought? Doesn't anyone ever think of joke? Death, madness—it's like living in the Chamber of Horrors. The sooner I get out the better."

She caught the look in his eyes and turned back to him involuntarily. "I'm sorry. I shouldn't have said that."

"You were right," he said quietly, and for the moment the sardonic expression had left his face, leaving it strangely tender. "I'm sorry, too. I hadn't realized you were feeling it so much. That's it, you see. One can't even see that in people. Your type don't show their feelings easily."

"Nor yours," she muttered, lowering herself shamefacedly into her chair again. That expression of his had brought about a swift change of mood in her. She had seen it on his face in unguarded moments before. She knew what it signified; she had seen it often enough on the faces of other men. But with Frank it was oddly different. For one thing it stayed in his eyes; it had never once found expression. She thought she knew why. There may have been other reasons, but she was sure of one. Her eyes lifted from his maimed leg to his gaunt face. She had often wondered what she would do if that long-hidden desire of his ever found words with which to speak. . . .

"Why haven't you ever married?" she asked suddenly, irrelevantly.

The familiar cynical grin came back to his face. "I? Who on earth would want an old crock like me?" Then quickly, as if afraid of her denial: "I'm too selfish. I can't afford the things I want for myself. Where would I be with a wife?"

"You'd make a good husband," she said. He looked away quickly, but not before his eyes had betrayed him again. "You're the dependable type," she finished, with a sudden perverse desire to hurt him.

The sardonic mask of his face covered his feelings well. He grinned. "Don't be damned insulting. You don't want dependable types. You want roués. You all like 'em a bit naughty. You nag 'em, but you hang on tight. It's the faithful types like myself who always get it in the neck."

Grateful he had taken her remark so well, she responded to his banter. "Faithful types," she jeered. "One year of marriage and you'd be as bad as the rest. . . ."

The door opened and Gwen appeared. Seeing Stella, her eyes flickered immediately over to the other chair, their suspicion dying at the sight of Frank.

"Ah, hello, Mrs. Ashburn," he said, rising.

"Hello. May I come in?"

"Of course."

She came forward. "I'm afraid something on the wireless just upset your brother," she told Frank. "He was sitting talking to me when that waltz of his, 'Delight', came over and it sent him into a shocking state. He jumped up, switched off the set, and went storming from the room. I do hope he's all right."

Frank nodded. "Don't worry. I'll go to him in a few minutes."

Gwen turned to Stella with some hostility. "Have you seen Mervyn anywhere?"

Stella was bent over the fire. "Yes," she said abruptly. "He was in here a few minutes ago. He came to find out if I wanted to go into town. He went off to write a letter."

"What are you doing? Are you coming now?"

Stella looked up. "Yes; I think so."

Gwen did her best to conceal her annoyance. "But I thought you said you weren't coming. . . ."

"I've changed my mind," Stella said.

"Well, don't be late, please. I don't want to miss my appointment."

Stella smiled coldly. "I won't be late. Mervyn will see to that. He'll give me a call when you're both ready."

Gwen's effort to smile at Frank was fraught with technical difficulties. She went out without another word.

"If I may say so," Frank said wryly, meeting Stella's eye, "there you have an example of the kind of thing I mean. Your brother-in-law—I hope you won't mind my saying it—is a mild example of the type of man we were discussing earlier. . . ."

"Mild?" Stella laughed. "Mervyn's a lecherous old rooster."

He shrugged. "All right. And so? His wife hangs on to him like glue. Doesn't it prove what I said?"

"Not altogether," she said harshly. "He's rich. That makes a difference, you know."

"So either way I lose," he smiled wryly.

She was about to reply when Mervyn came in.

"Come along, and brighten my morning," he winked. His eyes were only on Stella. He did not notice Frank, who watched him closely. Then he started.

"Oh, hello. I didn't notice you in that chair."

Frank nodded abruptly. "Hello," he said.

"Is Gwen ready?" Stella asked.

He grunted. "She's in the car, waiting."

"I'll run along and get my coat, then. Cheerio," she called to Frank.

"Bye-bye," he said. They went out, leaving him alone. He sat looking at the closed door for a long moment. Then, lifting his cigarette to his mouth he drew on it deeply and then ground it with unnecessary vigour into the ashtray by his side.

2

MARY was in the kitchen helping Mrs. Allister to prepare lunch when the door-bell rang. She hurried through, her eyes flickering on to the grandfather clock as she passed the open door of the lounge. Ten past eleven —it might be John. . . .

She tried to hide her disappointment at seeing Ethel in the porch. She forced herself to smile.

"Oh, hello, Ethel. Come in."

"Thank you." Ethel stepped stiffly into the hall. She was dressed in the same clothes she had worn on Thursday: a brown coat and hat and black, square-toed shoes. In her hand she was carrying a large, leather bag.

Mary closed the door. Ethel turned to her.

"Where's mother?"

"In the kitchen," Mary answered. "We're preparing lunch."

"Isn't Stella helping her?"

Mary shook her head. "Stella's going into town this morning. We can manage."

"I've never seen her in the kitchen yet," Ethel snapped. "With the maid away and her relations here, you'd think she would do a little to help."

"They are all eating out today," Mary said wearily, making a move towards the kitchen. "We're having a cold lunch and it is nearly prepared."

Ethel peered into the lounge, saw it was empty, then turned to Mary.

"I'd like a word with you privately, Mary, before I go through." Her voice was dour and fractious.

Mary hesitated, surprised at her own resistance. "I'm in rather a hurry, Ethel. I expect the doctor here any minute now."

Ethel bridled at this non-compliance in one so usually obliging. "It's very important, Mary. I shall not keep you long."

A shadow crossed Mary's smooth brow. Impatiently she stepped inside the room. Ethel followed stiffly, closing the door carefully behind her. She faced Mary, her legs apart, her hands securely gripped round the strap of her bag.

"Mother 'phoned me yesterday. Poor thing, she was almost out of her wits with worry. And no wonder. She got a big enough shock on Thursday night when she heard about James's operation—I do think she could have been spared the rest."

"What rest?" Mary asked coldly.

"This quarrel you had with James at some unearthly hour yesterday morning. Surely it could have been avoided. I realize full well that James is difficult these days, but surely it is up to us all to be more patient with him. If now and then he annoys us, we have to be sympathetic and blame his illness, not quarrel with him and make it worse."

Mary was astonished at the intensity of her anger. For a moment her desire to slap the prim, bigoted face before her was almost irresistible. Surprise that her normally placid nature was capable of such emotion almost overcame her astonishment at the other's words.

"Oh; I know you don't like being told this," Ethel went on. "But you have to pull yourself together. I know it has been a shock to you, too; but this is no time to think about money and careers. James's welfare is the only thing to consider; and each time you quarrel with him you are making him worse. You have to be told for your own sake as well as his."

Somehow Mary fought back the bitter words that trembled on her tongue. Her grey eyes, icy with anger, fixed on Ethel for a long moment; then she walked by her out of the room.

"You needn't look at me like that," Ethel shrilled after her. "You know I'm right. . . ."

Seeing she was addressing the door, she broke off furiously. She was feeling strangely disturbed. That expression of Mary's had come as a shock to her. Tears she had expected—not a look of cold dislike. The bully in her had suffered a repulse—she felt cheated.

Her thin lips compressed. It took events such as this to find out the true worth of people. The family had all taken Mary to be a quiet, good-natured woman—could that have been the cloak she had worn to cover other things? She, Ethel, had always felt that any girl who married a man as rich and famous as James must of necessity be regarded with suspicion. One could show friendship, but still retain one's vigilance. This she had always done and now it seemed her caution had been justified.

The sound of a car drawing up outside disturbed her thoughts. Peering from the window she recognized the ageing blue saloon of John Evans. Her face drew even tighter. The friendship of the doctor for Mary had not passed her unnoticed, and at this moment it grew in significance. Surely there was something almost indecent in a woman calling on an admirer to attend her sick husband! That John Evans was in love with Mary, she had no doubt. The thought was a powder train in her mind—it fizzed from one notion to a more alarming one.

On first seeing the car she had intended to leave the lounge and go through to her mother. Now she approached the door in sudden determination, opening it before the doctor could ring the bell.

"Good morning, Mrs. Cawthorne," he smiled.

"Good morning, Doctor," she answered frigidly. "Please come in."

After stamping his feet to remove the snow, he stepped into the hall.

"Awful weather, isn't it?" he offered.

"Yes; it is." She watched him glance into the lounge before addressing her again.

"I'd like a few words with Mary," he smiled. "Do you mind calling her?"

Ethel closed the door, then turned to him with determination.

"I will in a moment. But first I would like a few words with you myself."

John looked surprised but inclined his head. "Very well."

Ethel led him into the lounge, then faced him. "It's about James," she started. "Mary told us on Thursday night what you said, and now I want to discuss a few things with you."

She paused, obviously expecting a reply. He did not speak, although a troubled look appeared on his pleasant face.

Ethel went on with more confidence. "To begin with, it is absolute nonsense to say that James is insane. It's a shocking suggestion to make."

"Mary told you, then?" he asked quietly.

"Not directly. She told Frank and he told us. I've never heard anything like it. The poor boy is no more insane than you

210

or I. Quite frankly, I'm amazed that you, in your position, could say anything so libellous."

"Is that all you have to say?" John said quietly.

"Not by any means. I want to know if it is true that the specialists want the operation done within two weeks."

"It is true."

"What is all this about Mary having to give her consent? What has it to do with her? Surely James is the one to ask."

"James is not the one to ask, Mrs. Cawthorne. James cannot be asked for the reason you refuse to believe."

"James is my brother, and I should know him better than any general practitioner. I tell you James is not insane."

An impatient frown appeared on John's face. He made as if to speak, then checked himself.

"However, as you seem to have put everything into Mary's hands," Ethel went on grimly, "there are a few points I would like made clear. Is Mary agreeable to the operation being done?"

"We have not discussed it since

Thursday night, Mrs. Cawthorne. I am waiting to see her now."

"She spoke to us about it after you left. She stressed to us that there was some doubt as to whether James would be able to compose after the operation. Is that true?"

"It is a possibility, yes."

"Well, Mary gives both mother and me the unfortunate impression that she regards James's career as more important than his health and well-being. We feel she may be very reluctant to give her consent."

Worry merged into the frown on John's face. He spoke curtly. "She would naturally be distressed, Mrs. Cawthorne. If the worst should happen, she knows how severely he will feel the loss."

"We all know that, Doctor Evans," she snapped. "But our sense of values tells us how little music matters besides a man's well-being. Anyone would think, after hearing her on Thursday, that the two of them would end up in the workhouse. Actually, he has already earned enough to keep them both comfortable for the rest of their lives. Her concern is ridiculous. But that isn't all."

"Go on, please."

"Well; all this had upset mother quite enough, but the affair yesterday morning was the limit. Apparently James had risen early to do some work before breakfast, and Mary cannot have liked being woken up. Anyway, mother says she went down and simply flew at the poor boy. When mother went in to him he was in a shocking state of nerves. And this was just after she had told Frank that *we* must do nothing to upset him. . . . This isn't the first time it has happened; she's always nagging at him. I want you, Doctor, to instruct her to be more considerate and understanding with him in the future. She will probably listen to *you*."

John looked down at his watch, then at her. "Is that all?"

Her voice rose a full tone at his words.

"No, it isn't," she snapped. "Apart from that, there are a few things we have a right to know. Have you brought letters from the specialists regarding James's condition?"

"Letters?" he said in astonishment. "Of course not."

"Well; on a matter of this importance I think we are all entitled to see their opinions in black and white," she said. "And after we have seen them, the operation should be carried out at once. Have you made any arrangements yet to have it done?"

His flush deepened. "I have not."

"When are you going to arrange it?"

"When I have signed permission."

"By Mary?"

"Of course. Who else?"

"Who else?" she retorted. "Someone who puts James's welfare before the money he earns. If it is left to Mary the poor boy will probably be in his grave before she makes a move. I know. . . . I could tell from the way she spoke on Thursday. She'll have to be made to give her consent. That's your job and, as the patient's sister, I expect you to do it."

"She was given the specialists' report two days ago," he reminded her grimly. "And I myself gave her this time to recover from the shock."

Ethel's square shoulders set under her brown coat.

"If we can believe what you told her on Thursday, every minute is important. On your own words you have no right to waste time. If things are left and Mary goes on quarrelling with him, the poor boy won't last two weeks." Her voice rose resolutely. "I am speaking on behalf of Mrs. Allister, James's mother, as well as the rest of the family. Will you please arrange for us to see the specialists' reports at your earliest opportunity and in the meantime be arranging for the operation. And will you please tell Mary to stop provoking him? She has been doing nothing else for the last eight months. She'll listen to *you*, of course." Her words were uttered with deliberate meaning.

"Mrs. Cawthorne," he said coldly. "The only point on which we seem to agree is on the urgency of the operation. But I'm afraid I have neither the time nor the inclination to argue any further with you. There is such a thing as medical jurisprudence, and this matter concerns Mary alone. As your brother's next-of-kin she has the sole responsibility for any decisions

215

that have to be made, and I am answerable to no one else. As to your last request, I have only this to say. I have nothing but admiration for Mary's conduct and courage, and those are the only sentiments I am likely to express to her."

Ethel crossed over to the door. She was shaking with rage. She turned on him spitefully.

"Of course, I might have known what you would say. We all know how things stand between the two of you. We've seen it plenty of times in the past when you've come to visit her."

She noticed with satisfaction the flushed anger of his face before she slammed the door.

John stood a full minute before bringing his temper back under control. Then he went outside and pressed the front-door bell. Mary hurried out from the kitchen, stopping short at the sight of him. She noticed his stern face.

"Sorry I'm in," he said, trying to smile. "But your sister-in-law invited me inside and then apparently forgot to tell you I was here."

"She's through in the kitchen now,"

Mary said slowly. "We're not very friendly this morning."

"I gathered something of the sort," he murmured dryly.

She stared at him. "She hasn't said anything to you, has she? You're looking very stern."

"Oh; nothing worth talking about," he said hastily.

She drew him into the lounge. "Have you heard any more from the specialist?" she asked. Her eyes searched his face, pleading for news.

He nodded. "Yes; I had his report come through this morning. He has been in touch with the psychiatrists. I had another word with them myself yesterday."

"What is the general opinion?" she asked. "Do they suggest any possible cause?"

"I'll tell you in a minute, Mary. But first, what is all this about James having an attack on Friday morning? Why didn't you 'phone me at once?"

She did not answer immediately, and he knew why. Even to herself she was desperately trying to minimize the full seriousness of James's condition. He shook his finger at her.

"You should have 'phoned me at once, Mary. Exactly what happened?"

Reluctantly she told him.

"How is he now?"

"Oh; he is the same as ever again. What do the psychiatrists say? Don't they give any hope of avoiding the operation? Because, if they do, I'll refuse it, John. You should have heard James on Thursday night, before he broke down. He was telling me what music meant to him—oh; it was pathetic. If there is a chance of avoiding it, then I'll say no and hope for the best. You know that, don't you?"

His voice was troubled as he remembered what Ethel had just told him. "I know, Mary. But I can't give you that hope. All I have found out is a possible reason for his derangement, not an alternative treatment. There is no avoiding the operation. I told you that on Thursday night."

Her shoulders drooped. There was a world of despair in the slight gesture. He winced at it.

"Tell me, anyway," she said dully.

"Well, one of the most powerful agents in causing this type of neurosis is a deep-rooted sense of guilt. They believe this is true of James."

"Guilt!" she cried.

He shifted uncomfortably. "There can be other causes but the general opinion is that James's condition is due to some profound experience he has had—something that has shocked him to the soul. His history shows he has always had an instability, and because he has not been able to talk about this experience, or even bear to think about it, his mind has been affected."

She stared at him without understanding. "I don't follow you, John. Why couldn't he talk about it? What do you mean by guilt?"

Again he moved uneasily. "I can only give you examples. Suppose that during the war he did something of which he was later ashamed. Would that not prey on his mind?"

She frowned. "You mean he might have been afraid—shown cowardice somewhere?"

"It could be that," he admitted. "It

could be anything. I don't know what." He turned away abruptly. "God, Mary; I hate this job. I wish you had got someone else. I feel it my duty—it is my duty—to tell you everything, but none of it is going to help you at all. James must still have the leucotomy. There's nothing any of us can do to prevent that."

As she stood silent for a moment, he turned impulsively towards her.

"Let's go out—for a drive. We can't talk of these things in here. Fetch your coat and gloves and come out for an hour. James is all right, isn't he?"

"Yes. I looked in his study a few minutes ago and he was asleep on his bed. But there is lunch—I was helping mother—"

"Confound their lunch," he said in sudden irritation. "Let someone else do it for a change."

"It was nearly ready," she reflected. She made her decision. "All right; I'll come. I'll tell mother and collect my things."

Ten minutes later they were driving along the coast road, over the snow-covered cliffs. Through occasional gaps in them they caught glimpses of the sea below, hurling itself against the dripping rocks. The wind was bitter, driving bank after bank of clouds sullenly forward.

"How long have we got?" he asked. "Until one o'clock?"

She nodded.

"Then we'll go to King's Head," he said, ignoring the road on their left that led to Rombury, and continuing along the coast.

They sat in silence for a few minutes; Mary enjoying the wild scenery. She had been out of the house but once in the last week, and then only to Iveston. Gulls rose and fell over the cliff edge, like scraps of paper tossed in the wind. Far out to sea a lone ship tossed and plunged, at times vanishing completely in the trough of huge waves.

"Ethel said something to you, didn't she?" Mary said suddenly.

"Yes," he confessed. "That was why I wanted to get away." He paused, then went on reluctantly: "She is a natural trouble-maker. You will have to be very careful what you say to her. The less the better, in fact."

He made no mention of the rest of Ethel's comments to him. Mary had more than enough on her mind.

Half an hour later they saw King's Head looming up before them. It was a massive headland, rising nearly five hundred feet sheer from the sea, its precipitous sides the home of myriads of sea birds. Around its base, gouged out from the sheer rock by countless years of erosion, were a number of large caves, reputed to have been put to good purpose in the days of smugglers.

They passed through a small fishing hamlet bearing the same name that lay huddled in a shallow vale, and then they followed a by-road to emerge on the promontory itself. Although the vale had been well-wooded and fairylike in the snow, the top of the headland was bleak and desolate. Its few trees and bushes, stunted by a wind that always seemed to blow from the North, were like old men in their overcoats of snow, their backs bent double to the wind and the sea.

The view was impressive in its wildness. On a clear day the rugged coast could be followed by the eye for many miles. Today visibility was limited, but the clash below of grey waves and mighty rocks had a savage grandeur. Out at sea, where the rocky outworks tried to break up the assault before it could develop to the full, spray rose like depth-charge explosions. Reeling, but reforming rapidly, the onslaught continued, wave after massive wave hurling itself at the main fortress wall. The cliffs trembled under the assault and the sound was like thunder.

They sat in silence for a few minutes. Mary found a strange relief in the power and immensity of the scene. Its vastness seemed to dwarf all human problems, to mock in its puissance all human suffering and strife. For the moment she was content this should be so, and surrendered her mind to its wild fascination.

John waited for her to speak. He had admired her silence on James over the last half-hour. In spite of her anxiety to know all about her husband's case, she had seen his own need for time to regain his composure; and this time she had given him most admirably. Control and understanding such as this was a rare thing, and he found it beyond praise.

A gull broke the spell. It rose mewing

over the cliff edge, swooped down towards them, then wheeled, soaring high in the wind as it fought its way back to the sea.

Their understanding proved complete. She turned to him at that moment, continuing their conversation where they had broken it off in the house.

"So you think there is some guilt in his mind, and this guilt is torturing him to madness?"

"Yes," he answered quietly. "And whatever it is, it is having a more serious effect on him than it would have on a normal man. It would, of course. The more sensitive the mind, the greater the damage."

"You spoke of it being hidden. Does that mean that he no longer knows about it, that he has forgotten it?"

"Consciously, yes," he told her. "There is a theory that certain types of insanity are self-induced. A man has some shameful memory, so shameful it is painful to remember. So his mind buries it, imprisons it in the subconscious, and creates a warder in his conscious mind to keep it there. In certain cases the guilt is then forgotten, but it is still there and it festers in its prison, it grows more complex and powerful and so the conscious mind has to build up its own defences proportionally. The whole process then becomes automatic: the guilt grows more formidable and so does its jailor. And it is the jailor that ultimately destroys the mind. Like a Frankenstein monster, it grows beyond control, finally occupying the mind completely." He paused, then continued apologetically, "That is as near a non-technical explanation as I can give."

"I understand," Mary said steadily. "He has done something, committed some crime, and the guilt is too much for him." She started. "But wait. . . . Supposing I were to find out what that guilt was? Supposing it were shown to him—pulled out of that prison into the fresh air? Wouldn't that free his mind? There would no longer be any need for the jailor, and so his mind would clear. Isn't that what they do in psycho-analysis? Isn't that what you tried to do in the nursing home with drugs?" She clutched his arm in excitement. "Isn't that right? Mightn't that save him?"

He shook his head, hating himself, hating his words.

"How could you find out his guilt? He won't tell you; he doesn't even remember it now—it is too well locked away. Even under drugs his mind held tight. All he knows consciously is that he has some guilty secret, and that makes him doubly sullen and suspicious. If you were to ask him his guilt point-blank, his mind would almost certainly be shattered for ever—just at the thought that you knew of it. And even if you found out from some other source, it might still go when the guilt was explained to him. It's no use, Mary. He is too far gone. You couldn't hope to find out anything soon enough. You see, I can't leave him with you; it's too dangerous. He must be put under supervision, and he must have that operation. It is his only chance."

"But it *might* save him. You admit that. If we found out what it was, and then showed him he was forgiven, it might save his mind without the operation. . . ."

There was a brief silence before John answered. "No one can be definite about that, Mary. It might. There would be the one chance in a hundred, but the risks would be appalling. And I doubt whether there would be a psychiatrist in the country prepared to take the chance after seeing his case history. No, Mary. You mustn't even think of it."

"But it might work," she breathed. "It might, it might, it might . . ." Her eyes were shining with excitement. "Do you know of any particular . . . crime . . . that could have an effect like this on one's mind? Don't be afraid to tell me, no matter what it is."

"No," he muttered. "I can't think of anything in particular. But it would have to be something serious enough—in the victim's own mind, at least—to cause a profound state of regret and guilt." His voice rose harshly. "For God's sake, Mary, don't start building up dream castles. It would probably destroy his mind if you discovered it and told him, and in any case you haven't the time to find out. So don't even think about it."

Her eyes dulled, then closed. Her voice sounded far away.

"Guilt, regret: they aren't pretty words, are they?"

He could not answer.

"And I haven't very long, have I. . .?"

He answered that very gently. "No, Mary. I must be honest with you. You haven't any time at all."

She went on in the same, distant voice. "It's so funny. All the family except Frank think I don't care about him. That I put money before his health and happiness. They think I care about his career because of the money it brings . . ." She gave a sudden, retching sob. "Isn't it funny, John. . . ."

He caught her in his arms. "Damn them," he said savagely. "Damn their rotten, filthy minds to hell. . . ."

3

SHE lay in his arms with her head against his chest. He held her tightly while her body jerked in anguish. The paroxysm ended at last, but she did not move. Her voice came in sobs, muffled by his coat.

"Frank once said something . . . that put it well. He said when . . . you've grown up with a person from childhood . . . it's impossible to see them objectively. To you they are the sum total of all their faults and weaknesses. . . . You can see in them all the little things. . . . the inconsequential things . . . You never see them as an adult. And because of that you can never see them as others do."

"Go on," he urged. "Go on."

Her voice rose, became more protesting. "But I can. I didn't know James when he was a little boy in short trousers. I met him when he was a great composer, a world figure. I met him when he was complete. . . . Oh; I found out all his little faults—how he left soap in the bath, and dropped cigarette ash all over the floor of his study. But those things never meant anything to me. I saw the greatness in him, and after that I saw the man. And that's why today my loyalty has to be to James Allister the composer, not to the little boy they knew. My duty has to be that of a wife to a man, not a mother's to a child. And they can't see it, John. They can't see it. . . ."

His expression was akin to reverence as he looked down at her. "Let me tell you this, Mary," he said, very softly. "Let me tell you because it will not matter. I love you very much. And I have never loved you more."

She did not move for a moment, then her arms pressed warmly against him.

"I know," she whispered. "I know how all this must hurt. . . ."

John's voice was uncertain. "It does, but not quite the way I would have thought. It hurts because it hurts you. . . . But go on. Get rid of it all, Mary. It will help a great deal."

Gently she drew away, turning to the

side window so that he could not see her face.

"Yes," she said slowly. "I want to talk. I want to talk because I am afraid of myself. It's so easy to be selfish when one is one's own judge. I'm afraid, John. . . . You see, I want children. He wanted to wait until after the war, and like a fool I agreed. . . ."

"After the operation you can have children," he told her.

"I know," she cried. "Can't you see that is why I am afraid of myself? It is so easy for me to say yes—the family want the operation, you say it is necessary. . . . No one will blame me, no one will know. Don't you see?"

He nodded. "Yes. I understand."

"I have to watch myself so carefully. I have to be certain that my decision is the best for him, and him alone—"

"What about you?" he interrupted harshly. "Don't you owe anything to yourself? Doesn't your happiness count for anything?"

"It isn't quite as easy as that, John. It isn't as if I were married to an ordinary man. He doesn't belong only to me; he belongs to the world."

"Damn the world!" John muttered. "It isn't making any sacrifice. Think a little more of yourself. Your life still lies ahead of you. But why are you saying all this? You're talking as if you were going to refuse to have the operation done. You can't refuse, Mary. We can't let you refuse."

Her eyes pleaded with him. "You said the other night that no one could say how long he could last. He is composing powerful music now—he may go on for months, perhaps years yet. And a few minutes ago you admitted that there was a chance—however slim—if I could find out this hidden secret of his. Can't you see what I'm thinking? Shouldn't I wait, try to find out what he has done, and pray in the meantime that his mind will last? Isn't that my duty?"

He shook his head in alarm. "No, Mary. You can't do it. . . ." He turned away his face to avoid the agony in her eyes. "As a doctor I'm not able to let you wait. He is in a dangerous state. I can't allow him to go on walking about unattended. It is my duty to have him certified and put into safe custody."

Her head dropped. "Of course," she said dully. "You would be responsible if anything were to happen. It wouldn't be fair to you."

"I'm not thinking of myself," he said vehemently. "I'm thinking of you. Not only your happiness is in danger, but your very life—"

"My happiness," she said bitterly. "You talk of that! If he loses his talent, my happiness will be dead."

"What can I do?" he pleaded.

"Give me a little time," she whispered. "Give me a little more time with him to find out what he has done."

"But you mustn't ask him anything."

"I won't. I promise I won't. But he might let something drop by accident; he might give me some clue. If he is taken away I haven't a chance."

"It's hopeless, Mary. He won't let anything out. He can't; he doesn't remember himself. And all the time you would be in danger."

"Never mind the danger. Give me time. Delay the certification. Until that is done you can leave him with me. You know you can. He hasn't been violent yet."

"You don't realize what you are asking," he cried. "Apart from the physical danger to yourself and him, how will you feel if his mind cracks beyond all hope, and you know you might have saved him with the operation? You'll never forgive yourself. You'll never know a moment's peace for the rest of your life. I know you won't. You are going to ruin your life, throw away all chances of happiness for a chimera."

She turned to him and her smile was for his loyalty. "Listen to me, John. I'm one of the world's little people. I'm one of those who when they die will be forgotten. I'm a little woman married to a great man who will be remembered—*if he can go on composing*. He hasn't written enough music yet; he is still young. I want him to have that immortality. I'm very proud of him."

"But what is immortality?" he asked passionately. "Only a word. There is no such thing as an immortal work. Time is relative. If one of his works lasted a thousand years, that would be less than a second in eternity. Human happiness is the only thing that matters—things like your having children. . . ."

"His music may bring inspiration and happiness to millions," she whispered.

"If it did, the total of it all would be no more than your own. It doesn't increase or decrease according to the numbers. One man's pain is as great a thing as the pain of a million. And so is one woman's happiness."

Mary shook her head stubbornly. "Don't think I'm being altruistic, because I'm not. I'm just very proud of James. I'm a little woman married to a great man, and I can earn my own immortality—if I want it—by doing what other women before me have done—by seeing my husband finishes his work. And if I have to choose between his genius going out in one great crash of inspiring chords or being brutally slashed out by a surgeon's knife, what choice have I? What would he choose? What would anyone choose?"

She flung herself into his arms, burying her face in the rough tweed of his coat.

"Give me some time, John," she

sobbed. "Don't certify him yet. Give me a chance."

A welter of emotions as wild and turbulent as the sea below surged through him. He tried to hold them at bay, to reason with himself. James had not yet shown violence—could he find justification there? The wind soughed by the car, rocking them as it moaned past. He felt the warmth of her coming through his coat. Afraid to move, he sat motionless, looking down at her. His reply, when it came, was no reply at all. It was a statement of fact, and spoken very simply.

"Your happiness means more to me than anything else in this world, Mary."

"Thank you, John," she whispered. "Then you will do this for me?"

"Yes," he said slowly, his eyes now on the breaking sea. "Though I think it is the wrong thing, I will do it."

She clutched him more tightly, her voice muffled in his coat. "You do understand, don't you? If he were to lose his talent I could never be happy, not even with children. There would always be his eyes to see, empty or yearning. . . ."

He felt her shudder, and looked down

with sombre eyes. "I never knew you loved either music or him so much."

She moved closer to him, as if to help him bear the things she was to say. "I love them both, John. I love them very much. To have all the beautiful pictures or inspiring incidents we saw together turned into wonderful music was such an adventure. When I hear them again, all the memories come back. . . . Did I ever tell you how I first met him?"

His throat was dry. "No," he said huskily. "You never told me."

"It was just after the war started. I was making a visit to their house on behalf of the Red Cross. His mother let me into the hall and went upstairs for money. I heard music—someone was playing Beethoven beautifully. I guessed who it would be, and as the study door was open I peeped in. Just at that moment he stopped playing and put his head on his arms. I tried to tip-toe away but he heard me and looked up. Then he laughed. 'I don't know who you are,' he said. 'But let me tell you this —if I could write one work as wonderful as that, I would go to my grave the next day, happy.' That was my introduction to

James Allister. . . ." She paused, then went on in wonder: "What could a man like that do to have such guilt on his soul?"

Shyly she drew away and he felt a chill where she had been. Her eyes searched his face.

"How long will you give me?" she asked quietly.

"How long will you need?" he muttered.

She looked at him helplessly. "How can I say that? I have to find out what his secret is and I don't even know where to start."

John shook his head, half in anger at himself. "You're asking for a miracle, Mary, and they don't happen. Remember, even if you find out what it is, we still have to call in a psychiatrist, and I'm certain we wouldn't find one who, after hearing the history of James's case, would take the risk at this stage."

"Give me the time, in any case," she said dully.

"Then we will wait until next weekend and see how he is," he muttered. "But in the meantime do everything you can to humour him, and be careful. For God's sake, be careful."

"Thank you, John," she said quietly.

He started the engine and backed the car on to the road. They spoke little on the way back to the house; both were too occupied with their thoughts. As John pulled up the car on the gravel drive outside the house, Mary took his hand impulsively.

"Thank you . . . for everything. You've been wonderful," she whispered.

"I wish I had your courage," he told her.

She smiled wearily. "It's really born of despair, John. I think I am too much of a coward to face that look in his eyes when he knows what he has lost."

"Remember now," he warned. "Say nothing to him. Nothing."

"I'll remember."

"And if he does anything unusual—no matter what it is—let me know at once. And humour him, for God's sake!"

Mary nodded. "You will come to see me soon, won't you?"

"I'll be round," he said. "Don't worry

about that. Look after yourself, and be careful. . . ."

"Good-bye," she smiled.

"Good luck," he muttered, clearing his throat. Then she had gone and he was turning the car and starting down the desolate road to Rombury.

4

A LUXURIOUS car swung into High Street, the main shopping centre of Rombury, and half-pulled in to the kerb. Mervyn Ashburn pointed across the wide street.

"That's your shop, isn't it?"

Gwen nodded. She was in the seat beside him, Stella being at the back. "Yes; that's the one."

"What time will you be finished?" he asked casually.

"About one o'clock, but you had better be here well before that in case they finish early." Her voice was surly, suspicious.

"All right," he waved. "Don't worry. We'll be here on time." He leaned across her to open the door.

"You're going round, aren't you?" she snapped. "You aren't going to drop me off here?"

He muttered something under his breath, rammed in the gears, and drove round and up the other side of the street. He pulled up outside the shop.

"I can't take you right inside because of the shop doors," he grunted sarcastically.

Her face set as she picked up her handbag from the seat. "What are you going to do while I am inside?" she demanded.

"Oh; have a drive around," he shrugged. "Perhaps look in a few shops. And we can go somewhere and have coffee. . . ."

Gwen swung round on Stella.

"Aren't you going to visit your friend? I thought that was why you came in with us?"

"I don't think so," Stella told her coolly. "I'll see her this afternoon, while you are at the Hensons'."

Her inability to find fault with this plan did not improve Gwen's temper.

"Well; mind you aren't late, that's all," she snapped at Mervyn, as she fumbled for the door-handle. "There'll be a row if I'm kept waiting on the pavement in this weather, that I'll tell you."

She jumped out of the car, and trod gingerly across the pavement to the hairdresser's salon. She turned in the doorway, throwing them one last suspicious glance before passing inside.

"Thank heaven for that," Mervyn exploded. "She's out of the way at last." He grinned. "I'll bet that's the first hair appointment in years she has been sorry she made. She hated leaving us alone."

Stella laughed at his expression. He turned to her with a sly grin. "C'mon, now. We have a full hour to ourselves. Come in the front, and let's make the best of it."

"I don't like the sound of that," she murmured, moving into the seat beside him. "What is this surprise you have for me?"

He smirked. "You'll see in a minute. . . ."

The car pulled away. They purred down the main street and turned into one of the narrow lanes of the old town. Picturesque, crooked little shops, many dating back to Tudor times, leaned forward in sly supplication as they drove by over cobbled stones. With the snow on their roofs and their windows gay with holly and Christmas decorations, the shops resembled white-haired old men with cheery, red-apple faces. The scene could have come straight from a novel by Dickens.

"Pretty, isn't it?" Mervyn remarked, as they entered another old street lined with antique shops. "It's got a real Christmas look, all right."

She nodded. "Where are you going?"

"You'll see in a minute," he winked.

They came out from a side-street into a square. The cathedral towered before them, dominating the town in its size and conception. Snow lay in white drifts round the base of its grey walls, but, on the soaring pinnacles above, it clung only in the sheltered nooks and crannies, and the effect was hauntingly beautiful.

"Looks good with the snow on it, doesn't it?"

Stella nodded, turning to keep her eyes on the great building. The memory of her one and only visit to it came suddenly back, bringing a train of complex emotions. It had been an experience that had both awed and frightened her; one she had never succeeded in forgetting. She had just come to stay with the Allisters, and had gone into town alone one evening. It had been early autumn the leaves on the chestnuts round the square had been gold in the setting sun with a faint smell of woodsmoke elusive in the still air. The cathedral had loomed before her suddenly; she had had no intention of entering it. Suddenly it was there, and the impulse to go inside had been too strong to resist.

Wondering at herself, she had approached its massive porch. It had been twelve years since her last visit to a place of worship. Her parents, particularly her father, had liked her to go; and sometimes she had accompanied them. But since they had both been killed, in a car accident three years before the war, she had felt no call or need for religion. That evening something had drawn her, and she had wandered uncertainly into the dusky nave.

Once she had read of the effects cathedrals have on the minds of people. How some, on entry, feel a sudden sense of exaltation, an expansion of their inner being. How others are subdued, overcome by the spiritual aura and reduced to a feeling of grievous insignificance. How others again succumb to a sense of unreality, a feeling as if the mind were being detached from the body and gently lifted away. From the effect could be determined the character of the respective person.

The character analysis Stella could not remember, but she knew well the class to which she belonged. In a mild way she had been aware of the feeling since her childhood days. Even in churches she had felt it—a vague sense of unreality; a sensation of divorce between mind and body. It had been an indefinite thing in those days, diluted by the presence of her family and the congregation around, and she had always been able to hold it in check by an occasional comforting whisper to her father.

But on this evening in the autumn she had been very much alone. The vast nave had been empty; the silence a palpable thing inside the massive stone walls. Ahead of her, striking through the stained glass of one of the great west windows, the setting sun was throwing a shaft of trembling, iridescent light across the chancel arch.

She had moved towards this broad ray of slanting colour like one in a dream. The aisle along which she walked was clothed in velvet dusk, its shadows accentuated by the light ahead. At first her footsteps had sounded hollow on the stone floor, but gradually they seemed to die away, leaving her with the strange feeling she was no longer in contact with the ground.

She had stood for some minutes at one side of the great shaft of light, watching the dust motes changing in hue as they drifted from one coloured ray to another, listening to the awesome silence. . . . Slowly the purple darkness had grown around her until the walls and high vaulted Gothic roof were hidden in shadow. The stone floor had become a mystic, glowing pool whose light lapped warmly at her feet. She had felt a thing of dark obscurity, standing nascent and bewildered alongside the fount of all knowledge and understanding.

At last, and with the misgivings of one starting on a great adventure, she had stepped into the luminous pool. Its light had seemed to shine through her as if she were diaphanous, and in its passing to wash away all past regrets and sorrows. Her body had seemed to dissolve in it, giving her mind its manumission. The passions of the flesh had fallen away; in her unfettered freedom she felt as light and ethereal as the dust motes that floated by. The great shaft of light had seemed to draw her into itself and give her a sense of oneness with its glory. This renunciation of personality had both exalted and frightened her. She had stood, almost in oblation, for a timeless minute; and then, as the feeling had swelled irresistibly within her, lifting her mind on wings of wondrous grace and serenity, fear had savagely snatched her back to herself. With a sob she had turned and fled into the darkness.

She had not felt safe again until she was back in the busy streets. There, among the jostling, venal crowds, she had at last managed to shake off the profound misgivings about her life and beliefs that the experience had engendered. Her reaction had been violent; she had pushed herself into places where the crowds were thickest. She had wished desperately she had known people—people with whom she could drink and forget . . .

Now, as she watched the cathedral and

saw its graceful spires and pinnacles disappear behind rows of chimneys, the vague, unwelcome realization that she would have liked to have paid it another visit came upon her. Why, she could not understand —unless it was because the beauty of the great building was almost unearthly in the snow. The memory of her emotional experience that autumn evening was almost a palpable thing, bringing with it a train of harrowing, unresolved yearnings. Her reaction now was almost identical to her reaction then. She turned abruptly to Mervyn, suddenly aware he was talking to her.

"You look as if you'd never seen it before," he grunted, motioning in the direction of the vanished cathedral. "Don't tell me you are feeling religious this morning."

"Stop talking like a fool and give me a cigarette," she said sullenly.

He handed over his case, his eyes shifting uncertainly from the road to her. Stella lit her cigarette and inhaled deeply.

"Where are we going?" she asked again, as they left the narrow streets of the old town and entered the suburbs.

"I've got a surprise for you," he smirked. "We won't be long now."

She found his air of mystery both foolish and irritating, but made an effort to conceal her feelings.

"I thought we were going round the shops," she said.

He laughed, a triumphant, self-satisfied sound.

"Don't worry. You won't be disappointed in a minute."

Well, it's about twenty miles to the nearest shops in this direction," she remarked a few minutes later as the houses fell away and they entered the whitened countryside. "You aren't abducting me, are you?" she went on sarcastically. "You haven't suddenly taken the bit between your teeth?"

"It wouldn't take much to make me do that," he chuckled. It was obvious he was enormously pleased with himself, and in spite of herself, Stella found her interest growing. She feigned indifference, however, staring out of the window at the snow-covered landscape.

About three miles from town he turned the car off the main road and drove up a narrow lane between two wooded hills. He stopped when out of sight of the main road and turned to her.

She shrugged. "What happens now? Is this where you seduce me? Is that the surprise?"

"That wouldn't be a surprise, would it?" he grinned. His hand was fumbling with his coat pocket and she saw the trembling of his fingers. He eyed her with elation.

"Do you remember last Wednesday—when we came into Rombury? You and Gwen were looking in jewellers' shops, and you stopped outside one and pointed to something you liked. . . ?"

Her green eyes widened. "You mean Doretti's—the jeweller in Garrett Street—where they have all those expensive things?"

He nodded happily. His hand had emerged from his deep coat pocket with a small package. "That's the one. Do you remember the thing you liked?"

"Of course. It was a pair of ruby earrings and a brooch to match—all set in platinum. . . ."

"Well, there you are," he announced,

thrusting the package into her hand. "I've bought it for you."

Stella stared down in awe at the small box wrapped in fancy paper. "But that set I pointed out was over two hundred pounds."

"You don't have to tell me," he said. "Well, aren't you going to open it?"

With shaking fingers she untied the cord and opened the silken box. Rubies gleamed redly at her from their velvet background. With a shudder of delight she lifted the brooch out, turning it in her hand and watching its crimson stone glowing sullenly at her. She took out the ear-rings and held them against the light. They hung like frozen drops of blood. . . .

A heady delirium which she made no attempt to subdue came over her. She stretched her hand out to the driving-mirror over the windscreen and jerked it in her direction. Attaching the rubies to her ears she eyed herself in the glass, swinging her head this way and that, swirling the red stones against her flushed cheeks.

"They're beautiful," she muttered. Oblivious of his gloating eyes, she undid her high coat and held the brooch against her white throat. A surge of reckless abandonment swept over her as the icy fire of the rubies burned her skin.

Mervyn's face showed his satisfaction. Reaching forward he unlocked a receptacle alongside his dashboard, and pulled out a flask and two glasses. He poured into them, and handed one to Stella.

"There's water in it," he told her. "Drink it back and we'll have another."

She gulped down the brandy recklessly, feeling its fire reach out along her limbs. He filled her glass again, almost to its brim. She laughed gaily.

"It's an old trick, darling. I've had it tried on me dozens of times. You'll need lots of brandy."

"There's plenty more where that comes from," he said thickly. "Cheers."

"Cheers," she answered, drinking deeply again. The spirit was almost neat —she knew that and found herself unable to care. The mood that had taken her after sighting the cathedral had been reinforced by his gift, and she threw all caution to the winds. What did it all matter which way one went? Some became sinners and some became saints—and a hell of a world it would be if they didn't . . . Who would want to be a saint, anyway, if there were no sinners to throw punches at? Put 'em on their own and they'd start on one another in no time, and blow their heaven wide open. You couldn't have saints without sinners any more than you could have light without shade, white without black. . . .

The brandy brought a colour into her cheeks that matched the rubies at her ears. She laughed and raised her glass to Mervyn, her perfect teeth gleaming through the glossy redness of her lips.

"Stop looking as if you want to eat me," she said, her voice low and husky in her throat. "Drink up."

He put his glass down suddenly inside the receptacle. "By heaven; I do," he muttered.

He took the glass from her, put it away, then moved towards her. She made no move of protest or assent, but lay motionless with the brooch at her throat and rubies at her ears.

He reached out for her, his breath coming heavily.

"You're beautiful. I want you. . . . How I want you." His voice was almost a groan.

His lips were hot on her face. She felt his hands but made no movement of protest. She felt languorous and relaxed; his caresses were not unpleasant. His fingers were on her white throat where the ruby brooch gleamed redly. . . .

She could feel his body trembling with passion. His face lifted again, and his mouth crushed against her lips. She struggled involuntarily for a moment, then lay passive again. Pausing a moment he stared with inflamed eyes down at her.

"You can have anything you want," he muttered. "Anything. . . ."

Stella closed her eyes at the sight of his face. He bent his head again, kissing her like a man tormented to madness. His caresses grew more abandoned; yet she still lay motionless. The latent desire to be loved, so long suppressed, was being released by him, and passion was moving down her body like a long, slow flame. Her indulgence was purely physical; the caresses could have come from any man. By nature ardent, she had known three long, empty years, and her body was starved for affection. As passion grew within her, she remembered the last time, and lay with closed eyes, trying to link this moment with the other. It was possible while she could not see, but as he turned his heavy body to her, her eyes opened involuntarily and she saw his suffused face close to her own. The sight of it, so different from the sensitive one conjured up in her mind, sent a psychic shock through her that sealed up the well of her passion. She recoiled suddenly, drawing sharply away.

"No." She barely recognized her voice. "No. . . . Leave me alone."

With an effort she broke free and sat upright, drawing her coat across her body.

Mervyn lurched forward again, trying to put his arms around her. She pushed him angrily away.

"For God's sake stop being a fool!" she snapped. "I said no. Don't you know what that means?"

The sharpness of her tones chilled his passion. He drew back sullenly, resentment showing in his inflamed eyes.

She pulled off the ear-rings and brooch

and put them back into the box, which she then handed to him.

"I'm sorry," she said, and her words were sincere. "I shouldn't have led you on like that. It was my fault, and I'm sorry."

His discomfort was painful to see. Turning away she lit a cigarette, giving him time to compose himself. Then she reached forward and took up his glass of brandy. She offered it to him.

"Finish it off."

He drained the glass without speaking. He looked at the box in his hand, then held it out to her. She shook her head.

"Not yet," she said. "I told you before I wanted time to make up my mind. I still do."

Relief drove the resentment from his eyes. "You mean . . . you might still do it? You aren't angry with me?" He wiped his perspiring forehead, then turned contritely towards her. "I'm sorry about this," he muttered. "I couldn't help it— honestly I couldn't. . . . You affect me this way. Say yes, and I'll do anything for you, buy you anything you want."

"Don't buy me anything until I say the word," she told him curtly.

Mervyn thrust the box at her. "Keep these—please. No; I want you to. Gwen may find them, and start asking questions. Keep them—at least until you have made up your mind."

Half-gladly, half-reluctantly, she put the box into her handbag. He watched her in relief.

"I'm crazy about you, Stel," he muttered. "You aren't angry with me, are you?"

She eyed him speculatively, then her lips twisted. "No; I'm not angry. As I told you before—you're a dirty old man, but I suppose you can't help it. But remember —behave yourself now."

"And I haven't spoilt things. . . ? You won't hold this against me?" His voice was anxious.

"You're no worse than I thought you would be," she said coolly. "Now stop talking about it, and let's start back. We don't want a row with Gwen."

He gave her one last regretful look, and then turned the car. They drove back to Rombury.

"What's the programme for this afternoon?" she asked him, busy with her cosmetics.

He grimaced. "First lunch, and then I have to take Gwen to the Hensons'. We promised we would call on them today. Why don't you come round with us? Bill Henson is a good boy. He entertains well."

Stella shook her head. "No; I'd better not come. Gwen will start thinking things if I change my plans. I'll go round to this girl friend of mine, and you can call for me on your way home."

Before they reached the hairdresser's shop in High Street, Mervyn offered her a small pill. Stella looked at it in astonishment, then at his embarrassed face.

"What on earth is this for. . . ?"

"She'll smell the brandy otherwise," he muttered uncomfortably. "It'll save a row."

Bursting into laughter, she took it from him. "I was wondering how you were going to get round that," she said with amusement. With all his faults, she thought, there were things about Mervyn one could not dislike.

5

THE three of them arrived back at the house just after five o'clock that afternoon. Darkness had already fallen and frost made a hard crust on the snow. Stella opened the front door with her latch-key, and they entered the lounge. Mervyn, whose arms were full of parcels, grunted with satisfaction at the sight of a blazing fire.

Stella smiled. "That looks like Frank's work."

"Then God bless him," Mervyn said. "It's a welcome sight." He laid his parcels down on the table and marched over to the blaze, rubbing his hands before it.

"What do you think you're doing?" Gwen snapped. "Don't leave the parcels in here. Take them upstairs."

"All right; don't be in such a hurry," Mervyn grunted. "A man can get warm first, can't he? Let's sit down here for a while—nobody seems to be about. We can have a little drink."

From the unusual resistance he was putting up to Gwen, and from the shine on his flushed face, Stella decided he must have consumed his fair share of alcohol that afternoon. Gwen's tart reply confirmed her impression.

"You've already had enough. Every time you see Bill Henson it's the same. He is as big a toper as you. Where did the two of you go this afternoon?"

Mervyn winked slyly at her. "To the right place. Bill knows 'em all. You didn't think we were going to stay around with you and Joan, did you? You're worse than two old hens when you get together."

The drawing-room door at the other side of the hall opened at that moment, and Ethel appeared. She stared coldly into the lounge before turning towards the kitchen. Mervyn winked broadly at Stella, and then lurched forward.

"Hello," he called. "G'd evenin'. We are just thinking of havin' a snort before dinner. Would you care to join us?"

Ethel paused. Her eyes travelled up and down the slightly unsteady Mervyn. "A snort! What on earth do you mean. . . ?"

He moved nearer her, grinning. "Oh;

g'wan. Don't give me that. You know what a snort is. Everyone knows . . ." He lifted his elbow, pretending to swallow. "Ugh, ugh, ugh . . ."

Ethel stared at him, speechless with indignation.

Encouraged by her silence, he tried to take her arm, breathing heavily on her in the process.

"C'mon," he urged thickly. "It'll do you good. Make you feel human."

She snatched her arm away and jumped back. Her eyes threw knives at him. "Take your hands off me!" she gasped. "And don't you ever dare suggest such a thing again."

Bristling with indignation, she threw him one final glare and then marched off to the kitchen.

Somewhat sobered by the encounter, Mervyn turned back unsteadily to the lounge. He grinned sheepishly at the others. Gwen was furious, Stella laughing.

"I don't think she likes me," he muttered. "There's something in her voice—"

"You fool!" Gwen was almost choking

with rage. "What do you want to go annoying her for?"

"There's no harm in *asking* anyone to have a drink, is there?" he muttered. "She didn't have to jump down my throat."

"Can you wonder?" Gwen broke in. "I've been telling you for days that they all think we should go now that James is so ill. If you had any pride, we would be spared these insults."

He turned appealingly to Stella. "It isn't true, is it, Stella? You don't all want us to go, do you?"

"Of course we don't," she soothed. "Don't take any notice of the old crow. She can't help being that way."

"There you are." Mervyn turned in triumph on Gwen. "It's just that woman. Nobody else minds."

"She's the only one who'll come out with it, but all the others are thinking it," Gwen snapped. "It's most unpleasant for me. I've some pride if you haven't."

Mervyn muttered something under his breath. Morosely, he moved nearer the fire. Stella turned to the door.

"Oh, well," she yawned. "I think I'll run along and change. I'll see you both later. Thanks for the lift," she threw casually at Mervyn.

He looked up hopefully. "Won't you have a snort before you go?"

She raised her eyebrows. "A snort! What on earth do you mean?" With a laugh she walked gracefully out. "Later, perhaps," she called back.

Gwen watched Mervyn's eyes following her hungrily. Her lips compressed.

"We can't stay here any longer," she told him acidly as soon as the door had closed. "Everyone is looking at us, wondering just how thick our skins are."

"And yours is so confounded thin, isn't it?" he grunted sarcastically. "What are you bleating about? We were invited here for Christmas, for three weeks, and we've only been here one so far. . . ."

"Stella should never have invited us at all with that poor man in his condition."

"Stella knows more about the family's feelings than we do," he muttered. "She'll tell us soon enough if they want us to go. . . ."

"Will she?" Gwen sneered. "I wonder. . . ." She turned on him suddenly, waspishly. "What were you saying to her tonight in her friend's front garden?"

Mervyn's face dropped almost audibly at the sudden question. He stared at her, mouth agape. "Telling her? What d'you mean?"

"You know what I mean, all right. When we called for her tonight, why didn't you bring her straight back into the car? What were you saying to her in the garden? And why did you take hold of her hand?" Anger made her voice shrill.

Consternation spread foolishly over Mervyn's face. He began to bluster. "I don't know what you are talking about. What do you mean—holding her hand? I was probably giving her a cigarette or something. You're so suspicious you imagine anything these days. And how do you know I was holding her hand?"

"Because I was watching through the hedge, that's why," she informed him virulently. "It's no use your lying. I saw you."

He snatched at the opportunity to be indignant. "So you were spying on me. My God; it's awful, terrible! I'm not going to stand it any longer."

She ignored him. "It's because of her you want to stay on. I know!"

"Has there to be a reason for everything I do?"

"I've found there always has been one in the past," she snapped.

"So I couldn't be staying on because I'm enjoying myself?" he suggested bitterly. "There has to be another reason for it."

"There is another reason—a dirty one," she told him. "And I'm going to find out everything about it, I warn you. You aren't going to make a fool out of me. Do you think Stella cares a jot about you? She's only after your money, you fool. I know her better than you do."

Her remark stung him to fresh anger. "You know too damn much. Go to hell!"

"I'll find out," she threatened. "You'll find out you can't do this to me. You wait and see."

She stormed out, slamming the door behind her.

Mervyn groaned. He stood a moment in indecision, then, removing his overcoat and flinging it over a chair, he walked over to the sideboard and pulled out a bottle and a glass. He poured himself a stiff drink, added a little water from a carafe, then lifted the glass to his lips and drank deeply. He gave a grunt of satisfaction, topped up his glass, and returned to the fire. He was contemplating the flames morosely when Frank entered the room, a newspaper in his hand.

Mervyn started and turned, half-hiding the glass with his arm.

"Oh; hello," he muttered, relaxing again.

"Hello," Frank said, approaching him. "Have you just got back?"

Mervyn nodded glumly. "Yes; a few minutes ago. Like a drink?"

Frank shrugged. "All right. Why not?"

Mervyn went over again to the sideboard. Frank watched him with amused interest.

"Did you have a good day in town?"

"Not bad," Mervyn grunted. He raised the water carafe. "How do you like it—with or without?"

"With. That's fine."

Mervyn walked unsteadily back and handed him the drink with some solemnity. Then he slumped into an armchair.

"All the best," Frank said, raising his glass.

"Cheers," Mervyn answered moodily. "Cheers, and damn all women."

Frank grinned. "Is that how you feel?"

"That's just how I feel," the other grunted. He drained his glass with a gulp, then pushed himself out of his chair again.

"Have another," he offered thickly.

Frank shook his head. "Not for me, thanks. But you go ahead."

"You don't mind. . . ?"

"Of course not. Why should I?"

"You're all right," Mervyn grunted, busy with the bottle. "We should have got together sooner." He returned to his seat and leaned forward, peering heavy-eyed at Frank.

"How did you keep out of it?"

Frank looked at him in surprise. "Out of what?"

"Marriage," Mervyn said dolefully. "How did you dodge it?"

Frank grinned. "Oh; I don't know. I've never got round to it. Not enough money, I suppose, and then this thing doesn't help. . . ." He tapped his leg.

"Modesty," Mervyn grunted. "Sheer

modesty. You've been too smart." He lifted his glass in envy. "Anyway, here's luck to you. You're a smarter man than I am. A hell of a lot smarter."

Frank eyed him quizzically. "I take it that you have a grudge against women tonight."

"Tonight?" Mervyn stared at him vacantly, then gave a dismal laugh. "Not just tonight—any time. I've always had a grudge against 'em. They've got me into all the trouble of my life so far, and I've got the feeling they're going to get me into a good deal more yet. So damn 'em all."

"You seem to have a good case," Frank agreed. "Why don't you get away from them for a while? Give them a rest."

"I'm married," Mervyn pointed out with dejection. "But even if I wasn't I don't think things would be any better. It's all a matter of glands. . . ." He eyed Frank pathetically. "Glands; that's what it is. You've probably got normal ones, so they don't worry you. But I'm not normal; they work overtime with me."

"Do they, by jove."

"It's a hell of a thing," Mervyn assured him lugubriously. "It's like being hungry all the time. You can imagine it . . . Whenever there's a pretty woman about, I'm restless—my soul's not my own. It's hell."

"It must be."

"It happens all over the place. I might be on the beach, just settling down for a sleep in the sun, when one of 'em comes along in one of those nice, brief costumes —you know the sort of thing. . . ."

"I know," grinned Frank.

Mervyn took a quick, unhappy drink from his glass. "Well; that's the end of my rest. In no time I'm fidgeting and uneasy . . . You've no idea what it's like."

"You should try a doctor," Frank said, keeping his face straight. "A drop of medicine might help."

"I went to one once," Mervyn confided. "He said it was nothing to worry about— that it was only the creative urge in me. He said I should try to divert it into other channels—into art or business." He shook his head with dull finality. "But nothing helps. I think I'm to be pitied."

Stella entered the room at that moment. She had changed into a flared, apple-green dress that matched the deep russet of her hair. She sauntered over to them.

"Well, well," she said, eyeing their glasses mockingly. "This looks like a nice little party."

They rose, Mervyn with more zeal than balance. "It has all the makings of one, my dear," he said thickly. "Come and make it complete. Let me get you a glass."

She shook her head. "No, thanks. I've had quite enough brandy for one day."

He missed her meaning. "I can go upstairs and fetch you something else," he muttered, starting forward.

She seized his arm and led him to a chair. "No, thank you. I'd rather wait until after dinner. You two boys carry on. Don't mind me."

She took a chair offered by Frank. Mervyn dropped back with a satisfied grunt into his armchair. His melancholy had fallen away on Stella's arrival. He suddenly felt expansive.

"You know, we should throw a party here," he said to Stella. "One night this week. A few drinks, a bit of dancing— it would be just the thing. What do you say?"

She lifted her slim shoulders. "I don't mind. But we mustn't disturb James. . . ."

"Bring him along," he waved. "That's the idea—we can invite the whole family. It'll do him the world of good, and Mary too. . . . That's what they need." Excited by his idea, he turned eagerly to Frank. "You'll ask them for me, won't you?"

"I'll ask them," Frank shrugged. "Although it will be a miracle if they come."

"You ask 'em. Point out to Mary the good it will do him." He rubbed his hands. "Good show; then that's all settled. Let's make it Tuesday night. I'll fix everything up—it's all on me. It should brighten things up no end." He leaned back, pleased with himself and his idea.

"What were we talking about before?" he began.

"We'd better drop that subject now, hadn't we?" Frank grinned.

Stella opened her eyes in mock dismay. "You weren't telling jokes, were you?"

"No, we hadn't quite reached that stage," Frank said. The smile left his face as he watched Mervyn's eyes roving

272

shamelessly over Stella. Draining his glass, he set it down abruptly and rose.

"Very enjoyable," he said. "Now you'll have to excuse me. I have to run into Iveston for some aspirins for mother." He looked at Stella. "Is there anything you want bringing back?"

"I'm out of cigarettes," she told him. "Will you bring me a packet?"

Frank nodded and went to the door. He turned there, looking back at Mervyn. "That's something you should try," he said. "Aspirins. They might be useful in particularly bad moments."

"Eh?" Mervyn stared at him. "Aspirins? Oh, yes. Yes, I could try them. But they wouldn't help."

Frank laughed and went out. Stella stared curiously. "What's the matter? Have you a headache?"

Mervyn shook his head.

"Then what did he mean about aspirins?"

"Oh; nothing," he muttered. They heard the sound of Frank's car starting up outside. Its engine faded into the distance. Mervyn looked across at Stella, and half-rose to go across to her.

"No," she said firmly.

He sank back sullenly.

"She's suspicious enough now," Stella said. "Be careful what you say to her tonight."

"She jumped on me after you went upstairs," he muttered. "She saw me holding your hand in the garden tonight. She was peeping through the hedge. . . ."

Stella's expression turned to anger. "I told you to be careful. You know what she's like. . . . What did you say to her?"

He threw up his hands. "I said . . . oh, I don't know what I said. I can't take any more of her nagging. If you'd only say yes, I'd go straight to her now and tell her to go to hell."

"You won't do it in this house. I've told you—I don't want any trouble here. Maybe she is right—it might be better if you go. I can get in touch with you later. If you stay on here something is bound to burst sooner or later."

"Don't *you* start now. I've had enough for one day." His tone changed. "You don't want to get rid of me, do you?"

"I wouldn't have sent you an invitation if I hadn't wanted you to come. But I didn't know you were going to behave like this. So now it might be better if you go away until I make up my mind."

"I won't go until you've given me an answer," he said stubbornly. "If I go now, you'll forget all about me in a day or two." He lurched forward, his face flushed and reckless. "Why don't you say yes? What is there to keep you here? You aren't their sort."

Her red lips twisted bitterly. "Aren't I? Then whose sort am I?"

"You're my sort. You want to enjoy life, not let it rot inside you. Look at 'em all here—they spend their time digging holes to bury themselves in. A month here alone would drive me mad."

She spoke softly, as if to herself. "You don't understand. There's so much you don't know. . . ."

"I know I'm crazy about you," he muttered.

Stella heard voices coming from the kitchen, and put up a warning finger. "Ssh. Someone will be coming through in a minute. We'll talk about it later—when you are sober. Get those parcels up to Gwen now, or there'll be hell to pay."

He scowled, then gave in. "All right," he grunted.

She helped him to his feet, handed him his coat, then led him to the parcels, which she stacked into his arms.

"I'll see you later," he muttered.

"Yes, yes," she snapped impatiently. She pushed him through the door, closing it with a sigh of relief. There was a clatter of parcels outside, followed by muttered cursing. In spite of herself, she had to smile. After a few seconds she heard his unsteady footsteps climbing the stairs.

Thoughtfully, she returned to the fireplace. She would have to see he did not drink so much again, she told herself. In a state like this he was capable of anything. Perhaps it would be better if he did go. Gwen was growing more jealous by the day. Yet she had hoped to have them in the house for Christmas.

She sank into a chair, thinking of her last Christmas. Frank had been in London, and neither James nor Mary had yet come to live with them. There had been Mrs. Allister and herself, with Ethel and husband thrown in on Christmas Day for good measure. It had been an ordeal she had not wanted again—hence her invitation to the Ashburns. Of course Frank, James, and Mary would be here this year, but James's condition made no guarantee that things would be more cheerful.

She found her thoughts turning to Frank. In spite of his mask of indifference, she had known a long time his feelings towards her. Cynical of men, she had believed it only a matter of time before he made his affections known; but as the months passed by she had realized the war had left scars on his mind as well as his body. Although he rarely spoke of it—and then only as a jest—she was sure he was acutely conscious of his lameness. This, plus the fact he was fifteen years older than herself, was more than enough to keep his lips sealed, his admiration for her a thing locked within himself.

She had often wondered what her reply would be if he declared his affections for her. Looking back on her fifteen months with the Allisters, she realized that life would have been almost intolerable without Frank. Whatever his inner feelings, he had always acted as an elder, disinterested brother, giving advice when she had requested it, and keeping discreetly silent when she had not. With him she had always felt at ease. In his company, if she had felt like swearing she had sworn, and if she had felt like a drink she had had one—sometimes without water. She had never tried to be anything but herself in front of him—she had always felt those shrewd, crinkled black eyes would see through any disguise. For all his cynicism, he was a comforting person and a strong one. The whole family relied on him, but because his advice was unobtrusive and because he was so seldom found wanting, his worth was often overlooked. In his unassumption and reliability, he often reminded Stella of her own father.

The firelight shone on her face, darkening the shadow between her knitted brows. She was trying to lay her finger on the change that had come over her relationship with Frank during the last week. There was a subtle change somewhere. She had felt it, although why she could not say. He had treated her no differently. He had been the same Frank with his sardonic humour and derisive grin, laughing at the idiosyncrasies of others and grossly caricaturing his own. . . . Nothing outwardly had changed and yet his eyes had been often on her this last week and once or twice, when she had met them, she had imagined they held some mute message. Something he desperately wanted to tell her, and yet could not. . . .

A thought struck her suddenly. Was it because of Mervyn? Had Frank noticed the other's infatuation for her, and did he want to warn her against it? Or was it all imagination on her part?

The minutes went by and at last she heard the sound of Frank's car approaching. As he came into the room, she found herself regarding him with new interest. She could have sworn a glint of pleasure came into his eyes on seeing her alone; yet his face was the usual poker-faced, cynical mask as he threw off his coat and limped towards her.

He threw a packet of cigarettes on her lap. "They're not one of the best brands," he said. "But they were all I could get tonight."

"Thanks. I'll give you the money later."

"Forget about it," he said. "Excuse me

a moment. I'll just take these aspirins through to mother."

He went out, returning almost immediately. He dropped into a chair opposite her.

"Mary hasn't been in, has she?"

She shook her head. "No, I haven't seen her. How are things today? I meant to ask you earlier."

"James has had one of his days off," he told her. "He has been sleeping in his study most of the time. Evans came this morning to see Mary, but I haven't heard yet what he told her. She has been lying down this afternoon—I don't think she can get three hours' sleep a night."

"What about this party of Mervyn's?" Stella asked. "Are you going to ask Mary and James?"

"Why not?" he shrugged. "James can only refuse. And it might do him good if we can get him there and get a few drinks inside him. It might relax him; you never know."

She nodded. There was a short silence, then Frank motioned to the door with his thumb. "Where is he now?" he grinned.

"Has he gone upstairs to sleep it off? He was lovely tonight, wasn't he?"

"You mean Mervyn? Oh, yes; he went up twenty minutes ago. I think he'd had a good afternoon in town."

Frank chuckled. "Before you came in he was telling me how pretty women disturb him. It was one of the funniest things I have heard for a long time. He blames it all on his glands. I'm not letting him down, am I, by telling you this? You must have known it before."

Was that a warning? she wondered. His eyes were crinkled in humour, yet she thought she saw something anxious behind them.

"Oh, yes; I know all that," she said with indifference. "He's nothing but an old roué. He couldn't be faithful to one woman if he tried. . . ."

At least she could let him know that she had no illusions about Mervyn's fidelity.

His eyes seemed to clear. "He's certainly a character," he grinned. They both turned at the sound of determined footsteps in the hall outside.

Ethel entered the lounge. She was dressed to go home. Her hat was well pulled down over her bun and her coat was sitting stiffly on her squared shoulders. She was wearing them as a helmet and suit of mail. The black bag was swinging in her hand like a ball-and-chain. She looked extremely bellicose.

She marched across to Stella. "I've been trying to get a word with you all day," she said grimly. "But you are hardly ever in the house, and when you are, you are never alone. I want to talk to you about these friends of yours, the Ashburns."

Stella took a cigarette from the packet on her knee, and lighted it coolly. She blew smoke insolently through her nostrils.

"Well," she drawled. "What now?"

Ethel's face set. "You know what I'm going to say. I had a word with Mary on Thursday, but she hasn't the courage to speak to you. I suppose we have all been hoping your friends would have the decency to go once they saw how poor James was, but apparently that is asking too much. . . ."

"You leave my friends alone," Stella retorted. "And get on with what you want to say."

Ethel's grip tightened on her bag. "You

were here tonight when that ruffian tried to drag me into this room. I saw you laughing . . ." Her voice choked off in rage.

"He was offering you a drink," Stella said contemptuously. "And you were too sour to be polite."

"A decent woman isn't safe in the same house as that lecherous old beast," Ethel snapped. "The way he looks at one . . ."

"Don't worry," Stella sneered. "You're safe enough. Is that why you don't like him? Hasn't he made a pass at you?"

Ethel held on grimly to the last of her control. "I came in to ask you when they are going. Surely you can see how difficult it is for us to entertain them when we have this anxiety about James on our minds. . . ."

"Entertain them!" Stella broke in furiously. "My God! All you've done is be as unpleasant as possible. What do you want me to do—kick them out and get into a hair shirt? Is moping around with our tails between our legs going to help make James better?"

"On mother's behalf," Ethel went on grimly, "I'm asking you how much longer

283

they intend staying. It is her house and she has every right to know."

"Her house?" Stella cried, jumping to her feet. "Whose money runs it? If it wasn't for James and Frank, where would she be? Where would you be, for that matter? I've seen you sneaking food out in that black bag to feed that lazy brute of a husband of yours. You've probably got some in there now."

She paused, then hurled her packet of cigarettes down on the chair in rage. "You can tell the old girl this—the Ashburns will stay here as long as I want them to stay. They came for Christmas, and they'll stay for Christmas. And if you don't like it, you can all go to hell."

She pushed by the shocked Ethel and flung out of the room, slamming the door furiously behind her. Whatever happened now, she would keep Mervyn in the house for Christmas, even if it caused an earthquake, she vowed. She would do it to get her own back on that bitch downstairs. . . .

Back in the lounge, Ethel turned to Frank in dismay.

"Did you ever hear anything so dreadful," she gasped. "The girl's nothing but a guttersnipe. I should have smacked her face."

Frank nodded. "You should have done," he agreed.

Ethel stared at him in dislike. "Why didn't you do something?"

"I?" He smiled sardonically. "Don't drag me in. It's your quarrel."

"You're as bad as the rest," she snapped. "If it wasn't for mother, it would be a long time before I came into this house. . . ."

He eyed her mockingly. She flushed, then tossed her head back. "Well, why don't you say it? Why don't you say you wish I would stay away? Well, I won't." She stalked to the door, flinging her last spear from there. "I won't stay away. Someone has to look after mother's interests. One day, when she is dead and gone, you're going to be very sorry for this. You'll see. . . ."

A draught of cold air from the closing front door announced her departure. Frank shook his head ruefully. He was busy packing his pipe when Stella

285

returned, her green eyes still snapping with temper. He stared up at her.

"Hello! Have you come back for some more?"

"No; I saw her going from upstairs," she answered sullenly. "I came for my cigarettes. I left the confounded things here."

She picked them from the armchair, then turned to Frank.

"I know she is your sister, and I'm sorry about it, but she is a damn awful trouble-maker, and I'm not taking much more from her."

"I know what she is like," Frank said softly.

"She has never liked me," Stella said bitterly, moving towards the door. "I don't know why. I've never done her any harm."

His eyes were on her reflectively. His voice was still quiet, almost expressionless. "You're beautiful, Stella. That's why she doesn't like you."

"It isn't my fault she is an old battle-axe," she finished, closing the door and making for the stairs. She was in her room before the import of his words reached her. In that quiet matter-of-fact way as if he had been talking about the weather, he had said she was beautiful. It was the first time he had ever said that.

Standing before her dressing-table mirror, she drew back her red-bronze hair with her hands, and stood staring at her beauty, almost in wonder.

Tuesday Evening

1

"OH, please. Really, I shall feel an awful fool, sitting here with him listening to me. Won't he play. . . ?"

Mary smiled, answering for James, who was moving restlessly on the settee beside her. "We'd prefer it if you would play, Mrs. Ashburn."

Gwen rolled her eyes entreatingly. "But I'll be so embarrassed, really I will. Please . . ."

She was making her appeal from the piano-stool in the music-room on the following Tuesday evening. The room had a festive air; the walls and ceiling being hung with gay, if somewhat premature, Christmas decorations—a touch of Mervyn, as were the bottles imposingly arrayed on a table near the french windows. His projected party had materialized, as much to his surprise as to the others. Except for Mrs. Allister and Ethel, who had been "otherwise engaged", the rest of the family were present, all in evening dress. There was Frank, Stella, Mary and James.

Had it not been for Frank, the composer would never have been asked. Mary had hardly given the invitation a second thought until Frank had argued with her. Any change, anything at all that might keep him out of his study for an evening, was worthwhile. A party might slacken off his nerves; a few drinks might ease the tension in them both. Even when convinced of this Mary had been unable to find the courage to approach her husband, fearing his reaction. Frank had shown no such reticence, and the outcome had surprised them all. With the unpredictability that marked all his actions these days, James had sullenly agreed to be present.

In the acceptance, grudging though it had been, Mary had found cause for optimism. True, that very evening she had had to remind him of his engagement; but now, in spite of his preoccupied and ill-tempered appearance, she felt a lightness of heart that she had not known for weeks. Perhaps the skies were lightening at last.

Perhaps in the letter she expected on the morrow she would find the information she so desperately wanted. Perhaps all was going to be well, after all. . . . In this brighter mood Mary was more than willing to humour the Ashburns, to whom she felt she owed this resurgent optimism.

Inevitably, however, James's melancholy presence had had a depressing effect on the company. Mary had anticipated this by deliberately bringing him in late, so giving the others time to build up a certain alcoholic resistance to depression. The two of them had entered quietly, been made comfortable, and then sat almost unnoticed while Mervyn, a storehouse of anecdotes and jokes, kept the others amused. Only gradually had the chill of James's dejection been felt.

Mervyn had soon summed up the situation as the appreciation of his audience began to wane. He had quickly filled up the empty glasses and suggested a dance. On his instructions the chairs were drawn back, clearing the floor. He asked Gwen to play the piano. Her response was not enthusiastic, and was not due, as she was pretending now, to shyness in playing before James. She was a competent dance pianist and had played often enough on similar occasions. Her reluctance was based on less worthy sentiments. She had no intention of sitting for an hour or more at the piano, plugging out music which Mervyn would use as an excuse for holding Stella in his arms.

"Please," she said again, trying to conceal her irritation under a cloak of demureness. "I'll feel awful—really I will."

"Rubbish," Mervyn grunted, pulling a carpet aside. "You've done it dozens of times before. Stop being coy!"

The pleading smile Gwen was holding out to James grew stiff. With an effort she swallowed back her anger.

"I wish you would play," Mary smiled. She was growing anxious. If Gwen went on appealing to James she might easily upset him. "James is at the piano all day," she went on. "And I know you play well."

Gwen turned back to the piano to hide her annoyance. "All right," she muttered. "Just for a little while. . . . What do you want?" she called abruptly to Mervyn.

He approached her. "Oh, you know . . .

a few foxtrots, a couple of waltzes. Maybe a tango or two. . . ."

"I'm not sitting here all night," she breathed. "So don't think I am."

His face was flushed with alcohol. He grinned broadly. "All right, all right. . . . Don't get upset. We'll keep feeding you with drinks."

She eyed him spitefully, then jerked herself round and began a slow foxtrot. Her playing was mechanical but technically competent with good rhythm. Mervyn's heavy eyes began to gleam. They rested on Stella for a moment, before passing on to Mary and James.

"Come on," he invited jovially. "Support the pianist."

Mary smiled and turned to James. "Wouldn't you like to dance, dear? Try one and see how you feel."

He looked at her with dull eyes. She took his arm gently. He rose and they stepped out on to the floor.

"Good show," Mervyn called. He went over to Stella. She was sitting nonchalantly in a chair beside Frank, ravishing in a strapless evening gown of yellow silk organza. Her green eyes watched him mockingly.

"Come on," he said. "Loosen up."

She rose carelessly, aware of Frank's gaze on her. Frank grinned. "Go on. Give us a demonstration."

"We could, too," Mervyn winked. He swung Stella away. "This is the stuff," he grunted. "I feel human again."

"You be careful," she warned. "Gwen's gone sour. She'll be watching you."

"She's always sour," he grumbled. "Forget her." He pressed her closer. "Lord, you're beautiful. I could eat you."

"Stop it," Stella snapped. "And ease off the drinks. You've had too much."

"I'm enjoying myself. It isn't a sin, is it?" he protested.

Frank held a match to his pipe. His face was expressionless. He was watching the two couples on the floor. James was moving like an automaton, the paleness of his face accentuated by his evening dress. He had been a good dancer in the past and his feet were moving mechanically to the music, although it was obvious that his mind was far away. Mary was having to lead him.

The other couple were dancing beautifully. In spite of his heavy build, Mervyn was light on his feet and an excellent, though ostentatious, dancer. More than once Stella had to grip his ebullient arm to avoid a collision with the other couple. More than once she had to check that same arm for other reasons. . . .

Abruptly the music stopped. Mervyn applauded loudly. "More, more!" he called.

Gwen commenced again. Mary led James back to the settee. Mervyn moved to put his arm round Stella again but she checked him.

"Go to Mary now," she whispered. As he hesitated, she jerked his arm impatiently. "Go on."

"All right, I'm going," he muttered, moving across to the settee. Stella watched him go, then sauntered back to Frank after she saw Mary rise for the dance.

She stood beside Frank's chair. He was drawing on his pipe; both hands clenched round the bowl. He grinned up at her.

"Enjoying yourself?" he asked.

"So, so," she said. She stood, as if

waiting. Then she lifted an eyebrow. "Well? Do I have to ask you?"

His face twisted suddenly. It might have been with pain, but that was the risk she had to take.

"Ask me what?" he said. "For a drink?"

"For a dance," she answered.

There was anger in his eyes—she could see it now. They gleamed like dull metal, an alloy of anger and bitterness. For a moment she was afraid he would walk out of the room.

Stella lifted a glass by her elbow and drained it. "I shall not be put off easily," she murmured. "I never am after the third gin. Will you dance with me?"

Still he did not answer. She made her voice hard. To have softened it now would have been fatal.

"You're not refusing, are you?"

He put his pipe down deliberately into an ashtray. His face was pale. He rose slowly, grimly.

"No," he said quietly. "I'm not refusing."

His body was hard against hers,

unyielding. He stepped forward, deliberately exaggerating his infirmity.

Stella had expected something of the sort. A perfect dancer with excellent balance, she let her body swing with his, making almost a rhythm out of his lameness. In spite of himself, Frank was drawn forward.

"From the sublime to the ridiculous," he said, twisting his face to where Mervyn was dancing with Mary.

"Mervyn has been called many things," she murmured. "But never sublime."

He felt the supple lightness of her, the sway and glide of her body with his, and looked at her in wonder. Her hair was close to his face; its dark fire seemed to burn his cheeks. The perfume of her came to his nostrils, rare and elusive. . . . Slowly, imperceptibly, the stiffness went out of his body and limbs. His limp became less noticeable.

"I never dreamed James would come tonight, did you?" Stella asked.

"No," he muttered. "No, I never did, although I thought it worth a try. Although whether it is doing him any good or not is another matter."

Stella watched the composer as they passed by. He had not moved since Mary had left him. His eyes were fixed rigidly on the piano. He looked in another world.

Gwen made this dance last a long time. When it was over the bitterness had gone from Frank's eyes. There was appreciation and something more in them as they returned to their chairs.

"Thanks," he said quietly.

"Thank you," Stella yawned. "Now what about that drink?"

"Good idea," he grinned. "I'll go and get them." He went over to the table by the french windows where Mervyn was already busy.

Gwen turned round from the piano. "Is that enough?" she called.

Mervyn looked up in derision. "What do you mean—enough? We're just getting warmed up. What's the matter with you tonight?"

"You're not getting much more," she said, less successful this time in keeping the irritation from her voice. "Why don't you put on the gramophone?"

"Don't worry; we would have done if there had been any decent records,"

Mervyn told her. "Here you are; here's another drink for you. Now give us a waltz."

She glowered at him as he handed her the glass. "You're not getting much more," she muttered. "And stop drinking. Do you want them all to see what a toper you are?"

He made an exclamation under his breath and turned abruptly away. She glared after him, then lifted her glass and swallowed half its contents. Sullenly she turned back to the piano and began a waltz.

Mervyn went over to Stella. His eyes were bloodshot, heavy with drink.

"Come on," he said thickly. "It's my turn again."

She motioned him away. "Frank's getting me a drink. I'll have a dance later."

"Aw, c'mon. Don't be mean. Besides," and he jerked a thumb in disgust towards the piano, "she's going to pack it in soon. She's in a rotten mood tonight."

His voice was loud. Stella rose, to keep him quiet. "This is the last one," she said coldly.

"Don't tell me. . . . What's wrong with everybody tonight?" He swung her away recklessly. Stella tried to hold him off but his arm pressed her close, bringing their bodies tightly together. His breath was hot on her neck.

"Stop it, you fool!" she whispered angrily. "Everybody's watching us. Her eyes were fixed on Frank, anxiously. He had returned to his seat, her filled glass standing beside his own. His face was expressionless again.

"Let 'em all watch," Mervyn muttered. "I don't care any more. I'm crazy about you. Do you hear . . . crazy about you."

They were approaching the piano. As he brought her into a turn his arms tightened around her, bringing his lips into contact with her hair. Gwen turned her head at that moment. Stella wrenched herself away but not in time to prevent Gwen seeing the near embrace. Then their steps took them away across the room.

"You fool!" she gritted. "Gwen saw you. Have you gone mad?"

Not only Gwen, but the others must have seen them. Frank must have seen. . . . Her anger nearly choked her. Yet to pull herself away and leave him would be to accentuate the incident. The cold fury of her eyes sobered Mervyn; making him avert his ashamed face. They danced on in silence.

Gwen was playing automatically. Her jealousy was like a raging demon inside her, striking out blindly in its efforts to break loose and confusing her with its violence. Her conscious mind was not in control. It was a transient suspicion, barely considered before thrown aside, that now returned to govern her immediate actions. She did not consider the danger to others; she did not care. Her only desire was to punish; to strike out at everybody and everything within her reach. Quickly she rounded off the tune she was playing, ran through a modulation, and began another waltz.

Mervyn felt Stella stiffen in his arms. "What's wrong?" he muttered, staring at her suddenly frantic face.

"That tune," she panted. "She's doing it on purpose. . . ." She broke away from Mervyn. "Stop it!" she cried to Gwen. "Stop playing that thing." She caught up her dress and ran to the piano, but was too late. James was on his feet, a cry, a half-moan, breaking from his lips. His hands were holding his head.

"Don't," he groaned. "Don't. . . . For God's sake, don't. . . ."

Mary was clinging to him, her face ashen. "What is it, darling? What's the matter?"

"That music. That waltz. . . . Stop it. . . ."

Gwen had ceased playing. For the moment she was scared, fearful of what she had done. Frank was on his feet.

"It was your waltz," Mary faltered. "You wrote it. Can't you remember?"

"Remember. . . ." His face contorted as he swung round on her. "Did you tell her to play it?"

"No. No; of course I didn't. Why should I. . .?" She seized his arm frantically. "Sit down, dear. If you don't like it, Mrs. Ashburn won't play it again. I promise you she won't."

James was struggling for breath; his eyes wild and glaring. With a muttered imprecation he threw off her hand, turned, and stumbled from the room. With a hand at her throat, Mary stood a moment as if made of stone. Then she ran after him, followed by Frank.

They left a silence in the room. Gwen had swivelled in her chair to watch the others run from the room. Stella was a statue by the piano. Mervyn was standing in the centre of the floor, his bloodshot eyes dazed and vaguely frightened.

Slowly Stella moved. Her eyes were green slits of venom as they turned on Gwen.

"Why did you play it?" she whispered, hate in her voice. "You knew he couldn't bear it. You found that out last Saturday. Why did you do it?"

Gwen's lips writhed together in a smile of triumph. The malevolence in her eyes matched Stella's own. "Why darling; I was doing it for you. I forgot all about him. I remembered how you and David used to like it. It was one of your favourites, wasn't it?"

They stared at one another like two cats, eyes virulent and hating. Their emotions charged the air with life, making invisible things that crept coldly on the back and temples.

After a full thirty seconds Stella picked up her gown and swept from the room. Gwen's laugh followed her, shrill and exultant.

Mervyn was still standing agape in the middle of the room, like a large, bewildered dog. Gwen rose from the piano-stool and approached him. There was a strange air of jubilance about her, and Mervyn watched her coming with disquiet. He was uncomfortably sober again.

"What happened?" he muttered, his tongue running nervously over his lips. "Why did Allister go off like that? What the devil's going on?"

"Your party is over, dear," she said. "It's a pity, but I told you it would happen. The fellow's crazy."

His eyes lost some of their nervousness at her apparent amicability. He grunted dejectedly.

She took his arm, pointing to the bottles on the table. "Never mind. There's all the more for you. Come along, and I'll mix you something." Her laugh was high-pitched, a triumphant sound. There was a curious excited gleam in her eyes.

Mervyn stared at her heavily, trying to understand. Then, abandoning the effort, he turned and followed her to the table.

The Following Saturday

1

THE days passed by, and time moved in uneven jerks for Mary. In moments of tense anxiety, when James hovered dangerously on the brink of raging delirium, time was pitiless. It leered and sidled hatefully up to her; it yawned and sneered and mocked. . . . Seconds became hours, and hours haunted years. Then, with the crisis over, time stepped back with a jeer and took a great leap into the morrow—to bring the day when she would have to admit defeat and make her irrevocable decision twenty-four hours nearer.

So Saturday came round again. Saturday —and eight full days had passed since Mary had received John's report. Eight days—in which she felt she had run the whole gamut of human emotions. Hope, fear, love, despair, even hate. . . .

Yes, even hate, she admitted to herself with shame that Saturday afternoon as she stood before her dressing-table and brushed her black hair in an effort to soothe her overtaxed mind. That feeling of burning, searing bitterness that welled like vitriol within her each time Ethel made her accusations could be nothing else but hate.

Because of the pressure brought to bear on her daily, she had been forced to tell Ethel and Mrs. Allister of her decision to postpone the operation, but her reason she had been forced to keep to herself. The danger that one or the other of them might question James was too great. In any case, she knew that neither of them would have found any excuse for postponement in that reason. They would have been shocked at the suggestion that James held some guilty secret, and in all probability have accused John and herself of some plan to bring the composer into disrepute. By this time Ethel had convinced Mrs. Allister that Mary was in some way the cause of James's condition, and now her postponement of the operation brought new suspicion to their minds. Hourly their animosity grew.

James had appeared to grow no worse during the week. Except for his strange behaviour on the night of the party, which

Mary could in no way understand, he had suffered no major outburst of temper. Occasionally he had turned on her with angry eyes, and then time had paused and eyed her mockingly. But he had not actually crossed the borderline into delirium; there had been nothing comparable to the scene on the previous Thursday night. He had spoken to her seldom, and even then his words had been abrupt and sullen. His mind had seemed lost among the sulphurous clouds and steamy jungles of his symphony, on which he had worked almost ceaselessly.

Mary had tried to find comfort in this week of comparative calm, but without success. It had happened so often before. His mind was like a volcano—after a violent eruption it would settle reluctantly down again, its sullen exterior giving no indication of the time of its next outburst. What manner of things were massing inside it, what unbearable pressures were being developed, one could only imagine. And in the imagining there was exquisite torment and suspense. Like those who lie in huddled dread round the feet of a volcano, listening to its every sullen rumble and watching its ominous, shifting glow, so Mary waited, every second a barb that tore at her lacerated mind.

She brushed her hair mechanically, the gentle massage helping her mind to withstand the thoughts torturing it. She understood better now what John had meant by a hidden guilt driving her husband to permanent insanity. It *was* like a volcano, she thought. The guilt in his subconscious was building up giant pressures which were interfering more and more with the normal functioning of his conscious mind. While it was there, it represented a permanent and ever-growing threat to his life. At any time it could erupt and blast his mind beyond salvation in one mighty, irresistible explosion.

One way of escape was clear and incisive. The knife! The brutal knife which might save his mind but might also leave it bereft of its delicate genius. And the other way? A miracle. A miracle that would allow the light of reason and forgiveness to exorcise the evil things that were destroying him. A way that would leave his mind, with all its talents, intact and unharmed.

Her hand holding the hairbrush fell wearily to her side. She stood staring at her white face in the mirror. At times such as this, after her mind had found the strength to face her problem again and then exhaust itself in fruitless speculation, she found herself wishing she had not been given all the facts. It had been bad enough when she had heard what the operation might do to James: it was infinitely worse to know there was an alternative, a faint ray of hope. . . .

Hope. The word was a demon sneering into her face. What hope was there in trying to find out the secret of a man who would destroy his mind rather than tell it to a living soul? To whom could she turn for help? Not to James; he was the last person she could approach. And yet who else? She had been able to think of only one man who might be able to help— Colonel Briggs, who had commanded James's unit before and during the invasion of Europe. She had met the Colonel after the war—a bluff, hearty, ruddy-faced man who had thought highly of James, his third-in-command. The previous Saturday night, after hearing from John of the likely cause of James's disorder, she had written the Colonel. After begging his complete confidence, she had told him everything; and then asked him to be equally frank in his requittal. She wanted to know anything, however serious or trivial, that might have a bearing on her husband's present condition. . . .

The Colonel's reply had been sympathetic, but in no way helpful. Captain Allister's conduct during his association with the Colonel had been at all times exemplary. He had been a model officer. Of his private affairs during the war the Colonel could naturally say little, but he had no doubt they were managed as honourably as his military ones. Just before the invasion the Colonel had noticed a change in him—he had seemed more reserved and quiet—but what man had not grown more introspective as that fateful day approached? His capture had been most unfortunate. There had been a supply shortage up at the front, and he (the Colonel) had sent Allister forward to investigate it. The front was fluid at the time, and a probing enemy patrol had ambushed the small party. In the skirmish

Allister had been wounded and, as it later transpired, captured. From that day, of course, he knew no more of the other's affairs. The gallant Colonel concluded his letter with the sincere hope that her husband would make a complete recovery. If he could be of any assistance to her in the future, he was hers to command. . . .

The Colonel had been Mary's one hope. There was no one else to whom she could turn. She kept the cause of James's condition to herself until after his letter had arrived. It came in the late post on Wednesday; and that same evening she had told everything to Frank. He had listened to her tight-lipped, although without surprise.

"Don't tell anyone else, please," she had begged. "They wouldn't understand. They would say it was John who was trying to give James a bad name, or something awful like that. They might even go to James and question him. That could kill him."

"Don't worry," he said grimly. "I shan't say anything."

"Can't you think of something?" she

pleaded. "It doesn't matter what it is. Don't hide anything from me."

"I can't, Mary," he said regretfully. "Don't forget I hardly saw James during the war. I saw much less of him than you did."

"And yet you didn't look surprised when I told you. You didn't look surprised when I used words like guilt and regret."

"Quite frankly, I always thought it was something of the sort," he said quietly. "It was the obvious thing. Since he has been back from the war he has been in this condition, therefore something happened during the war to cause it."

"What am I to do now? Colonel Briggs was my one hope. Isn't there anyone else you can think of?"

He had shaken his head regretfully. "I can't, Mary. We could try to find out things about his prison life, of course, but it would probably take months. And we have no guarantee it would help us. And you say Evans couldn't give you long."

"No. He couldn't. I'm working on borrowed time now. . . ."

He had said nothing more to her except to offer his regrets, but she had read the expression in his eyes. There was sympathy in them, but there was also resignation. Like John, he saw only one hope for James, and that was to have the operation as quickly as possible. Both men feared that if she waited for the miracle that could never happen, her last chance to save him might be lost. She was also endangering John's professional career, for should James do something drastic in one of his outbursts, its repercussions might well harm the doctor.

She turned wearily away from her dressing-table. She had better go downstairs. Ten minutes ago Mrs. Allister had tapped on her door and told her in a querulous voice that she was going downstairs to make tea. If Mary did not join her, her absence would be made a further cause for complaint. As she walked from her room, she realized she had no alternative now but to consent to the operation. Colonel Briggs had been her one hope, and he had failed her. And miracles did not happen, no matter how one prayed. She made her decision. She would wait another day, twenty-four hours more, and then she would give her consent for the thing to be done.

Like one with only that time to live, she walked blindly downstairs.

The front-door bell rang as Mrs. Allister was setting out cups and saucers on a tray in the kitchen. Muttering to herself, the old woman pattered down the hall and undid the latch. Her face cleared at the sight of Ethel.

"Oh; come in, dear. You're just in time for tea."

Ethel stepped inside and pecked her mother on the cheek. "How are you feeling today, dear?" she asked solicitously.

Mrs. Allister's thin hands fluttered at the question. "Oh; just the same. But what can you expect? It's all this strain. . . . I really don't think I shall be able to stand much more of it."

Ethel led her into the drawing-room and into a chair. "I know, dear. It's dreadful, absolutely dreadful. I've been speaking to Dick, and we both want you to come and stay with us over the weekend. It'll be a nice change for you, and we can have a long talk about everything. Now don't argue," she said sharply, as the old woman's mouth opened in protest. "Dick is coming to fetch us later in the afternoon."

"It's so cold outside, dear," Mrs. Allister muttered weakly. "The wind is awful, and it looks like snow. And I really should be here in case something happens. . . ."

"You'll be quite warm in the car," Ethel said firmly. "And nothing is likely to happen in two days. Now don't say any more—it's all settled."

Having disposed of her mother's objections, she removed her coat and sat down.

"Well; has Mary said anything more to you?"

Mrs. Allister shook her head, reaching for her handkerchief. "No. Not a thing. Oh; isn't it dreadful! I think she must have lost her mind. . . ."

"It's that doctor," Ethel broke in savagely. "He is as bad as she is—I'm sure of it."

Mrs. Allister's eyes stared owlishly at her. "Doctor? Do you mean John Evans?"

Ethel leaned forward. "I've had this on

321

my mind some time, but I didn't want to give you more to worry about. . . . However, I've spoken to Dick, and he agrees it is only right that you know everything."

The old woman's handkerchief fluttered in anticipation before her nose. "Know what, dear? Oh; I can't stand much more, I really can't."

It seemed on this intimation they did not agree. Ethel went on without hesitation.

"John Evans is in love with Mary," she announced. "Don't you see what that may mean?"

"In love with her?" Mrs. Allister's voice was shocked.

"Of course. Anyone can see it. They grew up together." Ethel's voice dropped, became significant with meaning. "Don't you see. . . ? I've often wondered if James hasn't found something out."

There was a gasp. "You don't mean . . . her and Evans?"

"Why not?" Ethel asked triumphantly. "Wouldn't that explain everything?"

The old woman stared at her helplessly. "But how can we prove it?"

"We can't. But we can call in another doctor."

"But we discussed that the other night," Mrs. Allister wailed. "And Frank said that no other doctor would come unless John Evans gave his consent. They won't interfere with one another's practices, you know."

"I don't care what Frank or anyone else says," Ethel snapped. "Can't you see that if Evans is in love with her, he won't have the same interest in James that he should have?"

The old woman's eyes bulged in horror. "Good heavens; you aren't suggesting that he is deliberately leaving James to get worse?"

Ethel went on, a little nervous at what she had said but still defiant. "As things are, it stands to reason Evans hasn't the incentive to do his best. If he had, why hasn't he compelled her to give her consent? She would have done as he said if he had insisted on it."

"You think he has given in to her?"

"Yes; I do. He is as bad as she is. He is more interested in her than in his patient. And the more one thinks about it, the more alarming it gets. . . ."

Mrs. Allister broke into tears again. "Oh; I wish it were over. It's becoming too much for me, really it is. I envy your poor father for not having to go through it all. I'm beginning to wish I were at rest beside him. . . ."

"Ssh; you mustn't talk like that," Ethel said without emotion. "Everything will be all right once James has had the operation. But it must be done quickly. Mary must be made to agree—then Evans will be forced to make arrangements. We have to make her give her consent at once, or it may be too late. Where is she now?"

"She's in her room," Mrs. Allister whimpered, dabbing futilely at her nose.

"We must do it this afternoon," Ethel declared. "We'll force her to give an answer. I'm tired of evasions." She made a militant gesture with her hand and rose. "I'll go and call her now, and we'll get it over. We can't afford to put it off a minute longer."

"She'll be down any minute now," Mrs. Allister said nervously. "I called her for tea." She half rose. "I suppose I had better go through and fetch it."

"I'll come and help you," Ethel said grimly, helping the old woman out of her chair. "And if Mary doesn't come down, I'll go and bring her. We'll get this thing settled once and for all."

On her way to the drawing-room, Mary stopped outside James's study. Hearing no sound, she knocked timidly and entered.

James was sitting on his piano-stool with a manuscript on his knee. He was wearing an old smoking jacket and was without collar and tie. His hair was unkempt and there was a blue shadow of beard on his face. As she opened the door, he looked up and frowned.

"I'm sorry, dear," she said nervously. "I didn't know you were working. I couldn't hear the piano. . . . Tea will be ready in a few minutes. Mother is making it now."

"Don't bother," he muttered sullenly. "I don't feel like any at the moment. There's something here I want to finish." His eyes dropped again to the manuscript on his knee.

She hesitated. "There isn't anything else you would like? A cup of coffee, perhaps. . . ?"

His frown deepened. He waved one hand impatiently. "No. Nothing at all, thank you."

She nodded and went out, closing the door softly behind her. He appeared a little better today, she thought with relief. He was in the penumbra of his derangement, the shadow land between sanity and madness, and in its gloaming light he was stumbling along, his deviating path taking him at one moment near the light and in the next towards the darkness. Neither the Jekyll nor the Hyde of his personality was dominant at present, but beneath his sullen exterior one could sense their grim, mortal battle for supremacy.

Mary walked along the hall to the drawing-room. It was empty and she stepped inside. She waited a few moments and was about to go into the kitchen when she heard voices approaching. A few seconds later Ethel and Mrs. Allister entered the room, the former carrying a tea-tray.

Mary's heart sank at the sight of Ethel. She had not heard her arrival and thought

Mrs. Allister alone. She felt she could bear no more, and yet, from the tightening of Ethel's lips and the look of breathless expectancy on the old woman's features, she sensed another attack was to be made on her. The desire to turn and run from the room was almost irresistible. With a supreme effort she fought it down.

Mrs. Allister gave her a nervous, unctuous smile and then busied herself with the tea. Ethel sat opposite Mary, folding her hands on her lap. Mary seated herself and lit a cigarette, listening to the silence in the room. It was heavy and oppressive, drawing a tight band round her forehead. In it she could almost hear Ethel's thoughts as they grouped themselves for the attack. It came a few seconds later.

"Mother and I were just talking about you," Ethel announced coldly. "There is something we must have out with you today."

Mary's lips twisted. She lifted her grey eyes to the other's face.

Ethel shifted under the steady gaze. Then her body stiffened. She must expect defiance, she reminded herself. That scene in the lounge a week ago had been a warning what to expect from this woman.

"You know what it is, of course," she went on. "We've been asking you for days, and you've done nothing but ignore us. Well; we've finally made up our minds. We want a definite answer with no more evasions. When are you going to agree to James having his operation?"

Mary felt that hate for Ethel again. It came in white-hot waves that threatened to engulf her. Its very intensity was self-destroying; it burned in its purity without residue, leaving her shaken and bewildered. She turned to Mrs. Allister, who was trying to pour tea with a shaking hand.

"Surely you can understand why I'm hesitating, Mother. It's such a terribly final step—once it is done there can be no turning back. If he loses his talent, it will have gone for ever. I'm hesitating because I'm trying to find out what has caused his condition—so that I can perhaps help him recover without the operation. I'm praying for a miracle. Perhaps it is wrong of me but surely you, a mother, can understand."

It was as near as she had gone towards explaining to them her reason for postponing the operation. She dared say no more, nothing about his guilt—the dangers were too great. Even as she spoke, she realized the inadequacy of her words.

The old woman set down the teapot and clutched her handkerchief defensively. "I don't understand. I don't see how anyone who professes to love the poor boy can put his career before his happiness. If you want him well again, why don't you do as the specialists advise? I don't know what you are waiting for when you know any day may be his last."

Having delivered herself of her sentiments, she withdrew from a counter-attack behind a positive barrage of tears.

"That's the next one you are going to kill," Ethel said accusingly, pointing to her mother.

Bitterness drove away the last of Mary's constraint. Her voice was low but intense. "You aren't thinking about James, Ethel. You are thinking of yourself. You don't mind his being certified and operated on —if it is all done privately. You don't care what happens to him afterwards as long as he appears normal to the rest of the world. You're afraid of the publicity and scandal if his brain goes permanently. And you're jealous of me—you always have been. You're jealous of me because I am married to a celebrity and you to a nobody. You're so jealous you would be glad to see your own brother's greatness destroyed if it meant that I were pulled down with him."

The blows went home. Ethel's eyes turned into agates and the red spots burned like coals in her sallow cheeks. She quivered with rage.

"*You* dare say that. You, who are putting money before everything." She leaned forward threateningly. "You've kept us in suspense long enough. You've enjoyed torturing us. But this is the end of it. You're going to be made to do something now—made, do you hear? Perhaps we can't get another doctor because of your lover's obstruction, but there is one thing we can do. . . ." She paused, then went on deliberately. "I don't believe James is out of his mind yet—I believe it is all a tissue of lies to keep him ignorant of what is going on. I asked Evans for proof and he's never given it to me. So, if you don't agree to the operation at once, I'm going straight in to James to tell him everything. Everything, do you understand? About you and Evans, and about the specialists' reports. Then we'll see what *he* wants—whether *he* will choose music before his health."

Mary leapt to her feet in alarm. "You can't do that. He must be told nothing of the danger he is in. The shock might kill him."

"Would it?" Ethel sneered. "Or is it the story the two of you have invented between you?"

Mary stared at her in fear, then swung round on Mrs. Allister.

"She mustn't say anything to James, Mother. She mustn't, do you hear? It might drive him to violence, even to suicide. . . ."

"Something must be done," the old woman wailed. "Things can't go on like this. I want my boy well and happy again."

"But he wouldn't be happy," Mary cried. "Can't you see that? If he couldn't compose, he would be like a man without a tongue. And when he knew what we had done, he would hate us. . . ." She eyed them both bitterly. "No; not us. Me. Neither of you would share the blame. You'd both point your fingers at me. I can see it in your eyes. You'd blame me then just as you blame me now. And I feel it will happen. . . ."

Her voice broke off in a retching sob. "Oh, God; why do you want me to be his executioner?"

Mrs. Allister wept unheedingly into her handkerchief. "I want my son well again. I want him happy. How can you be so cruel. . . ?"

"Oh, God," Mary whispered again. She turned blindly for the door. Mrs. Allister raised her tear-stained face.

"Wait a minute," she sobbed, tottering over to the table. "There's a cup of tea here for James. Please take it through to him."

Mary looked back dully. "He doesn't want tea. He doesn't want to be disturbed."

The old woman stared at her vacantly. "What do you mean?"

"He doesn't want tea," Mary repeated wearily. "He is very busy."

Mrs. Allister's tears dried magically. Her lips compressed. "Doesn't want tea? I've never heard such nonsense. Very well; if you won't take it to him, then I shall go myself. The poor boy isn't going to go without his afternoon tea now."

"But he doesn't want it," Mary cried desperately. "I asked him when I came down. If you go in now you might upset him."

Mrs. Allister dug indignantly into the sugar bowl and dropped two lumps into the cup. "I've never heard anything like it. What harm can tea do him? Go on— you needn't bother to wait. I'll take it through to him myself."

"But you might upset him again. . . ."

"I'm taking him a cup of tea," the old woman snapped. "And that's the end of it."

Mary's shoulders slumped. Her eyes closed for a moment. Then she held out her hand. "Very well," she said quietly. "Give me the cup."

Mrs. Allister held it out to her triumphantly. "Take it straight in while it is hot."

Mary moved to the door again. As she reached it, Ethel rose from her chair.

"Wait a minute," she snapped.

Mary turned, meeting the other's malevolent eyes.

"Yes?" she said.

"You haven't given me an answer yet. Are you going to arrange for that operation or not? If you don't, I shall go in and tell James. I mean it."

Mary's face was deathly white in the shadows of the room. She spoke in a half-whisper. "I've already decided to have the operation done. I decided earlier this afternoon. But now I'll tell you this, Ethel. . . ." The very quietness of her words added to their intensity. "If you say anything to James—in fact, if you cause any more trouble at all, I think I shall kill you. . . . I don't believe I shall be able to help myself."

She turned and left the room. Ethel sat frozen for a moment, then turned with shocked face to her mother. The old woman had her mouth open, too startled to remember her handkerchief.

"Did you hear her?" Ethel's voice was high-pitched, frightened. "Did you hear what she said? She threatened to kill me. She's bad; she's worse than any of us have thought. She's wicked. . . ."

Mrs. Allister was too shocked to answer. She sat with mouth agape, her myopic eyes glassy behind her spectacles. In the silence that followed they heard Mary tap on the door of James's study. A pause followed, and then a loud, impatient shout. They heard Mary's voice, drowned a second later by a sudden crash of furious discords. Quiet followed in which Mary could be heard, pleading and imploring. Then all other sounds were immersed in a wild shouting that rose to a frenzy. A mad smash of crockery sounded in the uproar. Mary's voice came again, sobbing and pleading, followed by her footsteps running down the hall and up the stairs. The wild raving of the composer died slowly to a murmur as the two women sat staring at one another, stiff with terror.

2

JAMES ALLISTER stood panting by the door of his study, listening to the echo of his shouting dying away in the far corners of the room. The eruptions of fury that had welled up and burst in blood-red flashes in his brain began to subside in frequence and severity. With hands clenched and body trembling, he stood motionless, feeling the cold sweat running down his face and back. One last spasm of rage sent a flash of crimson light across his eyes and tautened again the steel wire that cut into his temples. The veins in his forehead stood out like cords. Then, as the paroxysm died reluctantly away, his shaking body relaxed and the pressure on his temples eased.

With a groan he dropped into a chair, spent by the fury of his passion. He sat head in hands, his eyes, which had burned with such unnatural intensity a few minutes ago, now staring dully down at the green carpet. An unfamiliar object lay at his feet, but at first he made no attempt to focus his eyes on it, being quite content to sit without conscious thought as the steel wire round his head slackened further and brought him blessed relief. He had no memory of what had happened; he was aware only of a sense of utter exhaustion, as if he had just passed through some great physical or emotional experience.

At last he found the strength and desire to examine the thing at his feet. A frown crossed his pale face as he stared down at it. A broken cup handle. A cup handle. . . .Where could it have come from? He moved his eyes and saw other broken pieces of china lying on the floor around him. The contents of the cup had already sunk into the deep pile of the carpet, showing a darker green patch on its surface.

The frown deepened between his eyes. A broken cup and saucer. Why was it broken? Why was it lying there? He looked at his wristlet watch. Twenty minutes to four. This was the time they usually had tea. Then where was his? Why had they not brought it? He rose, and was about to press his bell-push when he hesitated. Of course; now he remembered. Mary had come in to ask if he wanted tea, and he had refused her offer. He stared at the manuscript on the piano. That was it. He had been having trouble with that phrase, and had not wanted disturbing. Relief at the memory soon passed when he found he could not recollect what had happened next. Lapses of memory such as this he had sometimes noticed before. Not always—only when concrete evidence lay before him, as it did now in the shape of the broken cup and saucer at his feet. It looked . . . he paused and frowned. It looked exactly as if someone had brought him tea in spite of his request to the contrary, and it had been dropped at his feet.

The strain of trying to remember made the steel wire tighten again round his temples. His mind seemed choked by some noxious, shadowy thing that stifled thought. Black and nebulous, an evil product from the shadow world, its writhing tentacles squeezed and strangled his every conscious thought at birth. He did not realize the thing was his own creation: the monster he had unconsciously willed into being to save his mind from the torture of memory and self-condemnation. All he knew was that it lay over his brain like a dark shadow, lifting only when he was immersed in his music.

A nameless fear came over him as his mind struggled to remember. What was happening to him? Why did his mind balk like this whenever he tried to reason or remember? Irritability merged with panic, and the two threatened to derange his mind again. The tightness grew at his temples; he stood with clenched hands, fighting back the terror. When his fear had subsided a little, he made another desperate effort to remember.

He could not. His mind tried first one road and then another, and each time ran into a black fog of emptiness. His fear grew at his helplessness. What was the matter with him? He wanted to scream, but terror choked his throat. His nerves tightened as he tried to pierce the mist around him. It was this inability to think clearly that made him sullen and abrupt in conversation these days. Sometimes, very occasionally, the tension seemed to ease slightly, the mist to lift. But so seldom now. . . . If only he could relax. . . . If he could sleep like others who put their heads on their pillows and were granted the bliss of unconsciousness. Even the few hours of sleep given him were full of wild and hideous dreams. . . . To sleep, oh, to sleep on and on, and know only the cool and calm of nothingness. . . .

Groaning, he lifted a hand to his forehead and felt its feverish heat. He stared down at the broken china again, and vague, swirling visions writhed in the mist of his mind, mocking him. It was Mary. . . . It had something to do with her, but what. . . ? He did not know. Oh, God; what was the matter with him? Why could he no longer think? Why was his forehead hot, and what were these iron hands that were crushing his skull. . . ?

An acute melancholy, the after-effects of his rage, settled over him. The study suddenly felt like a prison cell, holding in itself every nameless fear, and thrusting them at him from its shadowy corners. Its heat stifled him; he felt he could not breathe.

Opening the door, he stepped out quietly into the hall. He made no attempt to collect his hat and coat from the hall-stand. He had only one aim—to escape from the fear that brought waves of heat to his burning forehead.

Instinct told him to walk out of the house warily. If he were seen he would be asked a hundred questions, where he was going, why he was going, why he was not wearing his coat; and he knew the hot anger that seared his mind and exhausted his body would erupt again. So he was careful to remain unobserved, leaving the house by the kitchen quarters. He skirted the garden cunningly, keeping behind the hedge, and then made for a column of concrete steps that led down the cliff to the beach. The bitter wind cut through his smoking jacket like a knife. His body shuddered in protest, but his mind, feverish and tormented, barely noticed the discomfort.

Descending the steps, he reached the beach and crossed over to the wet sand at the edge of the waves. There he paused, his feverish eyes staring out over the raging sea. The wind drove spray over him, soaking his clothes, and the breaking waves sent long tongues of white surf licking hungrily out. Some of the far-flung sheets of water reached him, overflowing into his shoes and soaking his feet, but he made no effort to retreat. Then his wild eyes shifted, to settle on a ridge of rocks that stretched out into the sea ahead. He stared a moment, then turned abruptly and made his way towards it, his body moving jerkily, like an animated puppet.

Reaching the slippery rocks, he climbed over them towards where the waves were pounding and thundering in savage frustration. He reached the first of three huge rocks that formed the end of the ridge and walked upright over it, stepping forward without caution although its surface was treacherous with seaweed and the wind a wild thing that made vicious attempts to overthrow him. He reached the second rock and there he paused. With body swaying in the wind, he stood gazing at the tempestuous sea.

His mind was without conscious thought. He stood absorbing the mad turmoil of raging wind and sea as if it were a great, pagan symphony. The mighty thundering bass of the sea and the shrill scream of the wind came to him in waves of shuddering, primitive sound that held him transfixed. Patches of crimson, like gouts of blood, lay among the dark clouds over the sunset, and his brilliant eyes were fixed on them. He stood motionless, unconscious of cold or discomfort. Great, passionate chords of pagan music, stolen from the gods of the wind and storm, were rolling in awful majesty through him. He stood in ecstasy, every nerve of his body vibrating in wild sympathy. Forgotten now was his fear of the black monster that was choking his mind and dragging him to hell. Content with his abandonment to the pagan gods around him, it had drawn back and was leering at him from the murky environs beyond his mind.

A sudden wave, larger than its fellows, hurled itself savagely at the rock. Its impact was like thunder, sending a tremor through the solid granite. A sheet of water, hissing like rain, fell over the upright man. . . .

The icy impact sent a psychic shock through his whole being. A blinding flash of light illuminated the dark recesses of his mind, and in the split second of its passing allowed him to see and remember again the thing of guilt that had festered there. . . .

He saw it clearly again, this thing of shame that had been buried for so long. . . .He saw it again in all its putrescence.

Gone was the ecstasy of the moment. His arms lifted in agony, imploring the dark monster to return and blind him again. It stirred, but did not act at once. It lay sneering, punishing him for his earlier reproaches, watching his agony pitilessly.

With his mind a tormented hell, James Allister staggered on to the end rock. Cascades of spray showered over him. Alongside the rock the water boiled and seethed. Strange creatures with white faces and long, green limbs writhed and twisted towards him. "Come," they cried in welcome. "Come, come, James Allister," they called. "Come to us, for we are peace and forgetfulness. Our sleep is dreamless; in our arms the past will never be remembered. Come to us; we are peace and we are rest. Come, come, come. . . ."

They rose high on the waves, their long green arms held out in supplication. They flew forward as if to embrace him, vanished among the spray, then formed again. They were peace; they were rest. Eternal peace, his screaming mind told him. He heard their call again as he staggered nearer the edge of the rock. It came on the wings of the eager wind, in the sibilant hiss of the falling spray.

"James," their voices sang, strangely sweet. "James, James. . . ."

Still the black monster refused to ease his agony. It lay crouching, gloating over his torment. His face was contorted as memory scored deep gouges in his bleeding mind.

"James . . . James. . . ."

He was almost over the whirlpool now. The creatures were below him, calling, writhing, waiting for the embrace. He paused. One voice was familiar. He stared down. No; it could not be. Down there was peace and oblivion. Nothing of the past could exist. . . . Nothing of it. Yet he heard the voice again.

"James. Stop. For God's sake keep still."

He turned then, and saw her approaching. Her face was wild and her red hair dank with spray. Another blinding shock ripped through his brain. The black monster saw her and moved reluctantly forward, although slowly as yet. James crouched, his hands hiding his eyes, his shocked muscles tensed and ready. . . .

"James," came her cry over the scream of the wind. "Keep still. Don't move. Don't move. . . ."

3

FRANK paused outside the open door of the music-room. Stella was standing by the french windows, staring out into the back garden. The winter sun had broken through the clouds, and she was standing in a yellow patch of light. Her hair glowed like dull fire, and her body was a silhouette of grace.

Frank made his decision. He stepped into the room.

"Come out for a walk," he said.

She started and turned around. A flicker of welcome showed in her green eyes.

"Hello," she greeted.

"Come out for a walk," he said again. "It'll do you good."

Stella noticed he was dressed in overcoat and wellington boots. She hesitated, giving a shiver.

"That awful wind is still blowing," she said. "It's worse than ever today."

"You won't notice it once you're moving," he told her. "Come on. You have been riding about in cars too much lately."

There was a challenge in his words. "All right," she said, suddenly. "Wait here, and I'll get my things."

His eyes lit up as she swung out of the room. He waited, quietly content. She returned five minutes later, clad in mackintosh and fur-lined boots.

"All right," she told him. "Lead the way. Find the coldest and bleakest spot you can. I know you will, anyway."

"You misjudge me," Frank grinned. "I want to blow your cobwebs away, not kill you."

Her lips curled. "It'll take a good deal more than your wind to kill me."

He laughed, pulling out his pipe. She stared at him. "What are you lighting that thing for? Aren't we going now?"

"I thought you would want tea before you went," he said. "Mother is in the kitchen making it."

"Who's the soft one now?" she taunted. "Can't you face a breath of fresh air without a bowlful of tea inside you?"

He stuffed the pipe back into his coat pocket. "Come on, then," he grinned.

"You've asked for it." He took her arm in a hand that was surprisingly strong, and led her laughing down the hall and into the snow outside the house. The wind stung their faces with needles of ice.

"Which way do you want to go?" he shouted over the sound of the wind.

"Let's try the beach," she shouted back. "The tide is out."

Frank nodded, and they went round the house and down the back garden to the cliff edge, where the steps took them down to the beach, nearly three hundred feet below. Although the tide was coming in, there was still a wide strip of hard, wet sand left on which to walk.

This was familiar territory to Stella. Although normally she had little liking for walks in this weather, in the summer this same beach had been her consolation. Here she had lain in the long summer days, tanning her body until it had seemed dusted with gold powder. Even in those days there had been only an occasional sunbather as company. Now the beach was desolate, a glistening wet strip between iron-bound cliffs and raging sea.

They turned to the west. In that

direction the sand stretched for miles, there being only one obstruction—a promontory of rocks which jutted into the sea like a natural groyne. Once it was surmounted there were three clear miles and more of flat beach. The east beach was impassable, the cliffs sweeping out and dropping steeply into the sea, which engaged them in both high and low tides.

They set out along the sand. The wind was as fierce as on the cliffs above, stinging their faces with spray torn from the huge waves. Salt had destroyed the snow here, the only traces of it were white streaks lying on shelves high up on the cliff face. The sun, sinking into a haze, was already a red ball that hung low over the sea ahead. Above it the sky was a smoky, pastel-shaded mixture of blue and grey and green, but on the horizon a long, black bank of clouds was massing like a sullen army. Once the sun set behind those clouds darkness would come swiftly, but neither of them cared. High tide was still hours away, and both knew the beach well.

They reached the ridge of rocks in a few minutes and climbed over it. Stella made no attempt to help Frank. Purposely she kept her eyes averted and climbed slightly ahead of him. Dropping on the sand at the other side, she stood watching the great, white explosions of the waves bursting at the end of the promontory until Frank reached her side.

"Some of those waves would be a photographer's dream," she remarked.

He smiled his agreement. He was panting a little from his efforts, and she stood a few minutes more, as if fascinated by the waves.

"Where are Mervyn and Gwen this afternoon?" he asked, stepping forward again.

"Mervyn went to football with his friend, Bill Henson," she told him. "I think Gwen was in her room."

He nodded without further comment. The beach stretched before them, fading into the distant mist. Although not walking quite as quickly as she would have wished because of Frank's lameness, Stella felt the blood flowing more warmly through her veins. She turned her face deliberately into the lashing wind and breathed its saltness deeply into her lungs.

Watching her, Frank saw a glow of colour spreading through her cheeks. Tiny drops of spray hung on her long eyelashes, like globules of dew.

They spoke little on their way out. The wind made conversation difficult, blowing their words away. An occasional, desultory comment was all they passed to one another, and Stella found this adequate. She was enjoying this walk, and there was something warm and comforting in the nod and smile of the limping man at her side. Frank was a restful person, she thought—a man one could be natural with. With him one could throw away one's cloak of sophistication, and sing. . . . She did sing, into the teeth of the buffeting wind, and found reward in her companion's slow smile.

The sun turned blood-red and half-sank into the dark clouds that rose like a second sea on the horizon. The pastel sky faded and a grey mist crept from the sea and hung over the beach ahead. The wind redoubled in fury, triumphant at the approach of the night. Over the cliffs a pale, wintry moon shivered at the sight of the clouds that welled threateningly upwards.

Frank met Stella's eye, and nodded. They turned for home, she laughing as the wind sent her stumbling forward. Conversation proved easier now with the wind partly at their backs.

"It looks like being a dirty night," Frank remarked, pointing to the approaching clouds.

Stella nodded cheerfully. She felt oddly happy. She made no attempt to analyse her feelings, to find out why she felt this light-heartedness after months of restlessness and depression. If she did, she felt the mood would be lost. She was content that it was so, and did not question its cause. Light, bantering snatches of conversation passed between the two of them as they made their way back along the desolate, windswept beach.

Frank had been teasing her, and she had been replying in kind. They were about fifty yards from the promontory of rocks when she gripped his arm. The animal rapture of perfect health made her forget everything except the sheer joy of being alive and using her limbs. She pointed to the rocks ahead.

"I'll race you," she challenged. "Last there buys a packet of cigarettes. Come on."

She had actually started running when she remembered. . . .Checking herself, she stood deathly still, not daring to look back.

Then she turned and saw his face. . . .

Only for a moment, the fraction of a moment, did she see the man behind the mask. Then he was waving his hand sardonically towards the rocks ahead.

"Go on," he said. "There's a useful fable about a hare and a tortoise. . . ."

She did not laugh. She looked straight into his smiling face.

"It isn't a disgrace," she said harshly, deliberately turning her eyes down to his lame leg. "It isn't anything to be ashamed of. Do you think people care? Do you think women care?"

He winced and went very pale.

"Don't be a fool, Frank," she said. "Don't be a stupid fool."

Only when they reached the rocks was she able to relax. He limped beside her up to them without speaking. Then, behind a huge boulder that gave shelter from the wind, he stopped and offered her a cigarette. His familiar, cynical grin was back, but through it his eyes shone with approving warmth. He struck a match, holding it to her with cupped hands.

"Congratulations," he said quietly. "You handled that . . . situation . . . with admirable roughness. I'm grateful."

"I'm not interested in your gratitude," she said curtly, to hide her embarrassment. "I'm interested in whether you believe what I said or not. If you don't, then you're a fool. Because it happens to be true."

"Does it?"

"Of course it does," she snapped. "You lost that leg fighting for your country. Is that anything to be ashamed of?"

His eyes turned bleak and sombre. "Sometimes I think anyone who takes part in a war has something to be ashamed of." Then he smiled cynically. "My sin is twofold. If I had been decent and died, all would have been well. I might even have been a hero. But I wasn't so considerate. I went on living and that was very thoughtless. Now I'm a liability on my country. Worse than that, I'm a war relic. People resent me just as they resent bomb stories. I'm a derelict that reminds people how damn uncomfortable they were a few years ago, and how damn uncomfortable they might be again. Sometimes I commit an even greater felony—I remind people what nice fat profits they made out of blood and death. So you see I have every reason to be ashamed of myself."

"That's all sheer self-pity," she said scornfully. "Nothing else. You should snap out of it."

Frank looked at her in amusement, then laughed soundlessly. "You're probably quite right. That is one of the things I like about you, Stella. You're no hypocrite. You don't lie."

Her lips twisted. "Don't I?"

"Oh; you'll have your moments. Everyone has. But not as many as most people. You haven't the need for 'em. Do you know what makes most people lie— ordinary people, I mean?"

She shook her head.

"Respectability. Propriety," he told her. "Ironical, isn't it? The desire to keep up with the Joneses—to appear well-to-do and refined. People will lie and cheat and perjure their souls to do it. They must, you see, because no one is respectable and refined all the time." He chuckled. "Now that is where you are different. You don't give a damn what people think about you —as long as they think you are beautiful. You'd lie for that, of course—you'd use two-way stretches and artificial thing-a-ma-bobs to keep your figure—"

"Now wait a minute," she broke in with a laugh of relief. "If you're suggesting that I—"

"I'm not," he interrupted with a grin. "I've seen you on the beach, and you're divine. But you will probably use 'em later. . . ." He went on hastily before she could interrupt again. "But apart from that one thing, you don't give a cuss what people think about you. Mother and Ethel —who are both hypocrites—would call it brazen and shameless. I call it good home-spun common sense. It keeps you natural and it keeps you healthy."

Her eyes were brooding on the cold rocks ahead as he was speaking. The beach beyond was hidden by them. The wind moaned over the boulder behind which they sheltered.

"I'm no more honest than anyone else, Frank," she said bitterly. "In fact, I'm a damn sight worse. I've got my secrets and some of them stink."

"There you are," he shrugged. "You'll even admit that. How many others would?"

Stella turned on him passionately. "For God's sake don't go thinking I'm a saint, Frank. Not you—I couldn't stand that. I've committed more than my share of sins."

"I know that," he said coolly. "I know you're no angel. You've got your share of faults, but you've got strength with 'em. And give me a strong sinner to a flabby saint any day. There's potential strength and goodness in one; there's nothing but cant in the other. There's more in you, Stella, than in ninety per cent of the 'good' people we hear about who use their goodness as others use money to buy themselves a snug place in heaven afterwards. You'll reach your God just as quickly the way you're going. Perhaps more quickly."

She looked at him in wonder. She had

never heard him talk like this before. He was sitting on a rock and she was standing before him. There was enough light from the sunset and the wintry moon above for her to see his face. She wondered why it was she had never noticed before the likeness between him and his brothers. There was the same high forehead, the same well-chiselled nose and lips. . . . It was his expression, she realized. It was the lines that pain and years of cynicism had cut into his features. The claw marks of life had scratched deep into a face that should still have been young. They gave him a tougher, more weather-beaten look. But underneath, as she realized now, there was the same sensitive nature of his brothers. He had used his face as both a mask and shield to hide his nature, and the shield had received many dents and scratches in its defence.

"Let's get back to you," she said. "Why don't you practise what you preach? Why do you care about what people think or say—or what you imagine they think? Why are you ashamed of that leg? Why aren't you honest with yourself? You don't think you are as good as other men because of it. That's true, isn't it? Isn't it. . . ?"

"Yes," he said bitterly. "That's quite true." He stared down at his leg. "Nature abhors maimed things. In the animal world they are destroyed by their own fellow creatures. Sometimes I think we humans would do the same thing, if there weren't laws to prevent it. But laws can't stop people from thinking or showing their thoughts. It's ugly, Stella, that look in their eyes. Their social conscience and their primitive shrewdness are at loggerheads, the one telling 'em it is their duty to be kind, and the other telling 'em to get on with their business, and not waste time with a cripple. It all comes into their eyes —into a hybrid look of exasperated pity that's nauseating."

"It's pure imagination," she scoffed. "Nothing else. You've got a complex about it."

He shrugged ruefully. "Perhaps I have. But I've always had a strong sense of independence—or is that a sense of inferiority? Whichever it is, it took a bad beating when this leg went."

She shook her head angrily. "I can't

imagine a more capable man than you. I've always thought you strong—someone a person could rely on. You aren't going to disappoint me now, are you?"

She saw that look of hungry yearning behind his eyes again. Even his smiling mask could not conceal its glow. Then he laughed, without sound.

"What are you laughing at?"

Frank rose, smiling sardonically. "I was just thinking how humorous it would be if you chose this moment to tell a lie, even if it was a white one. Wouldn't that be ironical?"

She stared at him fiercely. "I'm not lying. Why should I lie?"

He put his hands on her shoulders. They were firm and strong. This was the first time he had touched her in a moment of seriousness. She stood erect, meeting his gaze defiantly. A timeless moment passed, and then his eyes crinkled suddenly at the corners. Lifting one hand, he touched her cheek. It was a brief thing, barely a brush of his glove, yet it was a caress such as she had not known before. She stood very still.

"And you aren't," he smiled. "God bless you for it."

His hands tightened then fell away as he turned and started for the house. She helped him now over an occasional, steeper rock. He made no demur; his eyes were smiling now as well as his lips. Suddenly she wanted to tell him everything. The reason for her restlessness, her bitterness, her moods. So that he, just he, would understand. To have done this would have brought her unspeakable relief.

But, even as the wish came to her, her eyes dulled. It was not fair to him, or to others. The luxury of confession could not be enjoyed when others were involved and had to pay for its procurement. Frank had been right about her in that one respect, she admitted. Crimes she might commit, but without the punishment to follow she had always felt something about them was disturbingly incomplete. . . . But when confession meant punishment for others, was it not a still greater sin to confess? Perhaps there lay her punishment.

Either way it did not matter, she told herself bitterly. She was not such a hypocrite as to encourage his affection when he knew nothing of her past life. Yet to tell him all would still mean the end of his companionship, his understanding, the warmth of his slow smile. . . . They would all go because there was one thing he would never, could never, forgive. . . . So, either way, the roads led into the desert.

"What's wrong?" he asked her quietly as they reached the beach beyond the rocks.

Stella realized he had sensed her change of mood. "Nothing," she muttered sullenly.

The gladness in his eyes faded reluctantly. They started along the beach in silence. A movement on the rocks on her left attracted Stella's eyes. She saw a dark figure silhouetted against the fading sunset. As she watched, it moved again, making its way nearer the end of the ridge where the massive waves pounded and thundered. Frank followed her gaze and stiffened.

"Good God; who is that?" he muttered. "What is he doing out there?"

Recognition came suddenly to Stella,

and with it fear. She clutched Frank's arm.

"Can't you see who it is? It's James. James, your brother. . . ."

Frank's face went white. "My God; it is! What is he doing out there?" He started forward. "I must get to him," he muttered.

With Stella helping him, he clambered over the slippery rocks. The going was bad, a succession of slime-covered rocks interspersed with pools of icy water. Frank could not leap the pools; he was forced to wade through them, gasping at the shock of the bitter cold. Rocks hid James from sight for a moment; then, through a gap, they caught sight of him again. He had moved; he was nearer the end of the promontory, and as they watched the spray from a bursting wave half-hid him from sight.

They reached a higher barrier of rocks. Stella managed to scramble up them and leaned down to help Frank. He caught her arm, but even with its assistance was unable to make the climb. One foot slipped and he fell backwards, almost dragging Stella with him.

He rose, cursing his helplessness.

"Are you all right?" Stella called anxiously over the howl of the wind.

Seeing he was, she threw a glance over her shoulder and winced at the sight of James almost at the edge of the rocks.

"I'll have to go on," she called down to Frank.

"Be careful!" he shouted back. "For God's sake be careful!"

She nodded and ran on. There was thirty yards of boulders between her and the three large rocks which formed the end of the ridge, and she scrambled over them frantically. Dusk was approaching rapidly, and the rocks were black against the sky. The wind sprang and sprang again at her, screaming threats at her temerity. She could no longer see James for the hulk of rock ahead. Her foot slipped on a patch of seaweed, and she fell sidewards, scraping her elbow along a jagged rock. Biting back the pain she stumbled on, her fur-lined boots icy, sodden weights on her feet. At last she reached the first of the three rocks.

She clambered on to it, and peered

forward. James was on the third and last rock, and as she watched he drew nearer its edge.

"James," she screamed. "James, James. . . ."

He did not hear her voice over the exultant howl of the wind. His eyes were fixed on a maelstrom of seething water among the rocks below. His eyes never left it as he slowly approached the edge.

Desperately she ran forward over the slippery rock. The wind caught her bodily and threw her sidewards. For one fearful moment she thought she would be hurled into the raging water. Sobbing, she clutched at the wet rock and pulled herself upright again. She saw James clearly now through the curtains of spray. Agony was distorting his sensitive face, yet there was a look of yearning mingled with it as he stared down at the writhing, sucking water below. He had the look of a man tormented beyond all human understanding who has seen at last a way of escape.

"James," she sobbed. "James. . . ."

She was on the third rock now, and she was afraid. She dare not run forward to clutch him, although he was now on the extreme edge. Instinct told her that the sudden touch of a hand would be like a trigger to his mind. She approached him slowly. A wave broke over the rock and its icy water sent her reeling back, gasping with shock. For a second he vanished completely from her sight, then she saw him straightening himself, his wild eyes still fixed on the whirlpool below. He crouched, preparing to jump.

"James!" she screamed in terror. "Stop! For God's sake keep still. . . ."

4

FRANK made a last desperate effort to climb the barrier of rocks, and fell back with a groan. It was no use; he realized the impossibility of making the climb alone. Blood drawn from his previous efforts was trickling down one leg, and his hands were scored and grazed. Frantically he limped to an adjacent rock and dragged himself on to its flat top, from which he could see the grim tableau ahead.

Through the spray that kept sweeping across his vision, he saw Stella advancing slowly on James. He was near enough to see their expressions: the frightened whiteness of Stella, and the agonized raptness of James, who was staring in fascination at the maelstrom below. The composer had not seen Stella yet; he was balancing on the extreme edge of the rock and seemed about to hurl himself forward.

Frank writhed in his helplessness. He was like a man on the rack, his lined face drawn in torment and every muscle of his body strained to breaking point. He muttered wild, helpless curses.

He saw Stella draw nearer. The wind carried her voice to him. Still James did not move. Frank understood the girl's caution. He knew as well as she the danger to the composer of a sudden, abrupt move. As he watched, a deluge of spray hid them both from his sight. His hands clutched on the rock before him, he dared not look. The water splattered down, some of it reaching him. He opened his eyes fearfully, expecting to see one or both had vanished. His breath sobbed back into his lungs as they reappeared through the spray.

James was crouching, preparing to jump. Frank heard Stella scream and saw her run forward. Now his fear was for her. James had turned abruptly and his face was ghastly to see. There was more than shock in it, more than fury at the sudden interference. There was something else, something that made his face contort and his hands shut out his eyes as if he were being confronted by Medusa. . . .

Stella was at his side now, and Frank knew how near she was to death. If his brother clutched her in his frenzy and jumped, they would go to death together in the boiling fury below. He watched in agony.

He heard Stella cry again, although her words were lost to him. Her hand was on the composer's arm, resting on his dripping sleeve. James recoiled at her touch, his hands leaving his eyes. His feet were not two feet from the edge. She touched him again, pulling gently. Her lips were moving as she spoke to him. His eyes were on her face, his expression terrible to see, his body crouching as if to spring. For timeless seconds both were motionless, while behind them the waves leapt like hungry beasts trying to drag them down.

Frank averted his face. The dull boom of a large wave brought his eyes round in terror again. A curtain of spray hid them from sight. As it settled, he saw them once more. . . .

He let his breath out, suddenly conscious of the tightness of his chest. For a moment he relaxed weakly against the rock. They were moving away from the edge. . . . Six feet, ten. . . . James was advancing slowly under the pull of her insistent arm. His expression was changing, becoming dull again. They reached the second rock, the first . . . and then Frank was helping them down.

James came first and then Stella. Frank caught hold of her, his fingers biting deeply into her arm. Their eyes met . . . and she leaned suddenly against him. He held her tightly, feeling the deep shudder of her body.

His dry lips moved, searching for words. "You were wonderful!" he muttered. "Absolutely wonderful!"

Stella pulled away from him, sinking down on a rock. Her face was deathlike. She sat with her head between her knees.

"Go away," she said in a strangled voice. "I want to be sick."

He knelt beside her, watching her anxiously.

James was standing sullenly alongside them, staring around with moody, puzzled eyes. The black thing in his mind had taken full possession of him again and blanked out all memory of the past. The agony on his face had subsided, leaving it dark and sullen.

"Go away," Stella muttered to Frank.

His arm was around her. He held her tightly, ignoring the hand that tried to push him away. Her body heaved and retched violently. A minute passed before she was able to straighten herself.

"Feel better now?" Frank asked.

"I'm all right," she lied, rising unsteadily. She nodded to James. "We'd better be getting back or we'll all have pneumonia."

Between them, they led James back to the beach. He stumbled forward with bent head, speaking to neither of them.

Frank turned on him when their feet sank at last into the sand. "What the devil were you doing out there?" he asked roughly, reaction turning him to anger.

The composer gave him a dull resentful glance. "I came for a walk," he muttered. "I came for a walk, and then . . ." His brows drew together in sudden alarm. "I can't remember what happened then."

Stella motioned to Frank to say no more, and they hurried on in silence. The dark cloud had spread from the horizon almost to the winter moon above, and fine snow mixed with the spray from the oncoming waves. The wind pierced their wet clothes and cut them to the bone.

At last they reached the cliff steps and left the bleak, windswept beach behind. They had almost reached the top when Mary appeared, running down towards them. She was without hat and coat, and her face was frantic with anxiety. She stopped short at the sight of them, almost breaking down in relief at seeing James.

"Steady," Frank said, going up to her. "Everything is all right."

Pulling away from him, she ran down to James. Her eyes dilated in fear at the sight of his sodden clothes.

"There's a good deal of spray on the beach," Stella said meaningly. "We met James down there. He had gone for a walk and we all came back together."

Her tone warned Mary. She turned to James, trying to smile. "I didn't know you wanted a walk, dear. I'd have come with you, had I known. I felt like some fresh air myself."

"I didn't feel like company," he muttered, starting up the steps.

Mary looked at Stella in fear. Stella

shook her head and whispered, "We'll tell you everything in a minute."

Together they followed the two men up the steps, and into the house above.

An hour later Stella left her bedroom and made her way down to the lounge. She was dressed in a warm skirt and cardigan. A hot bath and a brisk rub down had taken most of the chill from her body, although an occasional shiver still ran through her.

Frank and Mary were in the lounge as she entered. Both rose on seeing her. Mary, with white drawn face, came over to her at once.

"Frank has told me what you did," she said simply. "I shall never forget it." She tried to take Stella's hand in her gratitude.

Stella pulled away abruptly and walked to the fire. "Drop it," she said shortly. "It was nothing."

The hurt in Mary's eyes died away as quickly as it came. "It was wonderfully brave of you," she said. "You might have been killed."

Stella shrugged. She leaned over the fire as another shiver ran through her.

"You should be in bed," Frank told her grimly. "You were soaked to the skin."

"I'm all right," she muttered. She heard a clink of glasses and, turning her head, saw that Frank was busy with a bottle of rum. She eyed him mockingly.

"Hello, where's this from? Your secret cache?"

"Correct," he grinned, bringing her a large glass. She smelt at it and shuddered.

"I can't bear the stuff," she told him.

"Drink it off," he insisted. "It'll take that chill out of your bones. I'm two up on you already." He turned to Mary, his voice suddenly gentle. "Come on, Mary. Sit down and have this first."

Mary turned from the door by which she was standing. She shook her head, managing a smile. "Afterwards, Frank. When I've finished."

He winced at the look in her eyes. "Let me do it," he begged. "You sit here and let me tell him."

"No," she said quietly. "I'd rather do it myself. I won't be long. . . ." She turned abruptly and left the room, closing the door behind her.

Frank stood motionless a moment, then

filled his own glass with shaking hands. He turned wearily to his seat. He met Stella's questioning eyes and nodded. "Be gentle with her, Stella. She has gone to 'phone Evans."

Her eyes widened. "You mean—about the operation. . . ?"

He nodded again. "I told her everything that happened this afternoon. She realized she couldn't afford to wait any longer."

Stella was staring into the fire. Her eyes had a bitter, distant look in them. "So that is the end of it," she breathed. "The end of it all. . . ." A shudder ran through her, and she lifted her glass and drank deeply. The strong liquor made her grimace. Her lips twisted at him.

"You over-estimate me."

"If you feel anything like me, you need a strong one tonight," he said slowly.

"Where is James now?" she asked abruptly.

"He's had a hot bath, and Mary managed to get him into the bed in his study. But he'll be up again before the night is over."

"How long do you think it will be before he has the operation?"

"Not long. I think Evans will have everything arranged. Once he gets the all clear, I expect him to move quickly. I wouldn't be surprised if they don't take James away tomorrow or Monday."

She shuddered again, and drained her glass.

"Have another," Frank said.

She hesitated, then held out her glass defiantly to him.

"Why not?"

He drained his own glass, and then went and filled them both. He returned and stood by her side, looking down at the loveliness of her. In the soft lamplight the swirls of her hair gleamed like red-copper pools. In the whiteness of her oval face, her grey-green eyes, with their long, curled lashes, appeared enormous. She lifted them to him and a wave of longing that was pure anguish swept over him.

"You were wonderful out there this afternoon," he said gruffly. "You took your life in your hands when you touched his arm." He lifted his glass, grinning to hide the fear his memory invoked. "Here's to those strong sinners we talked about."

Her face was averted; he did not see the

expression on it. She did not move for a moment; then turned towards him bitterly, lifting her glass.

"Here's to them. To all their rotten souls. . . ."

There was the ting of the telephone-bell in the hall as the receiver was put down. Footsteps moved slowly away and up the stairs. At the sound of them, Frank's mood changed.

"What a rotten business this life is. What a dirty rotten business." His words were accusing, a denunciation.

Stella looked up at him. His inflamed eyes were fixed savagely on the door. "It's like a death sentence for her," he said bitterly. "She feels she is his executioner. What damn justice is there in a world where such things can happen?"

Stella did not move or speak.

He pointed his finger to the door. "You know what she has gone through," he growled. "You know how much she cares about James. And what is her reward for all that love and devotion?" He laughed, an ugly harsh sound. "A kick in the belly. That's what she gets. Of all the people in the world, she has to be the one to give

her consent. And it doesn't stop there—
no, by God, it doesn't. Not if what she
fears comes true. Because then she has
either to see the reproach in his eyes for
the rest of her life, or the emptiness—
whichever Fate is kind enough to leave
her. Can you imagine a worse hell for a
woman? Can you believe in Divine justice
when such things can happen?"

A long, deep shudder ran through the
listening woman.

Frank stared down at her, almost
accusingly. "Anyone who loves is a fool,"
he told her harshly. "The moment you
love you give a hostage to Fate. There are
a thousand ways it can get you then. While
you are alone you are safe, and if you don't
give a damn about yourself, you are wholly
safe. It can't touch you. But love, and it
will torture the life out of you."

"You're bitter," she breathed. "You're
more bitter than I am."

He stared at her angrily. "You've no
right to be bitter. You're young. You
haven't seen men killing one another. You
haven't seen what filthy beasts human
beings can be. You haven't lived in mud
and blood and disease, and prayed to a

God that never came. You haven't seen your friends writhing with their guts hanging out, and then gone on living to see a world that makes bigger and better atom bombs. Damn it all to hell."

"There was something else, too, wasn't there?" she whispered. "Someone you loved?"

The veins were standing out on his forehead. He drained his glass, then leaned forward, his eyes full on her face.

"Yes; there was," he sneered. "Once I was a fool."

"When?" she asked quietly.

"During the war, when all men are fools."

"What happened?" she whispered. Then she could have bitten off her tongue. Suddenly she knew.

He did not spare himself. His words were cruelly deliberate. "Very little, really. She had made a slight mistake, that was all. She told me so when I came out of the hospital. She wanted someone with two legs. It's understandable, really."

"Damn the bitch," she said suddenly, savagely.

Frank shrugged, pouring himself

another drink. "Why blame her? It's all part of the unlovely business. That was my point."

She paused, trying to find words to say. They came at last.

"Down on the beach I said women don't mind these things. I meant it. They don't, at least ninety per cent of them don't. . . . You were well rid of yours. Can't you see that? You were lucky."

There was a mocking smile on his face as he lifted his glass to her. "Of course I see it. I have no hostage to Fate. She did me a favour. Here's to her dear little heart."

"And so you will never love again?" she asked slowly. "Is that what you mean?"

She saw his hand shaking as it held his glass. She rose and stood beside him. "Is that what you mean?" she asked again.

He stood motionless with the glass at his lips. "If I were not such a fool," he said harshly. "Yes. But people don't change. The same fool that was in me then is in me now."

"Go on," she breathed. "And what does the fool say?"

He turned to her then, and she flinched

at the raw pain in his eyes. His lips twisted. "The fool whimpers at me that he wishes I were rich and you were less beautiful."

"I were less beautiful. . . ." It was a second or two before she understood.

"Yes. But then I told you he was a fool," he sneered, draining his glass.

Stella spoke bitterly. "Yes, it might have been better for me if I were plainer. Don't worry about my looks. . . . Sometimes I think I hate them myself."

His voice was soft, distant. "Like all fools I worship beauty. I worship it from afar. And because of my worship I can't bear to see it in sackcloth and ashes and bound to a cripple. I don't like seeking larks in lime traps. . . ."

"You are a fool," she said vehemently. "A stupid fool."

He bowed mockingly. "Then we both agree."

The front door closed heavily, and a second later Mervyn entered the lounge. His walk was slightly unsteady, and his face flushed with alcohol. He waved an arm cheerily at them both, although his heavy-lidded eyes were moving over Stella.

"H'llo," he greeted.

Frank looked at Stella, his lips twisting. Then, with a sudden curse, he brought his glass heavily down on the table and limped from the room.

Mervyn stared after him, then at Stella. "What's th' matter with him?" he asked.

Stella turned away in disappointment. Mervyn came forward suspiciously, his eyes flickering to the bottle of rum and glasses on the table.

"He hasn't been makin' up to you, has he?"

"Stop talking like a fool!" Stella snapped, wheeling round on him.

His face became sulky. "I'm not being a fool. He looked damned disappointed to see me come in."

"What do you want him to do?" she asked sarcastically. "Leap up and kiss you?" Then she tried to make her tone more agreeable. "How was the football this afternoon?"

"Shocking," he grumbled. "We didn't stay to the finish. How about a little drink?" he suggested slyly, eyeing the bottle again.

"By the look of you, you've had enough," she told him.

"You sound like Gwen," he grumbled, pouring himself a stiff drink. He was reaching for the water carafe when his hand hesitated. There was the sound of acrimonious footsteps hurrying down the hall. He set the glass down in alarm. "That sounds like her now."

"You should have gone straight up to see her," Stella muttered.

The footsteps reached the door and Gwen stalked into the room. Her make-up had been neglected; the powder on her cheeks was streaked with dried tears, and lipstick had smudged along her thin mouth, giving it a torn, grotesque appearance. Wisps of dyed hair straggled down one cheek, and her dress was crumpled. She looked pathetically middle-aged. Her eyes were malevolent.

"So you're back at last," she spat at Mervyn.

He eyed her with trepidation. "I've just got in. I was just coming upstairs to see you."

"Lying won't help you now," she broke in viciously. "I know everything that's going on. Don't try any more of your bluffing."

Stella sank into a chair. Her body was tense and stiff. Faint lines of strain appeared alongside her nostrils and lips.

Mervyn's face was a picture of guilt and dismay. He tried to bluster. "I don't know what you're talking about."

Gwen's eyes stabbed at him in hatred. "You liar. You know what I mean all right. You dirty old . . ."

"Oh; I say. Please . . ." Mervyn lifted a hand in protest.

"Don't look so shocked," she said viciously. "You bring me to this house, telling me that because Stella is my half-sister it is our duty to be with her for Christmas, and all the time you came with one thing in your mind—to seduce her at the first opportunity. And she was waiting for you—everything was planned and ready. The little . . ."

Stella's green eyes glowed. Her voice was icy. "Don't go too far, Gwen."

"Keep quiet, you," Gwen spat. "I'm coming to you in a minute. And I'm going a lot further yet." She turned back on Mervyn. "I want to know why you are buying her presents costing hundreds of pounds. Are they a bribe for her favours, or are they in return for them?"

Very sober now, Mervyn looked at Stella in dismay and then at Gwen. He licked his lips nervously. "Presents," he muttered. "I don't know what you're talking about."

"Don't you?" Gwen sneered. She unlocked one of her tightly clenched hands to show a ruby brooch. "Do you recognize this? And there are two ear-rings to match it in her room," she went on, stabbing a finger towards Stella.

Mervyn was ludicrous in his dismay. His eyes goggled at the brooch.

"Where did you get that?' he muttered.

Stella jumped up like an enraged tigress. "How dare you!"

Gwen laughed triumphantly. "Neither of you thought of that, did you? You fools —you didn't think you could get away with this, did you, right under my nose? I found this jewellery in your pocket the same day you bought it," she told Mervyn. "I kept quiet at first, in case it was a Christmas present for me. But on Thursday night I found out it had gone, and I guessed who had got it then. But I waited to be quite sure."

"You waited until I went out and then searched my bedroom," Stella interrupted furiously. "You went in this afternoon and stole it."

"Don't look so shocked!" Gwen blazed at her. "It isn't much beside what you're trying to steal from me. I'll go a damn sight further too, before I let you get away with that." She swung round on the dismayed Mervyn. "You fool," she gibed. "She's only after your money. . . ."

White with fury Stella walked towards the open door. Gwen turned on her in a flash.

"Where do you think you are going?"

"There's a sick man in the study across the hall," Stella told her bitterly. "Your screaming will be heard all over the house."

Gwen sneered. "So that's the way you try to squirm out of it."

"I'm not trying to squirm out of anything," Stella said with contempt. "But for God's sake be decent. It isn't the family's fault this has happened."

Mervyn lumbered forward. "I agree,"

he muttered. "If we must have it out, let's go somewhere else to do it."

His intrusion was more than enough to set a match again to the gun-cotton of Gwen's temper. She turned on him in such a blaze of fury that he halted and stepped back in fright.

"You damned hypocrite!" she screamed. "You'll seduce your wife's sister and then start belly-aching about social proprieties. Decency! My God! Neither of you are going to get out of this so easily."

The door of the drawing-room opposite opened suddenly and Frank approached them with set face. His eyes went from one to the other of them, not changing in expression as they reached and passed Stella. He stepped inside the lounge, closing the door behind him.

His voice was stern. "I'm sorry to intrude like this, but I must ask you to keep your voices down. Something pretty serious happened this afternoon, and James is in a dangerous state. Any excitement might do him harm. You understand, don't you?"

"Of course," Mervyn muttered gruffly. "I'm damned sorry. Come on." He turned to go but Gwen ignored him. She pointed venomously to Stella.

"Do you know what she is trying to do?" she asked Frank.

His eyes were bleak. "Whatever it is, I am sure it is no business of mine," he said quietly.

Stella's face turned bitter at his words. She walked slowly away.

"Then it should be," Gwen retorted. "After all, she is your sister-in-law, and she is in your house. You surely can't approve of her trying to seduce my husband under its roof."

Mervyn came back desperately. "Gwen. For heaven's sake—"

"You cheap coward!" she shouted at him. "You never could stand up to anything. You'll lie and cheat, but you'll never take your punishment like a man."

Perspiration was rolling down Mervyn's florid face. He turned to Frank in misery. "I'm sorry, old man," he muttered. "We'll get out as soon as we can. That I'll promise you." He flung open the door and walked away hastily down the hall.

"You're the one that wanted to stay," Gwen yelled after him. "You dirty old swine!" She swung round on Stella. "You try and get him, that's all. See what happens. I'll drag out all the dirty washing I can find and hang it up for the world to see."

She met Stella's contemptuous gaze and the last of her control went. She turned to Frank in sudden decision. Her eyes were like hard stones, pitiless and vindictive.

"Now I'll tell you something you should know," she said between her teeth. "Something I had guessed, but wasn't sure about until the party last Tuesday when I played a certain waltz. . . ."

Stella's checks suddenly went ashen. She opened her mouth to protest, then her shoulders slumped. She walked over to the fireplace and lit a cigarette. She stood motionless with her back to them, staring down at the flames. Gwen watched her exultantly.

"I played it specially," she sneered. "Something happened in this room last Saturday morning that set me thinking. So I played that waltz when James was present—to see what would happen. And something did happen. You'll remember —you were there."

Frank was standing like a statue. He did not speak. Gwen went on pitilessly. "That waltz was a favourite tune of hers during the war," she said, jabbing a finger at Stella. "She was always humming it when she was staying with me. Well, I went away for a fortnight in '44 and left her alone in my flat. When I got back the woman who lives above told me a man had come home with her one night—a man who played the piano beautifully. She had heard him playing Stella's favourite waltz on my piano." Her voice was sly, insinuative. "Are you following me. . . ?"

Frank was staring at her in unbelief. His nostrils were pinched and white, and his breath was rasping through them. Suddenly he came to life and flung open the door.

"I want no more of this, Mrs. Ashburn," he said harshly. "Please be so good as to control yourself and leave this room."

Her eyes narrowed. She turned on him like a harridan. "So you've fallen for her as well, have you? She's made a fool out of you, too. You don't want to hear what a dirty little tart she is. You don't want a possible reason why your brother is insane, crazy with remorse. All right—but she isn't going to get away with it. If you won't hear it, then her mother-in-law shall. I'll write and tell her everything. She isn't going to get away with it, I tell you. . . ."

Frank motioned again to the open door. "You can't face up to it, can you?" she screamed. "You want to keep your family's nose clean. Well, go to hell! Go to hell with the rest of your rotten family!"

With a curse she walked out and slammed the door behind her. Frank stood transfixed, his incredulous eyes on Stella. She made no movement. She was still standing before the fireplace, head on arms, staring down into the flames. The sound of the grandfather clock was like a hammer, thudding in the heavy, motionless air.

When Frank spoke at last, his voice was part of the nightmare into which he had fallen. It was his voice, and yet he could not recognize it.

"Was that true?" he said. "Was it James?"

"Yes," Stella whispered, without turning her head.

"James!" he breathed. "You and James! My God. . . !" His face writhed with pain as if he had received a blow low in the stomach. He shook his head to clear the daze that deadened thought.

He moved slowly forward, one foot before the other. She heard him, and her body cringed away. Her face was hidden in her hands.

"Leave me alone," she whispered. "I've had enough. Go away and leave me."

Her slim body was twitching and jerking in torment. Even in that moment he was acutely conscious of his desire for her. The revelation came as a shock to him, choking back the words in his throat.

He reached an armchair and leaned heavily on it. He looked at the slim-flanked, full-bosomed beauty of her, and suddenly found himself cursing James and Mary and the world. Let her past lie where she had buried it. Why should he lose what he might yet gain? James's recovery was more than doubtful, whatever evidence came to light; but her beauty was real, it was the substance beside the shadow and he desired it madly.

"Go away," she breathed again. "Don't stand there looking at me like that. I can't stand it. For God's sake go away. . . ."

The sudden memory of Mary's face on hearing of James's attempted suicide came back to him. Its agony, its hopeless despair. . . . He took a deep, shuddering breath.

"I haven't told you this yet," he said slowly. "No one knows but Mary and myself. But the reason she has held off the operation is because the specialist believes James has some secret locked away in his mind. If Mary can find out what it is, there is a slight chance of saving him. Do you understand?"

Stella turned a dazed, uncomprehending face to him. "You say if Mary knew . . . it might save him?"

"Yes. It is his one chance. While the secret is locked up in his mind it is destroying him."

She laughed suddenly, a high-pitched ironical laugh that sent a jangle of discords through his strung nerves. "If Mary knew, it might save him. . . ! Oh, my God, that's funny! That's funny. . . !"

He saw the horror in her face, heard it in her laughter, and did not understand. She dropped her head back into her arms, her body shuddering in agony.

He made himself go on. "Is this secret you share with him enough to drive him insane?"

Her body stiffened, and grew still. The silence pressed on his temples. He felt his pulse pounding in his clenched hands.

It was a full half-minute before she lifted her face and he saw, almost with a shock, that it was tear-stained. He had never seen tears on that hard, lovely face before. But the tears were drying fast. He winced at the animosity in her eyes. Gone was their understanding, their friendship, so tardily won. She was an outcast again, and he, with all other men, was her enemy. An enemy to whom she must divulge a secret she would have died to keep. Such was his belief at that moment.

With twisting lips she reached out for her cigarettes. She lit one, her every movement now careless and cynical. She turned to him and gave her answer.

"Yes," she said. "Quite enough."

To the last he had hoped otherwise. His heart gave one great throb, and then became inert lead in his breast.

She blew out a cloud of smoke. "Sit down and let me tell it to you," she sneered. "It's a fascinating little story. . . ."

Frank moved one hand. "No," he said dully. "I don't want to hear. I only wanted to be sure. . . . Tell it to Mary; she is the one to know. It's her last chance to save James. Tell her everything. I'll send her in."

He turned and limped to the door. Her words followed him like wolves, snapping and tearing at his dragging feet. "Don't you want to hear first? So I'm no hypocrite, aren't I? I don't lie, don't I? You fool. You poor, stupid, lame fool. . . ."

He should have been glad. He should have been jubilant that he had made the one discovery that gave Mary her chance to save his brother's mind. But, as he closed the door and walked slowly across the cold, draughty hall, his triumph was dust and ashes in his mouth.

5

WITH haggard face Frank sat alone in the drawing-room. Beside him lay his pipe, cold and forgotten. Long minutes passed in which he sat motionless, lost in a bleak sea of sombre thoughts.

He started at the sound of footsteps and jumped to his feet a second later as Mary entered the room. He limped towards her, helping her to a chair. Her eyes were dazed; she looked at him, at the room, at the chair as if they were all suddenly things of fantasy. She sank down and sat a moment with closed eyes.

Frank stood before her uncertainly. Then she lifted her face up to him, replying to the mute question in his eyes.

"She has told me everything," she whispered, raising her hands to her temples. "And it's . . . incredible, Frank. I still can't believe it."

He moved to her side, to keep his face from her sight.

"Is it . . . what you hoped to hear?"

She gave one convulsive, hysterical sob; then gripped the sides of her chair as if her life depended on them.

"Yes," she said bitterly. "It was all I had . . . hoped for."

He dropped one hand on her shoulder and held it tightly until she had recovered. Then he limped wearily back to his chair.

"It's all clear now," she said. "She has told me everything. It was through James and her that—"

"No, please," he broke in harshly, one hand held out in protest. "I don't want to hear. Not the details. Please. . . ."

Her grey eyes stared at him in confused surprise.

"I'm sorry," he muttered. "But I would rather not know—not tonight. But are you quite sure . . . what you have heard. . . is the cause of James's condition?"

Pain welled back into her eyes. Her voice was bitter again. "Oh, yes. Quite sure."

"I know how hard it must have been for you. But you did want to know, didn't you?"

"Of course," she said fervently. "Don't

think I'm not grateful. I am. It's like a miracle, coming tonight when I had given up all hope. I'm unspeakably grateful. But it was a shock. . . . I'll get used to it in a minute or two."

"I know," he said gently. "I know how you feel. What are you going to do now?"

She stared at him as if surprised at his question. "I shall go in to James as soon as he wakes up, of course. . . ."

He stiffened in alarm. "You mustn't do that. You must 'phone Evans and tell him. He will arrange for James to see a psychiatrist."

Mary shook her head in determination. "No, Frank. That wouldn't be fair to John. He would never agree to my going in to James alone, and once he had refused permission I would be obliged to obey him. The responsibility would be his then, and he has risked enough for me already."

"But if he wouldn't give you permission, then it must be too dangerous."

"It's my one chance," she said quietly, "and I must take it."

"But why? You might ruin everything. Leave it to a psychiatrist; he will know exactly what to do."

Her answer was wistful. "I can't explain why, but I feel that if he goes to a psychiatrist, his mind is certain to go. I feel I am the only one with a chance to save him."

"Surely that is just fancy," he muttered. "A man skilled in these matters must have a better chance than you. It is a terribly delicate task—one wrong word could destroy him. . . . You must 'phone Evans."

"No," she said, with abrupt finality. "I won't bring John into this. In any case, I don't think he would be able to find anyone prepared to take on James's case. I haven't told you this, but they all think he is too far gone for psychoanalysis to succeed. No one would dare to take the risk."

Frank's alarm grew. "Then you mustn't take the risk yourself. You can't go directly against the advice of experts. You must think of yourself. It might be terribly dangerous. No one knows what he will do when he hears."

Her grey eyes appealed to him. "Wouldn't you do the same if you were I? It's my one chance to save him—to bring back the James we know. I feel I have been given this chance to use. If I don't use it, then his last hope has gone. I *must* go in to him. . . .I'm not afraid for myself."

"But a psychiatrist could make more use of the knowledge than you could," he argued desperately. "You must see that."

She shook her head stubbornly. "No. Even if one would take on his case, I would still think I had a better chance. Something deep inside tells me so. I *know*, Frank. I can't explain why, but I know."

"But it is so illogical. . . ."

"It isn't," she cried passionately. "There are some things that can't be weighed and measured by science. Some things are outside reason. I *feel* I am right, and tonight I put more faith in what I feel than what I think. I *know*, Frank, that I have the best chance of saving him. A psychiatrist is an impersonal creature, but I am his wife. A psychiatrist can't forgive him, but I can—at least for part of the thing he did, perhaps for all of it." She leaned forward pleadingly. "Let me tell you what it was, Frank. I must talk to someone. Let me tell you what he did, and then you will understand better. Why won't you let me tell you?"

A look almost of panic came into his eyes. He half-rose and then slumped heavily back. "All right," he muttered in despair. "Go on. . . ."

She looked at him gratefully and then sat silent a moment, grouping her thoughts. The sound of a car engine came to them. A few seconds later it receded down the drive, losing its identity quickly in the moaning wind. The Ashburns had gone.

Frank sat with half-closed eyes, waiting for the blow. His shoulders hunched imperceptibly as Mary began speaking, her voice halting and low.

"It happened in 1944, after Stella and David had been married for nearly a year. Stella was staying with Gwen, in a flat in London. At that time she had met none of your family. . . . She had not seen David for months, and she says she was bored and lonely. She wanted to join up, but the Food Ministry would not release her. A few weeks before D-day Gwen went away for a fortnight's holiday with Mervyn, who was up in the North somewhere, leaving

Stella alone in the flat. During that time Stella heard from one of David's friends that James was on leave. . . .

"I remember that leave well," Mary went on quietly. "James had only been given two days, and I was in Northern Ireland at the time. There was no chance of our meeting, and so he told me by letter he would spend the leave in London with some friends. I knew it was not his fault, but I was sorry. D-day was so near."

Frank nodded without speaking. His throat was dry and his heart beating heavily. He listened with bowed head as Mary continued:

"Stella says she had always wanted to meet James, and her friend arranged an introduction for her. She did not meet him as David's wife. She called herself Miss Lawson—"

Frank broke in with one harsh monosyllable. "Why?"

"She says she did it for a joke—that she meant to tell him later and give him a surprise. He took her to a night-club, and saw her home. And then . . ." Her voice faltered, then continued, bitterness lending it strength.

"Stella never told him who she was. And so . . . he stayed the night with her. It was during that night that he played his waltz for her on Gwen's piano. It was a favourite tune of hers. A neighbour in the flat above heard his playing, and mentioned to Gwen later what a beautiful pianist Stella had entertained."

Frank found words at last. He nodded heavily. "Yes; I see it all now. That was why Gwen played it at the party the other night. It was to test James's reactions. Something had awakened her suspicions last Saturday. I don't think she meant to tell me tonight. I think her idea was to hold the threat over Stella's head, but her jealousy proved too much for her. . . ."

"Stella said the same thing," Mary told him. "She said Mr. Ashburn wanted her to go away with him, and his wife found out. That was the cause of the quarrel tonight."

Frank hesitated, trying to choose his words carefully. "From what Gwen said to me tonight, I guessed something of the sort had happened between James and Stella." His voice was gentle. "I know how you must feel—what a shock it must have been to you. But . . ." He paused again, groping for the right words to use. "Bad though it is, I can't feel it is enough to turn James's mind—even when he found out she was David's wife. Some men are more sensitive than others, I know, but . . . to do this to him . . . I can't see that."

Her lips twisted bitterly. "I haven't finished yet, Frank. The worst has yet to come. You see, the next morning David came home on an unexpected forty-eight hours' leave."

"Oh, my God, no!"

"Stella doesn't know what happened after that. She went out and left them. There was nothing else she could do. When she came back they had both gone. She never heard from David again, but two weeks later he volunteered for a dangerous raid and was killed. Do you understand now?"

The blow had landed at last. Frank sat as if stunned. In one blinding flash all was clear to him. Stella's moods, her recklessness, her cynicism—all born of remorse. And James—the effect upon his hypersensitive mind must have been catastrophic, particularly when he had heard of his brother's death and knew he was the direct cause. Wounded himself shortly afterwards and captured, he had been incarcerated in a prison camp for twelve long months. Imprisoned with its guilt, his tormented mind had found its only escape.

Mary continued, her voice angry now. "I asked her why she had not told me before. She must have known what was wrong with James; she isn't a fool. And she laughed and said she hadn't realized it would help him to tell his wife of his unfaithfulness."

Frank forced his numbed brain into thought. "She didn't know what Evans had told you," he muttered. "She didn't know James's one chance lay in his guilt being exposed. She would think it better to keep quiet."

"Better for him or better for herself?" she asked fiercely. "Was she thinking of him at all?"

He did not answer. His head drooped wearily.

"Don't you see now why I must go to him?" Mary asked, her tone changing, becoming vibrant with hope. "It wasn't his fault that David died. He didn't know Stella was his wife. His only offence was spending a night with her. The rest wasn't his fault, it was hers. . . . If I can convince him of that, I might free his mind. A doctor might be able to show him what is festering inside him, but a doctor can't forgive him. I can, and if he still cares for me, it might save him."

Curious in spite of himself, Frank lifted his head.

"Hasn't this made any difference to your feelings for him?"

Mary stared at him almost impatiently. "It might have done once, but not now. Not now he is ill."

As she finished speaking, she rose and crossed over to the door. Frank stiffened in alarm.

"When are you going in to him?"

"As soon as he wakes up," came her quiet reply. "I'm going to my room now. When I hear his piano I shall come down."

He made his last plea. "'Phone Evans," he begged. "Explain everything and ask him to be here in case something happens. He'll come; he won't prevent your going in."

"No," she said vehemently. "He might. In fact, I'm sure he will. And even if he did agree, it wouldn't be fair to him. If anything . . . goes wrong, he will be responsible. No; I must do it alone."

"Where is Stella now?" he asked, dry-mouthed.

"I left her in the lounge. She said she would be leaving tomorrow."

"You must hate her for this," he muttered.

She hesitated, then turned to him. Her voice was perplexed. "Sometimes I think I do. And then I'm not sure. I can't forget her face as she was telling it all to me. She was smoking a cigarette and even smiling, but underneath she was in agony. I could see it. And I can't forget that she saved James's life this afternoon. She risked her own life more than we thought. If James had remembered who she was at that moment—if his mind had cleared—he would have killed her. They would have gone to their deaths together."

Frank's eyes closed. He was seeing again the expression on his brother's face as Stella had approached him on the rock. The look of wild shocked agony. . . .

James had remembered. And Stella had known, and still gone forward. . . .

"Yes," he said slowly. "She risked her life."

"It isn't only that. She has suffered, too. No one knows how much. She was young when all this happened—we all do foolish things when we are young. But perhaps we aren't all quite as unlucky as she has been. I don't think I can hate her, Frank."

"You are being very generous," he murmured.

"Perhaps it is only because I am so grateful for this chance," she said quietly. "Wish me luck, Frank."

Mary left the room, leaving him with his thoughts. Minutes passed and as his brain lost its numbness, his eyes grew fearful. He looked up at the clock on the mantelpiece and then rose suddenly. There was no time to lose, every second counted. James seldom rested long; he had already been asleep well over two hours. Mary must not go in to him without a doctor being present. Limping hastily into the hall, he picked up the 'phone and dialled.

Stella stood at the window of the lounge,

her hand holding aside the heavy curtain. Except for the firelight, the room behind her was in darkness. Through the window she could see the dark masses of the two elms that stood before the house, their trunks and branches silhouetted black against the night sky. Her eyes fixed on the nearest one. In a year a tree was like a life, her mind whispered to her. Its leaves were the fresh and joyous illusions of youth. Infectious in their enthusiasm, they danced in the delight of their rapturous, fanciful dreams. But how short-lived were those dreams. Before the cold wind of reality they withered and dropped away, with only a soft, rustling sigh to mark their passing. Life went on—the tree did not fall. But how barren and pitiful was the thing that remained. Her eyes reviewed it in distaste, then turned wearily away. She drew the curtains with a shudder and was returning to the fire when she heard the sound of footsteps in the hall.

One pair went tap-tapping by, implacable and unforgiving. The front door opened and closed with a slam. Gwen had gone. The heavier footsteps followed more slowly. There was a grunt and the thump of suitcases being dropped on a tiled floor. The lounge door opened and the florid, unhappy face of Mervyn peered into the firelight. He gave another grunt, of relief this time, at seeing Stella alone. He stepped into the room.

"We're going," he muttered. "Gwen's waiting outside in the car."

Stella nodded indifferently. He came nearer, his heavy eyes pleading.

"You aren't backing out, are you? You are going to come away with me. . . ?"

"I never promised anything," she reminded him bitterly. "You know that."

"I know—but after what has happened . . ." he mumbled. "You've seen for yourself what she's like."

"She'll come round if you play the game with her."

"I want you," he groaned. "I can't go on without you." Even at that moment his eyes were roaming hungrily over her.

She laughed harshly. "You'll forget me the very next time you see a pair of shapely legs." Then her eyes softened a little. "You can't help it, I suppose. It's the way you were made."

"I won't forget," he promised. "I'm crazy about you. Honest, I am. There's nothing I won't do for you." He was fishing clumsily in his inside pocket as he was speaking. "Look—here is my box-office number. I'll arrange everything when I get back and write to you. You send your reply to this address. Don't let me down."

She took the paper, frowning down at it. Then she crumpled it in her hand.

"I'll send the jewellery along," she told him. "And I'll let you know. Don't make any plans until you hear from me. Do you hear?"

Hope stirred on his unhappy face. "I'll do anything for you. Anything at all. Just say yes, and you'll never regret it."

"Get along now," she muttered. "And I'll let you know."

Mervyn came pathetically closer. "Give me one little kiss," he begged. "Just one. . . ."

"You fool!" she gritted. "Haven't we had enough trouble for one night? I've told you I will let you know later. Don't look so miserable." Her voice was harsh, bitter. "I'll probably have to say yes. You haven't left me much choice with your confounded blundering. But get out now, or I'll make sure I never see you again."

He backed away hastily at her words. "I'm sorry for what has happened, I'll make everything right for you later—honest I will. . . ."

She nodded wearily. "All right. Now run along."

"Cheerio, then," he muttered.

"Good-bye," she said thankfully. He gave her one last supplicatory look and then went into the hall. He dragged the suitcases outside and closed the front door behind him. She listened to his heavy footsteps moving reluctantly along the gravel towards his car, and for a moment felt sorry for him. She knew the merciless upbraiding he would receive from Gwen for this fortnight's work.

The sound of their car moving away reminded her with a shock that there was only Frank, Mary and herself left in the large house with James. Two women and one lame man. . . . And at any moment now the composer might awaken and Mary would go in to make her desperate bid to save his sanity. Her success could mean his complete recovery; her failure his complete and utter ruin, beside other things that Stella hardly dare contemplate. Her experience on the beach with James that afternoon had left its mark on her; she had realized for the first time the wild fury of the emotions burning within him. Once unleashed, they were capable of any violence. Mary would be risking her life in his study tonight. Her revelation that she had discovered his secret might well drive him to violence and even murder in an insane attempt to keep his guilt a secret still. It was imperative there should be someone in the house who could control him.

She heard a woman's footsteps passing along the hall. A few minutes later a door opened and the telephone-bell tinkled once as the receiver was lifted. She heard the sound of the dial followed by Frank's voice, too low for her to catch his words. A minute later there was a tap on her door, and he entered.

Stella raised her eyes, meeting his gaze fully. His face was pale.

He closed the door carefully behind him before speaking.

"Well," she said bitterly. "What do you

want? Have you come to tell me what a bitch I am? I suppose Mary has told you everything."

"Yes," he said quietly. "She has told me."

"And are you satisfied?" she sneered.

Frank ignored her question. "Did Mary tell you she is going in to James as soon as he wakes up?" he asked in the same low voice.

She turned away. "Yes; she told me."

"I asked her not to do it," he said. "I begged her to tell Evans but she wouldn't hear of it. She says he will stop her. . . ."

She swung on him fiercely. "I don't blame Mary. I'd do the same thing myself. Nobody wants half a man; nobody wants to be half a man. She's doing the right thing—I'm not worried about that. But I am worried about her," she finished sullenly. "James might do anything when he finds out."

"I know. But she won't listen. So I 'phoned Evans a couple of minutes ago."

"Is he coming?" Her voice was eager, relieved.

Frank shook his head grimly. "Unfortunately no. He has been called out to a farm to see a sick child. There isn't a 'phone there and I couldn't get through."

Her eyes dilated in alarm. "What are you going to do now?"

"That's what I came to ask you," he said quietly. "The farm is about fifteen miles from here and I shall have to find it first. . . . The round trip may take me the best part of an hour. Dare you stay alone with Mary? Will you help her if something should happen while I'm away?"

She stood quite motionless, the firelight on her pale lovely face. Her lips twisted scornfully.

"No, I'll run for my life."

"You realize the danger," he muttered.

Stella sneered. "Run along and do your errand."

"I thought it only fair to ask you first," he said slowly. "I could stay, but it will be better if Evans is here. It may prove imperative for him to be here. There's every chance James will sleep another hour or more yet. It should be safe. . . ."

"For God's sake, go! We'll be all right."

"If he does wake, try to make Mary wait. We shan't be long. Tell her she must wait."

"Hurry and go. I'll take care of her."

He paused at the door, his face suddenly wistful. "Tell me one thing. Would you have confessed if you had known before?"

She stiffened as if stung with a whip. Her eyes narrowed into slits. She laughed, a harsh, bitter sound. "Confessed? Do you think I'm mad, you fool? You could all have waited until hell froze over before I would have told you."

Frank turned abruptly away. "I'll be back as soon as I can."

She waited until he had gone, and then sank into a chair, her face in her hands. She sobbed without tears, her body retching and struggling convulsively, fighting against itself. The sound of Frank's car died into the night, its engine racing as if it were being chased by devils.

She lifted her agonized face at last. The coals were burning red now, staining the room crimson in their glow. In the corners dark shadows crouched like apes, drawing strength from the dying fire. She sat with ears strained for any sound from the study across the hall, her body cold with a sense of utter loneliness. The loud tick of the grandfather clock sounded like the beat of an anxious heart.

Outside the wind redoubled in violence. Up among the eaves and chimneys it sobbed and wailed like an earthbound spirit in torment. It cried of its loneliness, of the desolate wastes of the icy North from whence it came. Grim, terrible lands of green water and ice-bound mountains where elemental forces ruled supreme. It seemed to be tearing at the house, trying to find a way to the sleeping man and force its evil self into his unstable mind.

Half an hour passed, three-quarters of an hour, and the hunched black shadows across the room crept stealthily nearer as the firelight waned. The groan and swish of the great branches of the elms outside sounded through the howl of the wind. Stella wanted to switch on the light, yet found herself unable to move. Fear had drained the strength from her limbs. Fear seemed to possess the very house: it lurked in unholy purpose among the shadows and stank like a loathsome smell. It seemed as if the dark and vile thing in the wind outside had found ingress at last, and was moving through an aura of evil to its goal.

The very beat of the clock grew leaden in fear of what the future might bring.

A sudden gust of wind howled round the house like a great, exultant laugh, the house shuddering at the sound. Then it dropped a moment, to listen and gloat at its success.

In the hushed silence that followed, Stella listened and heard it, too. Her cheeks turned ashen and her limbs went rigid in terror. The wind, soft that she should hear, gibbered and simpered in glee outside her window.

From the study across the hall came the wild, pagan chords of the symphony. . . .

6

JOHN EVANS paused at the door of the bedroom and looked back at the drowsy boy lying in bed. Then he lowered his gaze and smiled at the small, anxious woman at his side.

"He'll be all right, Mrs. Prescott," he told her. "I'll be round to see him again tomorrow."

Doubt struggled with relief on the woman's face as she tried to smile back at him. She was in her early forties, drably dressed and careworn with iron-grey hair twisted into a bun in the nape of her neck. Worry had painted dark shadows under her eyes.

"Shall I leave the light on?" she whispered, motioning to the oil-lamp that flickered in the quaint old bedroom, shedding its yellow light on the lime-washed, sloping ceiling.

"You can," John told her. "It won't keep him awake."

She led him down a flight of narrow,

creaking stairs to the sitting-room below. There was all the warm, homely smell of the farmhouse: the odour of newly baked bread, the aroma of old leather chairs, the hint of tobacco smoke. A kettle was singing on a coal fire that burned in a high, old-fashioned grate. Alongside it was an oven, its door newly shined with black-lead. An oil-lamp hung on a chain from the ceiling, throwing a circle of thick, yellow light on a table below, which was covered by a flowered oilcloth. In the shadows round the walls, brass ornaments gleamed dully.

A tall, broad-shouldered man of forty-five rose from one of the leather armchairs as they entered. His rugged face, square-jawed and weather-beaten, was as anxious as that of his wife.

"Well, Doctor; how is the lad?" He spoke with the burr and drawl of the West Countryman.

"He has a touch of pleurisy," John told him. "Not a severe one, but you will have to keep him quiet and warm. I'll be round again tomorrow, and if he is any worse, we may have to take him away for a few days."

"You mean to hospital?" the woman muttered.

"Don't worry," John smiled. "I'm hoping it won't be necessary, but in any case we'd have him right in a week or two. Don't be upset if he sleeps heavily tonight —I've given him a slight injection of morphia to make him more comfortable."

The farmer put his arm round his wife's shoulders affectionately. "There you are, Ma. . . . Stop worrying now." He turned to John. "You be staying for a cup o' tea, Doctor, or a drink, maybe?"

John hesitated. A howl of wind outside, making the fire glow redly, made up his mind for him.

"A cup of tea will go down well," he smiled.

"Then sit down and the wife will make one now." John was steered into one of the worn, comfortable armchairs, his host sitting opposite him while Mrs. Prescott busied herself with teapot and kettle.

"When do you want to fetch your bicycle?" John asked the farmer. Prescott had cycled to his surgery in Rombury that evening and returned to the farmhouse in John's car, leaving his cycle behind.

"Oh; I don't know," came the reply. "Maybe tomorrow. It depends on the weather. Don't you worry about it. If it gets in your way, throw it out into the garden."

"It'll be quite safe until you want it," John told him. "You did well to get through on a bicycle on a night like this. Listen to the wind now."

"Aye," the farmer grinned. "It's a wild night, all right. But it wasn't as bad on the bike as you would have thought. The wind was behind me most o' the way, an' I went like a haystack on fire. But I wouldn't have fancied the ride back."

"I'll bet you wouldn't," John chuckled.

A quarter of an hour passed quickly in the warm, comfortable room. John put his cup aside reluctantly and rose.

"Thank you very much," he told Mrs. Prescott. "That was very nice. I'll be round tomorrow to see you. Don't worry about the boy. He'll be well again in a week or two."

They saw him to the door. The wind was savage, sweeping the clouds across the fitful moon.

"Sorry I had to bring you out on a night

like this, Doctor," the farmer muttered. "It's a wicked night."

"It's all part of the job," John smiled ruefully. "Good night, Mrs. Prescott."

"Good night, Doctor," the woman called out gratefully.

Accompanied by the farmer, John stepped out into the night. Their feet broke through a crust of ice to sink into the mire of the farmyard as they made their way to the car. A fringe of trees, flanking the untarred and rutted road to the house, were tossing and swinging wildly—grotesque witches with gaunt hair and spidery arms who writhed together in a spectral ballet against the sky. Their weird lament came eerily over the howl of the wind.

John jumped into his car and let down the window. "Don't wait," he shouted. "Get back inside. I'll see you tomorrow."

"Thanks again, Doctor," the farmer called back. Turning, he stumbled back to the house.

John backed the car to the muddy track and started back to Rombury. He had to drive slowly: the ruts were deep and his small car kept sliding into them. He had covered half the distance to the arterial road ahead when he saw the headlights of an approaching car.

There was no room to pass on the narrow cart-track. He drew up with his side wheels a foot from a deep ditch. The other car pulled up in the centre of the lane. John was opening his door when he saw the driver of the other car limping hurriedly towards him. He stared in surprise, his heart suddenly contracting at what the other's appearance might portend.

"Hello!" he shouted. "What's the matter?"

Frank reached his car and peered inside. His grim face relaxed in relief at the sight of the doctor.

"I've had the devil of a job to find this place," he muttered. "I thought I must have missed you."

"What's happened?" John asked again anxiously.

"Wait a second," Frank motioned, limping round the car and lifting himself into the front seat. He closed the door to cut out the noise of the wind, and then told his story in as few words as possible. John's face paled as he listened.

"But she 'phoned me just before I left to tell me to arrange for the operation," he muttered.

"I know. It wasn't half an hour afterwards that all the rest came out."

"Wouldn't Mary promise to wait until we arrived?" John asked anxiously.

Frank shook his head. "She wouldn't let me get in touch with you. She said you would never willingly agree to her going in to James, and it wasn't fair to ask you. She doesn't know I have come out."

"What happens if James wakes up before we get back?" the doctor asked abruptly.

"I asked Stella to try to keep her from going in."

"She won't be able to stop her. I know how Mary feels about this operation. She has been praying for a chance to avoid it, and nothing on earth will stop her now. We have to get there as quickly as possible," he finished grimly.

The urgency in his voice lent new alarm to Frank's fears.

"Do you think there is much danger, then?"

"Terrible danger," came the reply. "When he finds out his guilt is known, he is certain to turn violent. Quickly, man. There isn't a second to waste."

Frank was already out of the car and stumbling to his own. He heard the doctor's shout over the wind. "You'll have to back out to the main road. When you reach it, go like hell. . . ."

On the main road at last, they were able to open out their engines. Both drove recklessly with Frank leading the way, his headlights blazing into the darkness.

To both of them the journey seemed interminable. The road wound and twisted through dark woods and narrow villages, forcing them to keep slowing down. At last they reached the coast road and along this they were able to make better time.

Here the wind seemed almost a physical thing. Time and again John had his car blown half-way across the road and he had to fight to bring it under control. Yet he drove automatically; his mind was ahead of his body. In his feverish imagination he was seeing Mary entering her husband's study and saying the fateful words that would unlock the door to the secret, fetid cellar of his mind. In that moment of ugly truth, when the thing inside was dragged before him like a long-buried corpse, dreadful in its putrescence and decay, the shock to his mind would be beyond human understanding. In the intense white heat of the revelation, his mind might burn away the black monster that it had created to hide its eyes and blank out its memories. If this happened, the composer would fully recover his sanity. But if his mind, in agony at the disinterment, were to turn and make an offer of absolute surrender to the dark thing in a desperate effort to end its torment, then James Allister would destroy himself beyond all salvation.

But John Evans found his anxiety more for Mary than for her husband. Her hazards were even greater. By confronting him with her knowledge of his guilt she was risking her own life, as well as the life of the man she loved. And even if she emerged from the encounter without injury only to find James's mind shattered beyond repair, her self-reproach at having taken the risk might well prove too much to bear. The least it could do was haunt and blight the rest of her life.

Neither Mary nor the others realized fully the physical risks involved. They believed James would only resort to violence if the bid to save his reason failed. They did not know that he would run wild in any case until the savage conflict in his mind was settled one way or the other. In those seconds or minutes or hours he would be a raging madman, lunging out in frenzy to destroy those who had bared his secret. Perspiration stood out on the doctor's forehead as his feverish imagination raced on unchecked. What bitter irony it would be if James Allister were to kill his wife, only to recover his sanity later and realize he owed his salvation to the woman he had struck down! The tragedy would be the greater because her sacrifice would have been in vain—the musician would face a murder charge, his life would still be ruined.

In the racing car ahead, Frank's thoughts were as frantic, although more confused. Danger lay everywhere—to his brother, to Mary, and to Stella. . . . Surely to Stella most of all. If James became violent, who was he more likely to seek out and destroy than the woman who had been the cause of his years of agony? For the hundredth time that night Frank cursed himself for making Stella tell her secret. He should have waited until the doctor was present; he should have known what Mary would do.

He drove recklessly, with his foot hard down on the accelerator. The road ran near the cliff edge now; at one side was the tossing sea, at the other a snow-covered, desolate heath. His headlamps threw cones of light on the dark road ahead. Things shone abruptly and were gone—trees, bushes, a gate, a blinded startled rabbit. . . . On he raced. He was ahead of the doctor now; his car was the more powerful and he did not hold it back. The other's headlamps gleamed occasionally in his driving-mirror.

Lights shone ahead. First a red tail-light and then the arc of a lamp being swung at its side. For a moment he was tempted to ignore them and speed by until he realized to do so might mean running down the person wielding the lamp. With a curse he stood on his brakes, drawing in behind a stationary lorry.

The lamp swung nearer. Frank lowered his window and shouted to the man swinging it.

"What do you want? I can't stop. I'm in a desperate hurry." In the distance he could hear the hum of the doctor's car approaching.

"You ain't got no choice, mister," the man said with a chuckle. Tall and burly, dressed in cap and overalls, he was clearly the driver of the lorry ahead. "If you can get through, you're a better man than I am."

"What's the trouble?"

"There's a tree across th' road, up in front. My partner, Bill, nearly went into it. 'E's gone ahead to tell 'em in town and I'm stayin' 'ere beside the lorries."

Jumping out of his car, Frank saw there were two lorries ahead, one round a bend in the road. The headlights of the foremost were shining on a huge oak that had been uprooted by the wind and was now lying full across the road. There was no hope of passing it by car.

The doctor's car drove up and braked.

A few seconds later John was standing at Frank's side. His face was serious and drawn.

"There isn't any other way round to the house, is there?" he muttered, knowing the answer.

Frank shook his head. "Not for miles back."

"Wait a minute." John ran back to his car, returning with his medical bag. He seized Frank's arm. "Come on. We're only a couple of miles away, perhaps less. We can be there in fifteen minutes if we run. . . ."

He remembered the other's lameness then, and hesitated. Frank pushed him forward roughly. "Go on," he gritted. "Run, for God's sake. I'll get along as fast as I can."

John nodded. Jumping over the fallen tree, he ran madly down the dark road. Frank clambered over the gnarled trunk and followed him, his face racked with anguish. The wind howled taunts at him, tugging at his coat and jeering at his infirmity. He sobbed bitter curses into it as he limped painfully along. . . .

432

7

MARY sat in her bedroom, waiting. Silence lay about her, abnormal silence, as if the spirit of the house was afraid, and was itself listening and waiting. . . .The usual living sounds were absent: the distant murmur of voices, footsteps, a door closing, taps being turned on and off. . . .Tonight the only noises were inanimate ones: the creaking of windows, the groan of rafters, and others not distinguishable but all suggestive of a house besieged and stiffly afraid. Outside the wind alternately whined and snarled, scrabbling and nuzzling at the tiles at one moment, leaping and tearing at the walls the next.

In a sudden lull, Mary heard the sound of a car engine. She knew it was not the Ashburns; she had heard their exit a quarter of an hour earlier when in the drawing-room with Frank. She ran out on to the landing and from there to a front window. At first she could see nothing, but, as the clouds thinned for a moment and only a flying scud obscured the moon, she saw the dark shape of a small car turning and heading towards the main road.

Slowly she returned to her room. It had been Frank's car. Where was he going? Was he going to fetch John? It was possible; she had never thought to make him promise not to interfere. Yet why had he gone out in his car? If he had wanted John to come to the house, surely it would have been far quicker to telephone him. . . .

She sat down in a wicker chair beside her dressing-table. She could not deny to herself that she was afraid. She had been praying for a week for this chance, and now it had been given to her she was terrified. The fateful moment when James's mind would poise and sway on the knife-edge between sanity and permanent madness, to fall irrevocably one way or the other, was drawing nearer every second; and now, irrationally, she dreaded its coming. Once her revelation was made there could be no turning back, no calling to John to salvage what she had wrecked. If her bid failed James would be hopelessly and permanently insane; and to Ethel, Mrs. Allister and, no doubt, to the rest of the world, his madness would lie at her door.

She had given up trying to decide what to say to him. To prepare words meant knowing his reactions to those said before, and by the nature of things that was impossible. She could think as far as the moment she confessed to knowing his secret, but always at that point her mind shivered into hopeless confusion, like a mirror shattered by a stone. She had tried and tried again, waiting until the cold tremors of fear had passed through her limbs, but each time it was the same— her mind could go that far but no farther. Beyond there lay the unknown, the dark weald among whose mists creatures of horror lurked and schemed.

Was she alone with James? she wondered. Had Stella gone with Frank? Was that why he had gone—to take her into town? Perhaps she had decided to leave tonight. No; she had not been upstairs to pack her things. But she might have gone with Frank to John, if it had been Frank's intention to fetch the doctor.

The thought of John made her sit upright in alarm. If he were coming she would have to hurry. He would almost certainly be against her project; as a doctor he had no alternative. The most he could do for her was to call on the assistance of a psychiatrist; and instinct told her that if James had a chance at all, it lay in her revealing what she knew and then offering her forgiveness. Without the latter she felt nothing could save him. But the risks were appalling, and she could not ask John to be a party to them. To do so might well ruin him professionally. As it was, if anything happened to her he might find himself in serious trouble for not having certified James. She could not ask more of him.

No, it was better this way. There was no one in the house to stop her; no one to plead with her to change her mind. She would face it as she had always felt she would have to face it—alone. Life was a lonely thing, she reflected, her thoughts flying off at a tangent to escape the whirlpool of confusion in her mind. In pain, in comfort, in misery, in happiness, in despair, one was alone, always alone. Was not life one long, hopeless struggle to surrender and end this bitter individuality? Was not that the reason men lived in cities, and flocked to theatres and clubs and football matches? Was not that why men and women married, and in each other's arms strove frantically to end their loneliness, not realizing that the very flesh they tried to fuse together was the barrier that kept them apart? Was death the only escape? Did it finally allow the lonely of heart the bliss of oneness with the Universal Spirit? Was that why, in paradox, the wise left their fellow-men and lived in the wilderness?

Lost, in the sombreness of her thoughts she did not notice the passing of time. A shock of alarm ran through her as she looked down at her watch and saw that nearly half an hour had gone since Frank had left the house. If he had driven off to fetch John, they would not be much longer. . . .If she were going to face James, she would have to go soon. Originally, she had planned to wait until he awoke, but now there was not time.

Her limbs began trembling. Without Frank in the house, dare she go to her husband? If he—she made herself face the contingency—if he were to become violent and desperate, would she be able to control him? And if she could not, what would then happen to him? The cliff edge was near—if he fled from the house in his madness he might run to certain death. Ought she not to wait? And again—was it wise to waken him? Might it not upset him; would he not be more tractable to her influence on waking naturally?

She jumped to her feet—a physical effort to quell her rebellious thoughts. No. She would do it tonight while she was alone. She had been praying for this chance, and her prayers had been answered. She would never forgive herself if she faltered now. She stared down at her watch again. He had been asleep over three hours—longer than was usual for him these days. She would wait another ten minutes. If he did not awaken in that time, she would go to him. . . .

In her agony of mind she walked aimlessly up and down the bedroom. Her loneliness was intense; it grew until she felt she could bear it no longer. She felt like a spirit, chained by invisible bonds to the bleak, windswept house. A presentiment of evil grew on her, adding to her fear and sending a deep shudder through her body. With each passing minute she felt the strain grow; her nerves were being stretched on a merciless rack. "Go down now and wake him," one half of her mind commanded imperatively. "The others will be home soon; every minute is precious. . . ."

"Wait," another voice urged anxiously. "Let him sleep. It may be fatal to wake him. Let the others come. You need advice and help . . . you cannot do this thing alone. Think of the danger. . . ."

Oh, God, God. . . ! She threw up her hands and clutched her aching head. She wanted to scream and scream. . . . Outside the wind laughed and the aura of evil grew round her like a miasma.

Then, suddenly, the wind dropped, and the sound of the piano came to her. Her heart gave one great throb, and her face grew deathly pale. Without allowing herself to think, she turned to the door. The decision had been made for her; she could no longer hesitate. Like a sleepwalker she crossed the landing and started down the stairs, one hand on the banister and a sightless smile on her face. The future loomed ahead as an opaque mist; it closed its cold grey web around her hideously. Through it came the wild chords of the symphony, muffled and terrifying.

In the hall outside the study someone tried to bar her entry. Through the mist she recognized Stella. Stella! That was strange. She had thought Stella had gone. She saw the girl's lips moving but heard no voice. The piano was all she could hear: muffled though it was, its vibrations filled the world. Stella's lips moved again, pleadingly.

"No. I'm going to him," Mary heard herself say. "I must go to him." Her hand was on the study door when she felt her arm being pulled away. Without effort, without anger, without any feeling at all, she shook off the frantic girl and opened the door.

She did not pause. To have done that would have been fatal. James's pale face was staring irritably at her from his stool by the piano, and she walked straight towards him. She saw nothing else in the room. Only his face, and the brilliant black eyes that watched her with dislike.

She heard her voice again, and wondered at its strength and purpose.

"I've come to tell you that I know what happened," she said. "I've come to tell you that I know everything about you and Stella and David. . . . And that I can forgive you. . . ."

Suddenly, irrelevantly, his face seemed to change into a roulette wheel. It began to spin, faster and faster. But there were two balls instead of one—they leapt and danced over its surface and grew larger and larger. She watched them in terror. They became great black globes, glowing with an inner fire. As she watched, the fires developed at incredible speed. Pictures swirled in their bloodglow— pictures of rage and hate and fear. In crimson smoke they welled up, bursting and bursting again from the swelling eruptions below. She saw terror and stealth and shame, swirling and writhing as if in the smoke and fire of hell.

Her voice had not ceased; she had been speaking all the time. "You didn't know," she cried. "You weren't to blame. It wasn't your fault David died. You didn't know Stella was his wife. You must get it out of your mind. It wasn't your fault. Do you hear, darling? No one will think it your fault. . . ."

At her mention of others, the pictures suddenly changed. Hate gave way to Cunning; Cunning searched her with hateful eyes, then turned its head invitingly. And then something monstrous burst forward, hurling the other fiends of emotion aside. With awful challenge it faced her.

Under Mary's voice, in her mind, she was praying. Aloud she screamed. "No. Don't, darling. . . . There's no need to be afraid. You're not to blame. I understand what happened. . . . No. Please. No. . . ."

With its life threatened, the monstrous thing moved at lightning speed. Desperate in its black fury, it struck again and again. . . .

Stella had never known such terror as she felt at the first sound of those wild, though muffled chords. The shock was psychic; it clutched her mind in a hand of ice. The

442

chords came again, like a pitiless knell of doom.

It was a full thirty seconds before she overcame the paralysis of her limbs and was able to turn to the clock. Frank had been gone over half an hour; he should be back soon. If she could persuade Mary to wait a little longer, all might yet be well. But she must hurry. Mary would be downstairs the moment she heard the piano. Oh, God; if only her heart would steady down and her legs stop their trembling!

Entering the hall, she walked unsteadily towards James's study. The piano sounded louder here; he was striking the keys with unnatural violence. The music was as wild and primeval as the wind that howled and screamed outside, and her heart hammered in her throat at the sound of it. If only Mary would wait. She *must* wait. It would be madness to go into that room alone. What could two women do against a lunatic?

She heard the sound of descending footsteps on the stairs. Looking round fearfully, she saw Mary approaching like a woman in the grip of a nightmare. Her face was utterly without colour and her body rigid. One of her hands felt and gripped the banister as if she were sightless.

She reached the floor of the hall and turned stiffly towards the study. Stella watched her approach in terror. Mary's eyes were fixed straight ahead, but her purpose burned deep within them.

As she reached the study door, Stella stepped in front of her. "Don't go in yet," she said frantically. "Wait until Frank gets back. He has gone for the doctor. They'll be home any minute now. Don't go in on your own. It's too dangerous. . . ."

Mary appeared not to hear her. She tried to step forward to reach the door.

Stella's voice was harsh with fear. "For God's sake, don't be a fool. You don't know what he will do when he hears. . . . Two women can't stop him if he turns violent. You *must* wait. They'll be here any minute now—in fact, they're late as it is. Don't worry about them stopping you. . . . I'll see they don't do that. But wait for them—you can't risk it on your own."

Mary reached forward for the door. Stella clutched her arm frantically.

"Be sensible, for God's sake!" she sobbed. "He might kill you in there. Wait a few minutes longer."

Mary spoke flatly, without expression. "No. I'm going in to him. I must go to him." She pulled her arm away with surprising strength and opened the door.

"No. Don't. . . ." Stella tried to clutch her again, only to fall back in despair as Mary walked into the room.

From the doorway Stella watched the tableau in horrified fascination. James, his good-looking, sensitive face sullen at the intrusion, was scowling at Mary from his piano-stool. Alongside him was a small table on which was resting a pile of manuscript. He was wearing pyjamas and dressing-gown, and his dark hair was unruly. His face was flushed; he looked feverish. His black eyes flickered with vague dislike to Stella in the doorway, and then back to Mary. He did not speak.

"I've come to tell you that I know what happened," Mary began in an unnaturally steady voice. "I've come to tell you that I know everything about you and Stella and David. And that I can forgive you. . . ."

Stella did not hear the rest of her words.

Her whole petrified attention was on James as he listened to Mary's revelation. Nothing she had seen in her life, even in nightmares, had ever terrified her as much.

Although for a few seconds he did not move, his body seemed to swell with suddenly liberated fury. The veins on his forehead rose like swollen cords and his hands, still resting on the piano keys, stretched out into prehensile claws. But his eyes. . . . Oh, God; his eyes. . . ! The sight of them cut off her sob of fear in her contracting throat. They burned as if the furnace doors of hell had been thrown open and all its concentrated fury was flaming through two black windows. He gave a grunt, an inarticulate ghastly sound without meaning; and his eyes rolled dreadfully, to settle back on Mary again.

She was talking frantically. "You didn't know. You weren't to blame. It wasn't your fault David died. . . .No one will think it was your fault. . . ."

James sat watching her with those terrible eyes. He emitted another inhuman sound, louder this time. "Who told you. . . .? Who told you what I did. . . ?

Who told you I killed David. . . ?" His words died into a slobber. He sprang to his feet, his body bent and strangely twisted.

Mary was screaming wildly. "No. Don't, darling. . . . I understand what happened. No. . . . Please. . . . No. . . ."

His glaring eyes had searched round for a weapon and fixed on a ruler that lay on the table. Snatching it up, he sprang on her, striking viciously. She reeled back, screaming, screaming. . . .

"Don't, darling. . . . Oh, God; don't. . . ."

For a moment panic almost overcame Stella, and she turned to run from the scene of horror. A cry of pain and a thud brought her eyes round again. She saw Mary on her knees, trying to protect her head from the blows of the frenzied man above her; and something drove her forward. Running into the study, she clutched Mary round the waist and tried to drag her away into safety.

James's wild cursing ceased suddenly. He stopped raining blows down on his half-unconscious wife and turned to Stella. The silence was more dreadful than the noise had been. Through it, in some remote part of Stella's brain that was still functioning, she thought she heard running footsteps on the gravel outside the house; but in the next moment even that last island of resistance was submerged in an overwhelming flood of terror. The wild eyes glaring at her spoke their purpose as clearly as a voice. They had recognized her at last. Mary had unlocked the cellar of his mind and pulled out the reeking thing there for him to see; and in blind, frantic desperation he had attacked her. But now, with his forgotten guilt bared before his eyes, he saw and recognized the woman who had been the cause of his agony. *And now she had betrayed him.* . . .

His scream was a fearful thing that froze the blood. Stella pushed at the still dazed Mary, trying to steer her past the composer and out of the room. He saw her intention and turned swiftly, cutting off their escape to the door. The Hyde in him was in control, his very face had changed in appearance—it was wolfish with sunken cheeks and cruel mouth. His body was hunched, stooping, like a great ape.

The rest followed at lightning speed. With a howl of frustration he hurled the light ruler away. He glared round the study, his eyes falling on a walking-stick in the corner by the door. Before either of the women could move it was in his hand. His lips drew back; he crouched and leapt. Stella saw him coming at her and screamed. She caught his first blow on her arm, only for the limb to fall away in agony after the impact. Again and again he struck, grunting with the effort of each blow.

Stella collapsed on the floor. A shock of pain tore through her body. She rolled over in agony, hearing the thud of the stick on the carpet by her side. A man's voice came above the uproar, a voice she vaguely recognized. "Allister. Stop it. Drop that stick!"

The shadow of the frantic man fell over Stella again. She saw his eyes glaring at her . . . death was in them. . . . He drew the stick back, holding it like a spear over her head. The brass ferrule on its point glinted dully, and time stood still. Then he drove downwards, viciously. . . . She twisted away but agony seared her face. The stick rose again. . . . he screamed in rage as his arms were held. There was a struggle . . . curses . . . a woman's screams . . . then the shadows were reeling over Stella again. A foot trampled on her hand, but she felt no pain. Blood choked her mouth and nostrils. Then one shadow broke loose for a second; there was a wild, triumphant yell, followed by a crashing blow that hurled her into a sea of utter darkness.

Sunday

1

CONSCIOUSNESS came back to Stella like a shifting fog. At times it lifted sufficiently for her to see vague, hazy figures moving around her. Then it would descend into a blackness too dense for the eye to pierce, and she would see only things of the mind. Time played strange tricks. In one moment she was a small child again, standing by her father's side and watching his strong hands carving out the tiny dolls that had once delighted her so much. In the next moment she was older—a girl of fourteen returning to the house of her aunt in Hampstead, where she had been sent when her parents were killed. It was a dank house—her memories of it were always as she saw it now, half-hidden in the shifting fog, bleak, cold, unloving.

The pattern of time swirled and she was a child again, sitting in church with that light-headed feeling of unreality stealing over her. She turned for comfort to her father, but he was her father no longer. He was Frank, but his eyes were as gentle and her relief as great. He took her hand gently and held it. She closed her eyes, but when she opened them again it was not Frank who was holding her hand. It was a young man with bleary eyes and undone collar who was holding out a glass of champagne to her. As she sipped at it, the youth's features shifted and became those of Mervyn. He was holding a pair of earrings before her, and the mist grew crimson round his florid face. . . .

Now she was in the cathedral and standing by the glowing pool of light. Lifting her eyes, she saw Frank standing at the other side of the shimmering rainbow. He smiled and beckoned her to step forward with him. Gladly she obeyed. Wondrous colours glowed around her; great forces cleansed her mind. With Frank holding her hand she felt no fear this time, only exaltation. Gladly she surrendered to the broad, graceful wings that would carry them aloft. She felt no regret; nothing but ecstasy. They were rising together up the great, shimmering column of light when something seized her foot. . . .

She kicked and fought frantically, but the thing gripped like the jaws of a wolf. It tore her from Frank's arms and pulled her away into the darkness. Sobbing in despair, she was dragged along the stone floor towards the porch. She screamed at Frank to stay, but he relinquished the pool of light and ran after her. Then the thing holding her foot gave one great tug, and she was outside in the dark, bitter street. There was no sign of Frank. Tearing herself loose, she ran back frantically, but it was not the cathedral she entered. . . .

It was a bedroom, and there was James sitting on the bed in pyjamas and dressing-gown. It was the James she had known, handsome and debonair. He reached his arms out to embrace her, but as she approached a figure came between them. It was gaunt and long dead, but there was enough flesh left on its face for recognition. . . . She covered her eyes and screamed, but her fingers became transparent, and the dead face still looked at her. Then the fog swirled mercifully, to lift a second later. David had gone, but

James was still there. But the room and his face had changed. . . .His eyes seared her like coals. Vengeful, crouching, he lurched towards her. With a moan of terror she fled into the night. . . .

She was in London. She was walking down an endless black road. From the skies above sounded a dull throbbing. It grew nearer and nearer. There was an explosion, then another, and great orange fires burned in the mist. She turned and ran as the explosions burst nearer. . . louder . . . until they were bursting in her very brain. She saw a dark figure standing in a doorway, and she ran towards it. It turned its face and smiled, and she saw it was Frank. With a great sob she clutched him, burying her face in his coat. She hung there until an explosion blew them apart.

She was on the beach. Ahead a lonely figure was struggling among the rocks. It was Frank . . . she had to reach him. She ran among the water and strange green things tried to drag her down. Frantically she fought them off and reached Frank's side. Now she could help him . . . at last she could help him. She bent down to lift him to his feet, and the maddened face of James glared triumphantly up at her. . . .

She ran into the lounge. There was Frank at last, by the fire. . . . There was love in his eyes, she could see it. . . . He rose and held out his arms, and she ran desperately towards him, only to draw back in horror. Before her, like a row of pikes waiting to impale her trembling body, were pointing accusing fingers. There was Gwen, Ethel, David, Mrs. Allister, James. . . . The fingers came closer, closer . . . growing bigger, growing sharper. . . . Behind them, Frank's eyes dulled. Slowly he turned away, and the fingers struck, driving through her cheek to her brain. She felt a shock of agony, and warm blood poured down her face. . . .

Screaming she turned and ran upstairs to her bedroom, locking the door behind her. With a sob she turned . . . to see James lurching towards her with the fire of hell in his eyes and a pointed spear clutched in his hand. . . .

Fog, delirium, terror, in which time stood still and one night was an aeon of torment for Stella Allister. Until at last the mist lifted sufficiently for her to see a vague shadow by her bedside. She peered at it. Was it Frank? Its shape was familiar. . . . She tried to move, but her body was inert. If it was Frank she had to speak to him. . . . The fog descended, then lightened, and with the light came back memory. . . . She tried to speak, and her head exploded in agony.

When she opened her eyes again it was early morning. The greyness she thought mist was the winter light oozing like cold water through the drawn curtains. She recognized the man leaning over her. It was John Evans.

Memory returned more readily this time. She tried again to speak, and her lips would not move. She managed a whisper, as faintly sibilant as waves on a distant shore. He bent his head to listen.

"James. . . . How . . . is he?"

"You mustn't talk," he said in a low voice. "You must close your eyes and sleep."

Her eyes pleaded with him in agony. "Tell me . . . about James."

He hesitated, then answered her. "He's quite safe. Don't worry about him."

Anger welled up weakly inside her. "What has happened? You must . . . tell me."

"We don't know yet," he said abruptly. "We have to wait. Now close your eyes."

With a moan of disappointment she fell back, and the fog engulfed her again. Through it the glaring eyes of James burned in hatred. He was following her, following to have his revenge. She ran and ran, her screams dying stillborn in the cold, pitiless mist.

John Evans took a last look at the unconscious girl and left the room. At the bottom of the stairs he met Frank, whose haggard face searched his own for news.

"She has been conscious for a few minutes," John told him. "She'll be all right. Don't worry."

"What about her cheek?" Frank asked bitterly.

"I don't know. One can never say. They can do wonders these days."

"Surely the sooner they get to work on it the better. Can't you get her away this morning? It'll be a tragedy if it leaves a bad scar."

John spoke curtly. He was weary, unshaven, very tired. "I can't help it. She'll live; she's in no danger. What is a scar on one's face compared with what might happen in there?" He jerked a thumb to the closed study door. "If I send for an ambulance there'll be questions to answer, forms to fill in. . . .What am I to say—that she was attacked by an insane man I should have had certified? And that he is still lying in the house and may start the same thing all over again? I'm doing my best. I can't do any more."

"I know," Frank muttered. "Only it seems so tragic." His voice trailed off as he turned away.

"I'm sorry," John said wearily. "But, in any case, it is safer to keep her here until the effect of the concussion has worn off. I promise you I'll send her away as soon as I know how your brother turns out. Either way it won't matter then."

Frank nodded and went up the stairs to Stella. The doctor walked heavily to the study and entered it. The electric light was not switched on, and the iron-grey of the morning was coldly lighting the room. In bed, alongside one wall, lay the unconscious figure of James Allister. He lay supine, his aesthetic face pale in the dim light. His breathing was slow and shallow, almost imperceptible. Only a strange nervous spasm that ran at irregular intervals down one side of his face, lifting a corner of his eyes and twitching his lips, showed that there was life still within him.

Mary was seated at his bedside. Her face was as white as his, accentuating the dark shadows round her tired eyes. There was an air of unutterable weariness about her; she seemed to be keeping herself from collapse by will-power alone. Although an electric heater was burning at her feet and a rug wrapped round her legs, her body was in a ceaseless state of tremor, partly from nervous tension and partly from the strain of an all-night vigil by her husband.

Her eyes lifted as John entered. He walked softly to her side, occupying the chair beside her.

"Any change?" he whispered.

She shook her head. "No. He hasn't moved." She motioned to the table alongside. "Drink your coffee. Frank just brought it in."

461

He nodded, picking up the cup and sipping thankfully at its scalding contents.

"How is Stella?" Mary asked him softly.

"She recovered consciousness for a few minutes while I was with her. Her memory is all right—she wanted to know about James. I had to tell her we knew nothing yet."

He offered Mary a cigarette, and noticed with alarm the shaking of her fingers as she took one. "Go upstairs and get some sleep," he muttered. "It may be hours yet before he wakes up. You can't go on much longer like this."

She ignored his entreaty, her thoughts still on Stella.

"Is she going to be all right?" she asked anxiously.

He nodded. "Oh, yes. There's no serious injury. A fractured rib, concussion and this nasty gash to her face. None of them is dangerous. She'll be all right."

Mary shuddered. "It's her face I'm worried about. Last night, when you picked her up—her whole cheek was torn back. It looked terrible."

"Those injuries always look worse than they are," he said. "They're unpleasant, but they aren't dangerous once the bleeding has stopped. I've stitched it up—there's nothing to worry about."

"But John, she was so lovely. It's horrible to think of beauty like that being spoiled. Shouldn't she be getting attention? Get the best plastic surgeon you can—we'll pay for everything."

"I will as soon as I can," he said grimly. "Frank has just asked me the same thing. I've explained to him my problem. I can't move her by car because of the condition she is in, and if I 'phone for an ambulance I'll have questions to answer. I can lie about what happened, of course, but it will be pretty obvious I have lied if things turn out badly here," and he made an almost imperceptible gesture towards the unconscious James.

"I know," Mary murmured unhappily. "I know how difficult we have made things for you. You've been a good friend, John. You've risked a great deal for me. But you do understand how I feel about Stella? I must do my best for her. . . . Don't look like that, John. I'm grateful to her. She saved James's life yesterday, and perhaps mine last night."

His voice was bitter. "She was only squaring the debt. I can't forget what she did. If she had told you months ago things might have been very different today."

"But how could she know it would help James?" She clutched his arm. "Listen, John. Put yourself in her place. How could she know that by telling me, James's wife, of his unfaithfulness she was helping him? To her, the only decent thing she could do was keep quiet. She knew nothing about 'hidden complexes' and the subconscious mind. How could she? She isn't a doctor. Don't you see that?"

"I see you are turning what could have been a purely selfish motive into something chivalrous," he said. "Isn't it more likely that she kept quiet to guard her reputation and her position here? How do you know she was thinking of James at all?"

"I didn't know," she whispered. "At least, I wasn't sure until just now."

"Just now?" He stared at her.

"Yes. Frank told me a few minutes ago when he brought the coffee in. During the night, when he was sitting with her, she was delirious and she let out everything.

How she had wanted to talk and dared not for James's sake. Frank said it was terrible to see her state of mind. She had gone through agonies of remorse. Poor Frank, he was so relieved. . . ."

"Relieved? Why?"

"I hadn't realized it before," she said quietly. "I suppose I was too occupied with James to see anything. Frank is in love with her."

"Frank is?"

"Oh, yes. He hasn't said so, but I saw it in his eyes when he arrived back last night and saw her lying in that state. . . . It must have been torture for him when he heard all this about her and James."

"Yes," he muttered. "It must have been."

"So you see, I can't hate her," Mary said. "She has done all she could do to square the debt. No one can hate a person who is genuinely sorry and who does his best to make amends. That's why I don't want her to pay any more. . . ." She laid her hand gently on his arm. "You will see she gets the best attention, won't you?"

He nodded. "Yes, I will. As soon as we

know one thing or the other here, I will have her taken away."

Leaning forward he raised one eyelid of the unconscious man, and examined the pupil underneath carefully. Then he timed his pulse.

"How much longer before we know?" Mary whispered, watching him.

John frowned, his eyes on the spasmodic twitch that kept running across James's right cheek and temple.

"I can't say, Mary. I gave him a stiff dose of morphia—I had to. But he should be out of that any time. But there is bound to be tremendous nervous exhaustion after what happened. . . .He could wake any time, or he might be out for hours yet."

She brought her stub of cigarette to her mouth, inhaling deeply. A sudden deep shudder ran through her, and she turned her face away.

"What is it?" he murmured softly.

"Last night. . . . Oh, God; I don't think I'll be able to forget it for the rest of my life. His eyes, John. You should have seen them when I told him I knew his secret. They were like windows of hell. And his whole face changed; it became evil. . . .

I've never been so frightened in my life. I thought then his mind had gone for ever. I had lost all hope before you came."

He nodded gently. "I knew this would happen. Whatever his ultimate reaction, I knew he would become violent immediately he was told. That was why, when Frank told me what you were going to do, I got the shock of my life."

"You saved Stella's life," she told him. "I think you saved mine and James's too." She shuddered again. "Thank God you came when you did. Even then I don't know how you managed him."

"It was touch and go," he confessed. "It was fortunate I managed to get that shot of morphia into him in time."

She leaned forward, staring tenderly at the unconscious face of James. His sensitive features were almost boyish in their repose. Watching them Mary could imagine she was seeing the man she had known three years ago, lying with tranquil mind in dreamless sleep. Then, like a sudden gust of wind ruffling the surface of a peaceful lake, the nervous tremor sent a sudden convulsion across his features.

Looking closer, she saw there was a fine mist of sweat on his forehead.

"What is that?" Mary asked nervously. "Why does his face keep twitching in that way?"

"It's some nervous reaction from last night. I don't think it is symptomatic. But he has a temperature. It may be from the shock or from the soaking he had yesterday afternoon. I don't know."

They sat a few minutes in silence. Mary spoke first, her voice low and pensive.

"I suppose we are all the same—I suppose we all have guilty secrets locked away somewhere in our minds."

John nodded slowly. "Yes; we are all the same. We all have our prison cells where we hide the things we don't want to remember. We all have our cellars where we bury the memories we have killed."

"Don't," she shuddered, holding his arm tightly. "It's all too horrible. I'd never realized before what mental torture meant. I could never understand what people meant when they said that torture of the body was nothing beside torture of the mind. But after these last few months— after seeing James's suffering, after thinking, dreaming, worrying about him, after last night, watching his eyes mirroring all the agonies of hell—now I know. And I can't help thinking about Stella. She must be going through as much as James himself."

The morning dragged slowly by. Except for moments when John went upstairs to attend to Stella, who was now sleeping naturally, he hardly left James's side.

About noon the composer showed signs of regaining consciousness. He moved an arm, his body twisted restlessly and he made a muttered exclamation. Mary watched with bated breath. As he lay quiet again she turned to John.

"How much longer now?" she breathed.

"Not long," he told her tightly. His face was grim; lines of strain were drawing round his mouth and eyes.

"If he . . . if he does recover, what will he be like?" she whispered. "Will he be normal—will he remember everything again?"

"He would remember the times when he was normal. But I don't think he would recall anything of what has happened

469

recently—unless he remembered the moments when his mind was fairly lucid."

"You mean moments like last Thursday night when he came to me and spoke about the concerto?"

"Yes. Those memories might be clear. But if he remembered fragments of the rest, it would be in the way one remembers nightmares. They would be completely vague and formless. He would remember nothing of last night. I'm almost certain of that."

"Will he be all right physically? I mean, will he be sick and require treatment?"

"Oh, yes. He has used up a terrific amount of physical and nervous energy, and then there would be a shock effect."

"But he will eventually be normal in every way?"

"Yes. If he reacts favourably, there should be no permanent ill effects, although we should have to treat him and give him rest for a number of weeks, perhaps months." Then he turned desperately towards her. "Don't put your heart in it, Mary. For God's sake expect the worst. It was a hundred-to-one chance, and after what has happened you mustn't bank on anything."

"You haven't much hope, have you?" she said dully.

"No," he muttered. "And I can't let you have too much. It won't take much more to knock you out. I don't want this to be too great a disappointment."

She laughed jerkily. "A disappointment. Such a funny word to use, John. Such a funny word." Her laughter rose shrilly.

He caught hold of her arm. "Steady," he muttered. "Steady. . . ."

Her hysterical eyes looked at him dazedly, then slowly cleared. She lowered her head. "I'm sorry," she murmured.

"Promise me not to be too upset," he begged, "if the worst should happen."

She tried to smile into his anxious eyes. "Don't worry, John. I won't let you down."

He sighed heavily, turning his eyes back to James. As they watched, the composer muttered something and rolled sharply over on his side. Something in the abrupt movement brought terror to Mary. James lay still a moment, then flung one arm across the eiderdown. John pulled a hypodermic needle from a case on the table and knelt beside the bed. His face was grave; his body tensed and waiting. Beside him Mary sat huddled in her chair, fearful to move, fearful to look, yet finding her eyes held in awful fascination upon her waking husband. His eyelids fluttered and she stiffened. In minutes, in seconds, she would know the truth—whether her desperate bid to save his brilliant mind had been a success or a pitiless failure. In the hushed silence she heard irrelevant sounds: the tick of John's wrist-watch, the distant breaking of the waves, the hum of a car passing the house. Then she became aware of John's quickened breathing, the rustle of his clothes as he leaned abruptly forward. Then all sounds were lost in the wild tumult that was her heart, thumping like a madly beaten drum.

Her husband's eyelids flickered, flickered again, and then opened. His gaze roamed wildly round the ceiling and then fell upon them. . . .

BEFORE unconsciousness returned to Stella, she had wanted to ask the doctor about Frank, but the words had not come to her. Where was he? Had he not been to see her? Did he no longer care? She had wanted desperately to know, almost as much as she had wanted to know about James, but speech had failed her and in the black mist there were no answers. In it, as she fled from the vengeful figure of James, she kept hearing Frank's voice calling to her, offering her succour, offering her strength. Once, as the gloom lifted, she thought she saw him by her side; but before she could run to him the mist had fallen again, hiding him from sight. Frantically she tried to reach him, to find him by his voice, but no matter which way she turned it grew fainter and fainter. . . . What was the use? He was taunting her; he hated her as much as James who was stalking her in the nightmare of cold and fog. She heard a sardonic laugh that echoed hollowly on all sides. With a sob of despair, she ran blindly away into the darkness. . . .

It was early afternoon when she awoke again. The window curtains were drawn, and a pale ray of winter sunshine was touching her bed. Needles of fire stabbed her eyes as she gazed at it. When the pain had subsided she looked at it again, watching the dust motes rising and falling gently, and her confused mind thought her back in the cathedral again. . . .Then memory began to return, and sorrow was its companion. Her eyes moved swiftly to the chair by her bed, faltered, then fell away. It was empty. . . . Bitterness touched her briefly, and was gone. What else could she expect? What other reaction could a man have for the woman who had caused the death of one brother and the ruin of another? Her punishment had come late, but the mills that grind slowly grind exceedingly small, she reminded herself.

Her head throbbed agonizingly. She became aware also of pain and stiffness at one side of her face. Lifting a leaden hand she explored the tape and thick bandages strapped over one cheek. Memory, fully returned now, sent a shock of terror through her body. Again she saw James standing over her with the brass-bound stick in his hand, and then driving it madly down at her face. . . . Her fingers searched her cheek in agony. Oh, God; no. Not that. . . .

Perspiration broke out all over her body. She wanted to scream and only a muted sob broke from her. She lay motionless, numbed by her discovery. Minutes passed while she fought the bitterest battle of her life. But at last her eyes opened, and they were unblenched again. The thing was done, it was conquered. It could be faced now. . . . Footsteps sounded on the landing outside her room, familiar footsteps. She turned her eyes and her heart gave a great throb.

He limped forward, his eyes eager, while she lay afraid to move in case it was another dream.

He bent over her, his voice gentle. "Hello. How's the hangover?"

She tried to speak, but no sound came from her stiff lips.

"Does it hurt to speak?" he asked softly, bending to listen.

"Not much," she managed. "Not very much."

"Good," he smiled.

There was something in his face, in his eyes, that made her hope against things that were hopeless. She took a deep breath, setting herself.

"Is there any news yet of James?" she whispered.

He nodded. The world suddenly stopped moving, and she closed her eyes tightly. There was a sound of rushing water in her ears. His voice sounded a million miles away.

"You can open your eyes, Stella. James is going to be all right. . . ."

Stella's heart would not let her speak. It struggled in her throat like a captive bird. For the moment the implications of Frank's message were beyond her. She knew it was good news; she knew it was wonderful news. But her mind had been frozen, devoid of hope. Feeling would return to her later and there would be pain with it, such being the nature of things.

But now, like a frozen creature placed before a fire, she was aware only of a pleasant tingling, a languid feeling that was in itself infinitely satisfying.

James was safe. James would be well again. That was good. Somehow, that was wonderful. The warmth of the fire sank deeper. Then Mary would be happy again. Mary would smile and laugh. . . .Mary had done the right thing. . . .

Her blood began to flow again, although slowly at first. With its movement came the pain. Mildly at first, a thin twinging, a warning of what must follow.

Now the blood was rushing through her veins in long, warm spurts, and the pain began in earnest. Pain at the thought of what might have been. If she had known the situation and told Mary earlier, might not Frank have forgiven her then? If he had not thought, as he must think now, that she had kept it all a secret to guard herself. . . . But what difference could that make? David was still dead. Nothing could bring him back. Nothing. Not remorse, not sorrow, not even a miracle. He was dead, and he had been Frank's brother.

The pain was agony now. She did not

know it for what it was—the resurrection of hope. She lay and offered her mind and body in sacrifice to it.

Frank watched the torturing train of emotions passing behind her eyes.

"Isn't it good news?" he asked softly.

"Yes," she breathed. "It's wonderful news."

"I think I know how you feel."

"Nobody could ever know how I feel. Nobody on God's earth. . . ." She tried to rise, caring no longer about pride, caring nothing about pain. "Where's Mary? I want to see her."

Gently he made her lie down. "She's with James at the moment," he smiled. "You can see her later."

"I want to see her now," she sobbed. "I want to tell her how sorry I am. . . ."

"You don't have to tell her that. She knows."

She tried to stop, but the floodgates were released and words poured from her lips, some of them incoherent.

"I was young . . . and such a fool. I wanted to meet James . . . but I didn't mean it to go the way it did. . . . But he was so much like David . . . only a stronger David, like you. David seemed a mere shadow beside him, and David had been away so long. . . . It wasn't as if I fell in love with James—I seemed to have been in love with him all the time, through David. And the war was on . . . and you know what war does to people . . . to women. . . ."

He dropped into the chair beside her, his eyes on her face.

"Don't think I'm making excuses," she whispered. "I'm not. Only Mary might feel better if she knew everything. . . . It wasn't sordid . . . it wasn't! At the time it seemed almost beautiful. . . . Oh, God; if I had known all this was to happen . . . to David and James and you and Mary. None of you have done anything to deserve it: Mary least of all . . . I wanted to die last night. I wanted James to kill me. I still want to die."

Her sobs were both a relief and an agony, racking her aching head unbearably. The bandages round her face were soaked in tears. She wiped her eyes dry.

"I'm sorry for that show," she muttered, almost sullenly. "It was all self-pity. You'll have to blame it on the knock I got on my head last night."

"It's not new," he said. "You've said it all before."

She stared at him. "What do you mean?"

"You said most of it last night while you were delirious. I was sitting here eavesdropping," he smiled.

So that, at least, had not been a dream. He had been by her side during the night. . . .

"You shouldn't have been listening," she muttered. "People say anything when they're delirious."

"You were *you*," he said intensely. "All the veneer and cynicism and sophistication had gone. You were a little, frightened girl."

She lay watching the sunbeam, afraid to believe. . . .

"You were looking for your mother and father," he said with a strange catch in his voice.

"You said I wasn't a hypocrite," she whispered. "And yet I've been living in this house all these months knowing full well what I did. You couldn't get greater

480

hypocrisy than that. . . ." Her lips twisted painfully. "Poor Frank—how wrong you were."

"It's no use pretending now," he said. "You told too much during the night. I know why you kept quiet."

She spared herself nothing. "There's still David," she said, watching the tremor of pain in his eyes. "I killed him—as surely as if I had shot him. I killed him, and he was your brother. . . ." The words were drops of blood squeezed from her heart.

He lifted his bowed head, remembering Mary's words. "We all do foolish things when we are young. But we aren't all as unlucky as you have been."

"It wasn't foolish. It was wicked. I killed him, Frank."

"'Each man kills the thing he loves'," he quoted slowly. "'Some do it with a bitter look; some with a flattering word.' You did love David, didn't you?"

"Yes," she faltered. "I think I did."

His eyes were intent upon her. "What was it about him that you loved?"

"I don't know. Something inside. . . . Oh; how can one ever say?"

"Had James that something, too?"

"Yes," she whispered. "That was it. That's what I tried to explain. They were alike, somehow, although James was more vital. . . ." She wanted to go on, to tell him that he, Frank, was the strongest of all the Allisters, but her words ran back into her throat, choking her.

"I killed him, Frank," she said again dully. "Nothing can change that."

"'Each man kills the thing he loves'," he quoted softly again. "'Yet each man does not die. . . .'"

"It's no use," she sobbed. "It will always be there. There is no removing it. . . . Oh; I'm not going to do away with myself. I'm not going to commit suicide or anything like that. I'm not that sort. I haven't the courage. But I do know what I've done."

"You've always known," he broke in harshly. "That's why you have been so bitter and cynical. . . . It was to hide the frightened child in you that was crying for comfort. You poor kid. . . ."

She fought back her sobs until the blood roared in her ears.

"You've gone through as much as

James," he said fiercely. "The same memories have been poisoning you, although in a different way. You have to put it all behind you now. You have to make a fresh start. Do you hear?"

The pain began to ease. She knew it would come again, but for the moment it was warm and comfortable, lying with him by her side, listening to his voice, watching the sunbeam. . . .

"What did I say last night?" she murmured, keeping her eyes from him.

His voice was soft. "You were a frightened little girl," he said again. "And you were crying for someone to comfort you."

She wondered if she had called him by name. He did not say so. Instead he asked a question.

"Tell me, Stella. This thing in the Allisters—is it in me, too? Or am I the odd man out?"

"Oh, no," she breathed. "It's very strong in you."

A light of life itself flooded into his tired eyes. He clutched her arm, a hungry movement. She checked him, lifting a hand to her bandaged face.

"Wait," she whispered. "Do you realize what this may mean?"

His face flinched in pain. "No. No, it won't . . . it can't! Evans is arranging for an ambulance. It should be here soon. We have told him to get the best plastic surgeon he can find. You'll be all right. . . ."

Her hand lingered briefly on her cheek, then fell away as if in farewell. "Somehow, I don't think so. I feel it is part of the price I have to pay. . . ." With the look of one who has discovered a great truth, she lifted her eyes to him. "There is a price to pay, you know, Frank. There's a price to pay for everything. I know it now. We don't pay it . . . afterwards. We pay it here, on earth. I don't mind. I'd rather have it that way."

"You'll be all right," he muttered again.

"And if I'm not?"

He was ready for her question. "Then I shall think that the wish I made last night has come true."

She turned and pressed her face passionately against his hand. "Oh, Frank. . . ."

She lay motionless a moment, then stirred feverishly. "You said last night that anyone who loves gives a hostage to Fate. Then what about me. . . ? It will be even worse." She touched her cheek again, disdainfully now. "A scar isn't punishment. There'll be worse to come, Frank. I don't mind, but what about you? If you live with me—if you care—you'll suffer as I suffer, and that wouldn't be fair. I don't want that. Do you hear, I don't want that. . . ."

He eased her down to her pillow gently. "Go to sleep now. You'll feel better tomorrow."

"I'm not delirious," she sobbed. "You said it. You know you did. . . ."

"I was a fool," he said contemptuously. "A cowardly, selfish fool. Oh; I was right enough in what I said. It's true—one always takes a risk in loving someone. But I was wrong when I said only fools did it. Because one should take risks, one should suffer."

"I don't want you to suffer," she sobbed again. "You'd feel it so much."

"Stella; a man who has never suffered has lived in vain," he said quietly.

"Suffering is the fire that burns out our pride and arrogance and greed. It purifies us for the thing that comes next."

Her wide eyes fixed themselves wonderingly on his face. "Comes next?" she breathed.

"Yes. I don't think death is the end. I think there is another taxi waiting, but one has to have one's feet clean to be allowed in it. If they are dirty, perhaps one has to wait."

"I know what you mean," she whispered. "Yes; I know. . . ." A deep shudder racked her body. "And I'm afraid, Frank. I'm terribly afraid."

He leaned over the bed and put his arms protectingly around her. "You've paid your debt, Stella. I'll swear to it. But if you haven't, we'll pay off the rest together. We'll finish it more quickly that way."

Her body rose trembling to him. "I can love you very much, Frank," she sobbed. "Oh, God; I can love you."

"Get well again," he said. His happiness was a living thing; it was peeling the harsh years from him, leaving his face strangely youthful in the sunlight. "Get well again soon, Stella Allister."

Downstairs in the study the curtains were half-drawn, and in the dim light Mary's eyes shone like stars. It was over three hours now since James had awakened, and still she was hardly able to believe the miracle that had happened. She sat at his bedside, watching his sleeping face in wonder. Her happiness was too great a thing to be contained inside her; it kept welling up and overflowing in joyous tears, in words, in gestures, and sometimes, as now, in wordless prayers of thanksgiving.

The door opened and John, wearing his overcoat, motioned her into the hall. With a last look at her sleeping husband, she followed him.

"Well," John said as she closed the door quietly behind her. "Are you happy now?"

Her eyes flooded with tears. "Happy? I'm giddy with it, John. I can't believe it yet; it's like a miracle. Are you sure this isn't just a temporary recovery?"

"Yes; I'm almost certain he will be all right now. The crisis is over; the guilt is in his conscious mind at last. He'll recover, Mary. But you're quite right about the miracle. Do you know what I believe helped to bring this about?"

She shook her head.

"That attempt of his to commit suicide. His condition was low and the physical shock of the icy water would be most severe to him—it may in fact have contributed to his high temperature. It has been found that severe physical shocks, even diseases, often bring improvement in mental cases. That experience plus your revelation so soon afterwards has pulled him round."

"I don't know what to say to you, John. How to thank you for all you've done."

"You've nothing to thank me for," he said quietly. "You did it all yourself."

She shook her head passionately. "No; that isn't true. You gave me the time I needed; you risked your career for me. I'll never forget, John. Never."

He smiled at her. "I'm going to run along now and make arrangements to get a bed for him. I want him to get the best of treatment until he has fully recovered."

"Is it safe now to talk to him of the past?"

"Not just yet. Wait until he is stronger. But actually I think you will find he will bring it up first. It is in his conscious mind now; he will want to talk and relieve himself of it. And when he does, you can make quite certain that he realizes he was not to blame for David's death."

"You'll be coming round to see us often, won't you?" she asked wistfully.

"Yes. I'll drop in now and then." His voice was steady.

She hesitated, trying to find words. "You've got the key of the garage?"

"Yes."

"You needn't hurry about bringing back the car. Any time will do."

He nodded.

Her lips moved helplessly, searching vainly for the right thing, the one thing, to say. There was a faint cry from the study.

"Mary. Where have you gone?"

She ran to the door and threw it open. "I'm here, darling. I won't be a moment."

John had turned away. He was at the

front door as she ran after him. She threw her arms round him tightly.

"Thank you, my dear," she whispered. "Thank you for everything. If I could only say what I was feeling. . . ."

Her face lifted suddenly and he felt her lips warm on his own. He stood motionless, his face white. Then she was gone, running back to the study. She paused at the door and waved back to him. Her happiness was too great a thing to conceal; it made a shining glory of her face. As she turned into the study, the hall became very dark and empty.

He opened the front door and walked slowly round to the garage. He took the car out and drove down to the main road. He did not look back at the house on the cliff as he turned for Rombury. A hundred emotions, each cancelling out the other, made his mind a blank and his face without expression. Afraid at last of this vacuum inside him, he willed himself into thought and his thought became her face, radiant in her newly found joy. The memory brought feeling back into his limbs and life to his heart. She was happy again, and that was good. That was everything. For the moment he thought no more but drove rapidly on, the dullness in his eyes giving way to an abiding contentment.

THE END

GUIDE
TO THE COLOUR CODING
OF
ULVERSCROFT BOOKS

Many of our readers have written to us expressing their appreciation for the way in which our colour coding has assisted them in selecting the Ulverscroft books of their choice. To remind everyone of our colour coding— this is as follows:

BLACK COVERS
Mysteries

*

BLUE COVERS
Romances

*

RED COVERS
Adventure Suspense and General Fiction

*

ORANGE COVERS
Westerns

*

GREEN COVERS
Non-Fiction

FICTION TITLES
in the
Ulverscroft Large Print Series

The Onedin Line: The High Seas
                                      Cyril Abraham

The Onedin Line: The Iron Ships
                                      Cyril Abraham

The Onedin Line: The Shipmaster
                                      Cyril Abraham

The Onedin Line: The Trade Winds
                                      Cyril Abraham

The Enemy	*Desmond Bagley*
Flyaway	*Desmond Bagley*
The Master Idol	*Anthony Burton*
The Navigators	*Anthony Burton*
A Place to Stand	*Anthony Burton*
The Doomsday Carrier	*Victor Canning*
The Cinder Path	*Catherine Cookson*
The Girl	*Catherine Cookson*
The Invisible Cord	*Catherine Cookson*
Life and Mary Ann	*Catherine Cookson*
Maggie Rowan	*Catherine Cookson*
Marriage and Mary Ann	*Catherine Cookson*
Mary Ann's Angels	*Catherine Cookson*
All Over the Town	*R. F. Delderfield*
Jamaica Inn	*Daphne du Maurier*
My Cousin Rachel	*Daphne du Maurier*

Enquiry	*Dick Francis*
Flying Finish	*Dick Francis*
Forfeit	*Dick Francis*
High Stakes	*Dick Francis*
In The Frame	*Dick Francis*
Knock Down	*Dick Francis*
Risk	*Dick Francis*
Band of Brothers	*Ernest K. Gann*
Twilight For The Gods	*Ernest K. Gann*
Army of Shadows	*John Harris*
The Claws of Mercy	*John Harris*
Getaway	*John Harris*
Winter Quarry	*Paul Henissart*
East of Desolation	*Jack Higgins*
In the Hour Before Midnight	*Jack Higgins*
Night Judgement at Sinos	*Jack Higgins*
Wrath of the Lion	*Jack Higgins*
Air Bridge	*Hammond Innes*
A Cleft of Stars	*Geoffrey Jenkins*
A Grue of Ice	*Geoffrey Jenkins*
Beloved Exiles	*Agnes Newton Keith*
Passport to Peril	*James Leasor*
Goodbye California	*Alistair MacLean*
South By Java Head	*Alistair MacLean*
All Other Perils	*Robert MacLeod*
Dragonship	*Robert MacLeod*
A Killing in Malta	*Robert MacLeod*
A Property in Cyprus	*Robert MacLeod*

MYSTERY TITLES
in the
Ulverscroft Large Print Series

Henrietta Who?	*Catherine Aird*
Slight Mourning	*Catherine Aird*
The China Governess	*Margery Allingham*
Coroner's Pidgin	*Margery Allingham*
Crime at Black Dudley	*Margery Allingham*
Look to the Lady	*Margery Allingham*
More Work for the Undertaker	
	Margery Allingham
Death in the Channel	*J. R. L. Anderson*
Death in the City	*J. R. L. Anderson*
Death on the Rocks	*J. R. L. Anderson*
A Sprig of Sea Lavender	*J. R. L. Anderson*
Death of a Poison-Tongue	*Josephine Bell*
Murder Adrift	*George Bellairs*
Strangers Among the Dead	*George Bellairs*
The Case of the Abominable Snowman	
	Nicholas Blake
The Widow's Cruise	*Nicholas Blake*
The Brides of Friedberg	*Gwendoline Butler*
Murder By Proxy	*Harry Carmichael*
Post Mortem	*Harry Carmichael*
Suicide Clause	*Harry Carmichael*
After the Funeral	*Agatha Christie*
The Body in the Library	*Agatha Christie*

WESTERN TITLES
in the
Ulverscroft Large Print Series

Gone To Texas	*Forrest Carter*
Dakota Boomtown	*Frank Castle*
Hard Texas Trail	*Matt Chisholm*
Bigger Than Texas	*William R. Cox*
From Hide and Horn	*J. T. Edson*
Gunsmoke Thunder	*J. T. Edson*
The Peacemakers	*J. T. Edson*
Wagons to Backsight	*J. T. Edson*
Arizona Ames	*Zane Grey*
The Lost Wagon Train	*Zane Grey*
Nevada	*Zane Grey*
Rim of the Desert	*Ernest Haycox*
Borden Chantry	*Louis L'Amour*
Conagher	*Louis L'Amour*
The First Fast Draw *and* The Key-Lock Man	*Louis L'Amour*
Kiowa Trail *and* Killoe	*Louis L'Amour*
The Mountain Valley War	*Louis L'Amour*
The Sackett Brand *and* The Lonely Men	*Louis L'Amour*
Taggart	*Louis L'Amour*
Tucker	*Louis L'Amour*
Destination Danger	*Wm. Colt MacDonald*

Powder Smoke Feud

William MacLeod Raine

Shane   Jack Schaefer

A Handful of Men   Robert Wilder

THE SHADOWS
OF THE CROWN TITLES
in the
Ulverscroft Large Print Series